PERPS

PERPS

A SHORT STORY COLLECTION

EDWARD WELLEN

Five Star
Unity, Maine

Five Star First Edition Mystery Series.
Published in 2001 in conjunction with
Tekno Books and Ed Gorman.

Set in 11 pt. Plantin by Minnie B. Raven.

Printed in the United States on permanent paper.

Library of Congress Cataloging-in-Publication Data

Wellen, Edward.
    Perps : a short story collection / by Edward Wellen.
        p. cm. — (Five Star first edition mystery series)
    ISBN 0-7862-2997-7 (hc : alk. paper)
    1. Detective and mystery stories, American. I. Title.
II. Series.
PS3573.E4566 P4   2001
    813′.54—dc21   2001018145

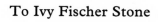

To Ivy Fischer Stone

CONTENTS

FINAL ACQUITTAL

Sweat shone like gilt on Byrne's brow. Without moving his head he knew the sudden stir and hush in the courtroom meant the jury was returning from its long deliberation. He tried to maintain his air of impassiveness, but as the jurors filed in he was stiff with willing them to look at him. Somewhere he had heard that when a returning jury avoided looking at the defendant it was because the jury had made up its collective mind to convict.

Now, however, when members of the jury did in fact eye Byrne it gave him no comfort. He still could not tell. He was unable to read the eyes behind the glittering glasses on the grave face of the butcher who was the foreman. The fixed faint smile on the face of the woman smoothing her skirt beside the foreman might be a smile she meant to be reassuring, then again it might be a smile of gloating.

Byrne looked no further. In any case, the judge's gavel was drowning out his heartbeat. Hogan, his defense attorney, nudged him to stand and face the jury.

The judge leaned forward slowly. "Ladies and gentlemen of the jury, have you reached a verdict?"

The foreman balanced himself by pressing his thumb on the railing. "We have, your Honor."

"What is your verdict?"

The foreman hammily let a pause weight the air. "We find the defendant not guilty."

Newsmen charged out. Byrne's knees gave, but he held himself up. The prosecuting attorney, voice trembling with anger, demanded a poll. The judge gaveled down a babble, permitted the polling, discharged Byrne, rather coldly thanked the jurors and discharged them—but that was all a blur to Byrne.

He sat down heavily. For a moment he had a job focusing, then he turned to his lawyer. He took Hogan's hand in both of his, thanking him silently. Hogan freed himself and began stuffing papers into his battered briefcase.

The courtroom was emptying except for a few friends making their way toward Byrne. His late wife's aunts had stopped by the door. Meed was with them, looking embarrassed because he was a friend of Byrne's and yet a second cousin, or something of the kind, and business associate of the women.

"Justice!" the tall thin one said, looking right at Byrne.

"A mockery!" the other said.

They wheeled and stalked out. Meed awkwardly followed them, throwing back a don't-get-me-wrong look of appeal at Byrne.

Byrne smiled wryly. The smile faded as he caught Lt. Harris of Homicide watching him. Lt. Harris, the man who had arrested him and testified against him, stood leaning against a pillar, a twisted smile on his face. Then people were between them, blocking Harris from Byrne's view, friends coming with uncertain eagerness through the gate from the spectators' section.

Byrne stood up. His legs were still weak but he knew he was able to proceed under his own motive power. A surge of need told him to get far from this place and its sickening associations. Yet now that he could leave, could step outside and breathe the sooty air of freedom, he hesitated.

His friends were crowding around uncomfortably, trying to keep out of their eyes that they were wondering how to word their congratulations.

"I knew you had to get off."

"Of course. Absurd to think you could ever have . . ."

"We all know you loved Madelon too much to . . ."

Byrne found his voice. "You stood by me, that's what counts. I can't thank you enough." His face twisted, but in a smile. "Don't worry, I'm not going to get sloppy. Except maybe sloppy drunk."

They laughed, but their laughter had a forced, hollow sound in the courtroom, where so many voices had wrung the most out of rhetoric throughout the trial.

He saw Meed returning. He looked down at Hogan pounding the briefcase on the table to settle the papers and make room for more to be placed crosswise on top. Then Meed was at his elbow.

Keeping his eyes on Byrne, almost defensively, Meed nodded toward the outside, where he had gone with the aunts. "I was just seeing them to a taxi. I had to come back to tell you I never for a moment believed you murdered Madelon."

"Thanks." Byrne glanced around at his friends hovering in an uneasy arc. Abruptly he took a step toward the door. "How about all of you coming up to our—to my apartment for a few drinks. Say in an hour; give me a chance to get ready."

All but Hogan accepted, nodding almost too eagerly.

Byrne eyed Hogan. "How about it?"

Hogan snapped, his briefcase shut. "I don't make a practice of socializing with my clients." Then he seemed to come to a decision. "But I'll be there." He smiled a rare smile that transformed his gray face. He said for Byrne's ears alone, "Frankly, Byrne, you puzzle me." His smile widened. "I can afford to say that now."

A court attendant, eyeing Byrne with curiosity, showed him out through a side entrance. The door closed. No one passing paid Byrne any mind. He breathed deep—it was fine to be alone, unwatched, free. Then farther along the block he saw a weary-looking Lt. Harris getting into a police car. Byrne quickened his step, came alongside just as the door slammed.

"Hello, Lieutenant."

Harris eyed him bleakly.

Byrne received heartier greetings when his friends showed up. They were almost too hearty. To do them justice, they were trying hard to be cheerful and nonchalant, to accept him unquestioningly, to pretend the death and the trial had never been.

Hogan sat quietly to one side, his eyes never leaving Byrne's face, trying to strike through the mask of flesh. Meed, too, sat apart, eyes for the most part on the drink in his hands, like a man watching a gauge. The others milled around.

Their keynote was gaiety, but there were warning looks from one to another, irrelevant comments on innocuous topics, sudden silences and sudden spates of talk, and much reaching for glasses. They watched Byrne out of eyecorners, plainly thinking, *the man's been through a great nervous ordeal; he won't want to talk about it, at least not right now.*

Yet he did talk about it. He had been upending his glass, seemingly without stop, and now began commenting mockingly on the judge, prosecuting attorney, and jurors.

They eyed him in polite puzzlement, as though witnessing a stranger. They had never known him to drink like this or talk like this; but then, hadn't his ordeal earned him a measure of forbearance? Hadn't it warranted a certain amount of license? They tried to relax understandingly, but they fell silent.

Byrne's nostrils whitened. He looked around. He was holding himself in but it was like holding in a steel spring.

"Come on, this isn't a wake. It's a reawakening. Let's celebrate."

They laughed uneasily.

Byrne lifted his glass. "To my loyal friends." He tossed it off, then grinned suddenly. "People usually suspend judgment—like a sword."

This won him a round of unsure smiles and nods.

Byrne refilled his glass sloppily. "There'll always be suspicion in the minds of some." He swayed slightly. "Let me put your minds at rest."

They tried to wave him down deprecatingly, but he seemed blind to them. He gazed past them, through the French doors which opened on the balcony, at the night and at the dim reflections of all of them in the room.

He said almost casually, but pronouncing the words with care, "I got away with murder." A bright, wild look flared in his eyes as though he knew he was overdoing it but didn't know when or how to stop. He said into the silence, "I killed Madelon."

They sat in shock, wanting to disbelieve, but believing.

He started to go on. "I can speak freely, without fear of further prosecution . . ."

Rising almost as a jury about to retire, they drew back from Byrne, set down the drinks with great care, and fumbled getting their coats and hats, their faces saying they were already gone.

Hogan was first to the door. He stopped and faced Byrne, examining him crossly. "I knew I shouldn't have come. I suppose this was the very thing I was afraid of." He left without pausing to put on his hat and coat, his face set, it seemed, more in anger at himself than at Byrne.

The others left silently, in various degrees of disgust. Everyone left but Meed.

Meed sat twirling his glass and gauging it with an odd smile.

Byrne turned on him challengingly. "How come you didn't pull out with the rest?"

Meed looked up with a sorrowful, understanding smile. "Because I know it isn't true." He put up a forestalling hand. "Oh. I know why you said that. Not to shock us; not to get back at society that put you on trial for something you didn't do."

"No? Then why?"

"Because you *feel* guilty. It's only human. All of us have at one time wished someone else dead. And if that person dies we feel—even if we had nothing to do with the death—a kind of guilt."

Byrne eyed him mockingly. "Oh? You think that? Well, think again. I murdered Madelon—really murdered her. And I got away with it."

Meed eyed him narrowly, with a thin smile. "Either the strain you've been under has cracked you or . . ."

Byrne leaned back easily, something between a sneer and a smirk on his face. "Or what?"

Meed shook his head. "No, I think that's it. You're just giving way to aftershock and alcohol. You've been under too much tension and you've had release."

Byrne grinned crookedly. "Meed, you're wasting your breath playing psychoanalyst. Murdering Madelon put no strain at all on my conscience."

Meed gazed into his glass. "Go right ahead. But when you're cold-shivering sober you'll wish you hadn't shot off your mouth."

"Speaking of shots—" Byrne downed his drink and reached for a refill. "That one was for Madelon. Poor Madelon. I done her wrong."

Meed said very quietly, "You'd better lay off the drink and that kind of talk. How do you expect to pick up the pieces of your life here?" He looked thoughtful. "Maybe it's too late already. You saw how the others took it."

"Maybe I just don't give a damn about anything, now that I've got away with murder. After all, you can't do much more than that in life, can you? You're right about one thing: I've a great feeling of release."

Meed gave a short explosive laugh. "I can understand how you might've been driven to feeling like murdering Madelon. I'll admit the woman could be trying. But that doesn't excuse your empty bragging."

Byrne raised an eyebrow in a leer. "Empty bragging? Shouldn't what I say loosely here be more credible than what I said under oath for my life?" He smiled smugly.

A shadow crossed Meed's face. He breathed hard, then he smiled. "What do you think you're proving? Only that you're irrational."

Byrne took a sizable swallow and came up looking sly. "You're trying too hard to be broad-minded. But I think down deep you're taking it like the others. What you're really angry at is not my guilt but my bad taste. Here I am boasting of my guilt just after a jury of my so-called peers has found me guiltless. Come on, confess. Isn't that it?"

Meed stood up abruptly, his eyes hostile. "You're damn right it's bad taste." He set down his glass savagely. "I should've left with the others." He snatched up his coat and rammed his arms into the sleeves. "I don't know why I stayed, except to see how much of a fool you'd prove yourself to be."

"Fool enough to get away with murder." Byrne eyed Meed disdainfully, turned and walked with great precision to the French doors, flung them open, and took a deep breath. He turned back with an evil smile.

Meed's eyes glittered. "I don't know why I should be so angry. I know you're not responsible. You're foolish drunk."

Byrne laughed. "I know what I know. I got away with murder."

Meed swelled with fury. "You damn blowhard, they let you go because they couldn't find the weapon. They never found it because I threw it into the quarry just outside town."

He stared in amazement as Byrne turned again to the night, moved nearer to the balcony railing, and took a deep breath.

"Didn't you hear me, Byrne? I'm saying *I'm* the one who murdered Madelon." He came up behind Byrne. "You poor drunken fool, you won't know what hit you either. I'm telling you because they're going to say you couldn't live with the guilt you admitted here tonight. Listen to me, damn you. I'm saying *I* did it. I was tired of her, but she threatened to make the end of the affair messy, and so—" Hands drawing back to push, he advanced on Byrne, watching him intently.

Lt. Harris stepped between them out of the darkness on the balcony, handcuffs gleaming. Meed froze till too late; the cuffs clicked fast.

Byrne turned slowly and saw the gleams as webbed blurs, like stars burning in mist. His vision cleared and he saw Lt. Harris eyeing him with a twisted smile.

"So I was wrong. I still don't know why I went along with you on this. I thought sure you did it—even up to just now." He shoved Meed toward the door. "Good night, Mr. Byrne."

"Good night, Lieutenant." He turned again to the night. He heard the door close. He took a deep drink of night. Night would soon fade. He would take a deep, deep drink of dawn.

INSIDE EVIDENCE

The window of Mr. Ricord's office looked out over acres and acres of junk—valuable junk. Detective Hertz mopped his face, wiping off the scowl that had come with seeing Mack calmly at work out there stripping wrecked cars, and turned back to Mr. Ricord. The detective raised his voice over the groaning and shrieking of scrap steel yielding to heavy machinery.

"Like I say, Mr. Ricord, I'm just checking up to see if Mack is breaking parole. Lots of these guys give us names of employers and never show up for work."

Ricord gave a gray gesture in keeping with his years. "As you can see for yourself, he's right on the job."

Detective Hertz grimaced. "Yeah. Well, have you seen him in the company of known felons?"

Ricord lifted an iron-gray eyebrow. "Known felons? Do known felons wear labels?"

Hertz shifted his stance. "Well, you know what I mean."

"Yes, I know. And I know you're checking up on him. The man has told me how all of you on the force have been hounding him out of one job after another with tactics just like these." The words might be harsh and almost angry, but the tone was soft and almost sad. "If you're hoping I'll turn in a bad report on him to satisfy whatever motivates your vengefulness, you're wasting your time. All I can tell you about him is that he puts in a good day's work. The aim of parole is rehabilitation, isn't it? Returning to society someone who's paid his debt to society. Period. End of sentence. But it seems you just won't let it end."

"Rehabilitation! Listen, Mr. Ricord, this Mack is strictly a

17

no-good guy. He got away with murder and now he's going around laughing at us. He hasn't paid his debt by a long shot." Detective Hertz stopped short of grabbing Ricord by the lapels. "I'm going to tell you something about Mack you must not have known or you never would've hired him in the first place.

"Maybe you're right about our vengefulness, because it involves a brother officer. But I know in my heart I'd feel the same and do the same if it had involved a civilian. Still, it does involve civilians—women and their relatives. We believe Mack is the Stocking-Mask Rapist."

Hertz stopped and looked as though he were waiting for that to hit Ricord hard.

Ricord maintained his composure. "Yes, I heard you. The Stocking-Mask Rapist. And you expect me to get rid of Mack in horror because you know my granddaughter was one of the Stocking-Mask Rapist's victims?"

Hertz looked discomfited. "Well, I was counting on you to show some feeling."

Ricord spread his hands. "I might show some feeling if you were able to prove Mack is the man. Can you?"

Hertz reddened. "We never were able to get a positive make on the man because he always wore a stocking mask. But we suspected Mack because he has the same build as the man and because we always found him near the scene of the attacks and because he was out on parole—this same parole—for a similar offense.

"Then one night a cop caught the Stocking-Mask Rapist red-handed—almost caught him, that is. Because the man started to run. The cop saw the girl was in shock but otherwise all right, so he gave chase. The cop drew his gun and called on the man to halt. The guy only ran harder. He had a good lead and was outdistancing the cop. It was either fire or let him get away. So the cop fired. The guy fell down.

"The cop was a rookie and he made a bad mistake. He felt sure he had killed the guy and thought it was safe to walk up to the body. He bent to lift the mask off and get a look at the guy's face. But the guy wasn't dead. The girl saw him grab the cop's gun and shoot the cop dead with the cop's own gun, then drop the gun, get up, and stagger away into the night.

"A half hour later we picked Mack up at a hospital emergency room. In gunshot-wound cases hospitals have to let us know right away. X-rays showed a bullet had lodged in between the fifth and sixth ribs of the left side where the bottom of the heart beats against the chest wall. If the bullet had moved even a little bit more, it would've penetrated the heart and finished him.

"Mack said he was shot in a holdup—he claimed some guy had stuck him up and shot him when he put up a fight. When he realized that we were waiting around to match the bullet in him with the bullet in the dead cop and that we could prove they came from the same gun—the cop's—he refused to let the doctors dig for the bullet. They warned him the bullet was only this much"—a pinch of air—"below his heart. He still refused.

"They patched him up, since they couldn't go in, and when he walked out that ended it for them. But not for us. We took it to court, trying to force him to submit to an operation to remove the bullet. That was the only way we could prove our case. But the courts upheld him.

"And so he's walking around with the evidence inside him. I ask you, Mr. Ricord, would an innocent man refuse to let them take out something that threatens his life? Now what do you say?"

The junkyard sounds seemed to swell in the silence. Then Ricord sighed. But he spoke firmly.

"I say a man is innocent till a jury says he's guilty. Isn't that what society is all about? What kind of world would this be if we ignored due process and played judge, jury, and executioner?"

Hertz threw up his hands. His eyes blazed.

"I'll tell you what kind of world it would be! It would be the kind of world it already is. Where the wolf preys on the sheep. You bleating do-gooders turn my stomach." He and his voice shook with fury. "I'm tired of waiting for the sheep to band against the wolf.

"Mack is just lying low till the heat dies down, then he'll be up to his old tricks. Well, I'm an old dog. I'm going to keep snapping at his heels. At the first sign he's breaking parole I'll pull him in and at least he'll do the rest of his time. Even if I have to make that sign myself. Just between the two of us, Mr. Ricord, do you have any idea how easy it would be for a cop to plant stolen goods or a few ounces of pot on his person or in his room?"

For the first time Ricord let emotion show. "You can't do that! Why don't you fellows lay off? Look at him work."

They looked out at Mack, who was sorting auto parts into bins.

"I'm looking. So?"

"So he's doing fine. I've been planning to move him up. Any day now I'm going to raise him to working with that. I'll break him in myself."

Detective Hertz's gaze followed Ricord's pointing finger to the huge electromagnet that lifted tons of scrap metal at a snatch. Their eyes met in understanding. Sooner or later Mack would be standing under the magnet when it was switched on. The sudden massive pull would shoot the spent steel-jacketed bullet into Mack's heart.

Hertz nodded. It struck him that you needed steel inside to make good in the junk business. "You're right, Mr. Ricord. I guess it's about time we laid off."

THE ADVENTURE OF THE BLIND ALLEY

Feeling his way through the pea-soup fog, Police Constable Cooper paused at the noise of a struggle. He stared hard to hear. At the first outcry and the noise of scuffling his hand had whisked to his whistle. But before he could blow a blast to frighten off the attacker, he heard the sickening sound of a cosh on a skull, then the thump of a falling body.

He withheld the blast and with heavy caution, in order to catch the assailant red-handed, he lifted his boots toward the rough breathing and the tearing of cloth.

P.C. Cooper smiled tightly to himself. He knew this to be a narrow cul-de-sac and himself to be between the attacker and escape. He had the culprit all but in his arms.

He winged out his cape and moved slowly but steadily into the blindness of the alley. But a curb leaped out of nowhere. P.C. Cooper's stumble and his muffled oath warned the attacker. The constable blew a savage blast. "In the name of the law, stand fast!"

P.C. Cooper heard fleeing footsteps, the ring of a hobnailed boot striking an iron mud-scraper, then the creak of a door and the snick of a latch. The culprit, then, was a denizen of this unsavory alley.

The constable swore under his breath. He had his man—and yet he did not have him. He knew there were a half-dozen doors on either hand. Unless the constable located the right door straightway, the culprit would have time to change from his wet outer clothes and to hide what he had stolen from the victim.

The victim. A dozen paces deeper into the alley, and the constable saw the shape of the victim on the cobblestones.

Feeling sudden clamminess and chill, P.C. Cooper stood over the fallen man. He eyed a familiar hawk-like profile, a bloodied deerstalker cap, a still-clutched violin case. Rents showed in the victim's clothes where hurried hands had torn away a watch chain and snatched a wallet. That the mighty man-hunter should have fallen prey to a common robber!

The victim stirred. A word came forth. "Constable . . ."

P.C. Cooper knelt, careless that his knee touched the wet stones. The blood-blinded face had not turned toward him. How had the man known to call him constable?

The whistle, of course. The habits and skills of a lifetime would not have failed him even in the direst of moments. Though stunned, the great detective would have taken note of some clue, and most likely clung to consciousness now solely to impart that clue.

"Sir, did you see your assailant? Can you describe him?"

A painful shake of the head.

"Do you know where he ran to?"

A painful nod.

P.C. Cooper's heart surged, but the man had only consciousness enough to point vaguely and gasp, "A flat . . ."

The constable grimaced in disappointment. The great detective had told P.C. Cooper only what P.C. Cooper already knew.

A flat, indeed! This was an alley of rooming houses—nothing but flats.

P.C. Cooper removed his cape and wadded it under the great detective's head as a cushion. Then the constable rose and duty took over. His whistle guided answering whistles.

Each blast, each echo, ached. It hurt him to think that his colleagues would find him simply standing there, waiting, while the culprit was safe behind one of those unseen doors.

A flat . . .

P.C. Cooper shook his head. Why should those words keep ringing in his mind? They had originated in the poor stricken mind of the great detective.

A flat . . .

Pounding boots pulled up. P.C. Cooper recognized the figure of P.C. Lloyd.

Lloyd was a Welshman, and Welshmen are famous for having perfect pitch.

Swelling with authority, Cooper seized Lloyd's arm and pointed him.

"Man, hurry and kick the mud-scrapers with your great hobnailed boots and find the one that sounds A flat."

IT AIN'T HAY

He flashed his tin. She unchained the door and let him in.

"Lieutenant Harding. From the Bunco Squad. Miss Colum?"

She nodded. She cocked her head to one side, making her an even more birdlike little old lady. He looked around with a practiced sweep and caught the open drawers and the half-filled trunk. He lifted his eyebrows.

"Seems like I'm just in time. Planning to leave?"

"Yes, I hope to get away this afternoon. You see—"

He frowned her to a halt. "I was counting on you to help us." Then he cleared his face. "Well, it won't take long. Maybe you can still help. What time do you leave?"

"I'm hoping to make the 5:09."

"Ah. Plenty of time. This job won't take more than a half hour."

She cocked her head the other way. "I don't understand, Lieutenant. In what way can I possibly help the police?"

"You can help the police and yourself at the same time. It's in connection with the two young women who took you for eight thousand dollars two weeks ago."

Her eyes widened. "But how—"

He grinned. "No; I wasn't there when you came in to report it. And I haven't read the report. But I can tell you almost word for word how it goes. You've just left your bank after making a sizable deposit. A stranger, a nice-looking soft-spoken girl, comes up to you on the street. She begs your pardon for accosting you but you have a kind face and she's unfamiliar with this part of town; and has a problem and doesn't know where to turn.

"She has just found an envelope full of bills and doesn't know what to do now. She looks around, takes you to one side, and opens the envelope for a peek. She shows you a packet of brand-new thousand-dollar bills. She says she's counted them and there are one hundred and twenty of them. One hundred and twenty thousand dollars! More money than you knew was in the whole world."

He gave her a mildly reproachful look. "You should've known right there. The U.S. Treasury no longer issues one-thousand-dollar bills."

She laughed ruefully. "Lieutenant, I'm afraid I'm not familiar with anything larger than a twenty-dollar bill."

His eyes flashed. "That's what gets me about these parasites. They pick on those least able to lose large sums." He drew a deep breath and let some out. "Anyhow. The girl tells you she has a retarded child, or something like that, and can sure use the money. While you're talking, another girl appears and gets into the conversation.

"It turns out that this second girl works for a lawyer. She'll ask his advice. She makes a phone call and comes back. The lawyer has advised her that the large bills most likely mean the money is mob money. The crooks who lost it would never dare claim it if the girl who found it turned it in to the police. They would have too much explaining to do to the tax people.

"So, as it would come back to the girl who had found it anyway, after six months, there's no sense turning it in now. The lawyer has also advised that, since the three of you know about it, the three of you must share the windfall . . . on condition that each of the three be able to show she can live for six months on what cash she already has without dipping into the 'hot' money.

"In the meanwhile, through his connections, the lawyer

will arrange to have the thousand-dollar bills changed into smaller bills that you can deposit without raising suspicion.

"Both girls are overjoyed, and so are you. You can certainly use forty thousand dollars, which would be your share. The others quickly come up with the evidence that they can live for six months on what they already have. The one who found the hundred twenty thousand can show a check for an insurance settlement, which is what she has come to town to collect. And the other just happens to have on her the proceeds from some bonds her recently deceased father left her. Now it's up to you.

"You return to your bank, withdraw eight thousand dollars in cash, and come out and show the sum to the others. They look at it and if it's not already in an envelope they put it in an envelope and give it back to you.

"Now the three of you head for the lawyer's office. Once you're in the building, the girl who works for the lawyer says that the lawyer's partner knows nothing about this and that what the partner doesn't know won't hurt him, so the lawyer would like you all to come up one at a time and not in a bunch that would attract the partner's attention.

"The first girl goes up in the elevator. Then the second girl. Then it's your turn. Only, when you reach the right floor and the right office number, you find nobody there's ever heard of the lawyer. There ain't no such animal.

"You feel sick. You force yourself to look inside your envelope. You almost faint. That's right, they've switched envelopes on you. Your eight thousand dollars is gone and what you have is a one-dollar bill on top of a stack of funny money or just plain paper cut to size."

He looked at Miss Colum and with a weary smile shook his head slowly. "And that's when we come in and try to pick up the pieces."

Miss Colum's hands flew to her face. "It sounds so silly now, when you tell it. And to think I let them take me in with a story like that." She lowered her hands and stared at him with owlish earnestness. "But the thing is, when they're talking to you it all seems so plausible. You have no idea."

He grinned. "Oh, I know how it is, all right. Confidence is the name of the game. They win your confidence. That's where the name comes from. And these people are slick. You weren't the first they've taken in." He sighed heavily. "And I'm sorry to say you won't be the last." He sharpened his voice and gaze. "Unless you help us."

"Me? What can I do? I've already done all I can. I gave the best descriptions I could of the two girls."

He smiled and his voice rubbed its hands. "Well, now, you can do even better than that. We've located the two girls and we want you to identify their pictures." He drew two pictures from an inside pocket and held them out for her to see. "Are these the two girls?"

She rose up out of herself in high excitement. She pointed at the two photos. "They're the ones! They're the ones!"

He gestured for her to calm herself, but she was shaking.

"This brings it all back. The worst of it wasn't the money though I couldn't afford to lose it. The worst of it was, I felt so *dumb*." She stared through him. "I looked inside the envelope full of bills and the bills were funny money—they pictured a jackass and had the horselaugh words 'It Ain't Hay.' And I did feel just like a jackass."

"Well, now, Miss Colum, here's your chance to get back at them. You'll help us put them away and get your money and self-respect back."

Her face tightened "How?"

"Now you're talking, Miss Colum. That's the way." He eyed her keenly. "Do you remember which teller you went to when you made your deposit earlier that day?"

She thought, then nodded. "Yes. He had a little moustache and long blond hair."

"Good. Excellent. We believe the girls and the teller are working together. He gives them the high sign when he spots a pigeon—excuse me, a prospective victim—such as yourself. You can help us trap him."

Her face tightened another notch. "How?"

He smiled. "I see we're going to have to hold you back. Only kidding, Miss Colum. We want them as much as you. Here's how we'll work it. You'll go to your bank and to that teller's window. You'll withdraw most of your remaining money—in cash, which he will count out several times so his fingerprints will be sure to be on the bills. Ask for all new bills—that will insure that his prints will be the freshest and clearest on them. You'll wear gloves and so will I. We won't take any chances.

"I'll have another detective watching to see who he gives the high sign to this time. We want the whole rotten crew. But you don't have to worry about that part of it. Your part will be over. I'll be waiting to give you department funds in exchange for the bills the teller handled. We'll need those for evidence but you won't have to be out one red cent.

"Then, too, after we arrest them all, we may be lucky and get your original amount back."

"You really think so?"

"Be honest with you, they may have spent some of it. With them, it's easy come, easy go. They like to live high and fast. But we should get some of it back."

"Well, anything would be nice. I'd given it all up."

He got brisk. "Then let's get started. The sooner we start the sooner we finish. I'll drive you to the bank and then either myself or another detective will drive you straight back here and you can wind up your packing. You'll make the 5:09 with time to spare."

She looked suddenly flustered and indicated her clothing. "But I have to change and I have to find my bankbook."

"Sure, take the few minutes."

She started to leave the room, then stopped. "I must seem to you a terrible hostess. I'm ashamed of myself. Our parents brought us up to behave better and I'm letting them down. Here, do sit down. You'll have a cup of coffee while I get ready? You don't mind instant?"

"Not at all."

It took her little more than an instant to bring him his coffee. He sipped it, made a face after she had left the room, but found nowhere to dump it. He sipped on, not wanting to hurt her feelings and risk losing her compliance.

Much more than an instant passed. He pulled his arm up to look at his watch. The hands dragged time along slowly. What was taking her so long? His eyes started to shut. He snapped them open and looked up sharply. But his head grew heavy, lowering to his chest. His heart beat crazily, noisily. He didn't have the strength to shove to his feet. He could not move anything but his heavy, glazing eyes. What had she put in his cup?

When he forced his eyes open again she was standing gazing down at him.

"Now, *Lieutenant,* shall I tell *you* how it goes? You and the girls are a team. They make the first encounter with the pigeon and take her for as many thousands as they can. Then after a few days you come into it, pretending to be a detective from the Bunco Squad.

"You tell the pigeon you have a make on the two girls and need the pigeon's help to trap their bank teller accomplice. Of course there's no bank teller accomplice. You only want her to withdraw her last few remaining dollars and hand them over to you for another funny-money switch.

"This is the 'comeback.' That's what you call this, isn't it? The comeback? I know you're a fake because it's my sister you came looking for and my sister did not go to the police with the story of her victimization.

"I feel half guilty myself because a few years ago, when the same thing happened to me, I was too ashamed to tell my sister I had fallen for a con game. It might have saved her if she had known. At least she wouldn't have been too ashamed to go to the police.

"She didn't want even me to know, but I got it out of her before she died. I got word she had collapsed and I rushed here to see her. We didn't have long together. She faded fast. The shock of being made a fool of had killed her. But before she passed away I learned from her that she had been the victim of a con game.

"Now I'm winding up her affairs. And that includes you. Excuse me a second." She stepped into the kitchen and came right back carrying a length of clothesline.

"The police—the *real* police—will have a few charges outstanding for all three of you, I should imagine. The girls' pictures should prove very helpful in locating them. Is *your* mug shot on file? Are you wanted anywhere?"

His blink gave him away and she nodded with satisfaction.

"Then there's impersonating an officer. That should hold you awhile. And so should this." She held up the clothesline. "I have to go out to use a phone and I want to make sure you'll be here when the police come."

Before tying him up she made as though trying to pull the clothesline apart with a snap, showing him its strength.

"It ain't hay."

THE PLAN OF THE SNAKE

Far out on the veldt one hundred years of weather have scoured and scattered the bones of the Bantu, the Boer, and the snake. If the bones have changed, the pebble half-buried amid them has not. The wind and the sun have worked on the pebble, but it is the sun's beam that takes a polish and the wind's glassiness that gets scratched.

When the bones of the Bantu wore flesh, it was the Bantu who found the pebble. The earth in its long travail had worked the pebble to the surface. The pebble winked at the world in vain who knows how long till the Bantu happened by on his hunt for springbok.

The Bantu abandoned the springbok's spoor to answer the blinking call of the pebble. He stood staring down at it, then hunkered and picked it up. The hand holding his assegai went suddenly slick on the weapon's wooden shaft, and the hand cupping the pebble weighed it in wonder.

He had heard of these pebbles and even seen a few, but never in the wildest tales had there been talk of one this size. With it he might, if not cheated, buy a hundred head of breeding cattle, and much land for a kraal, and more than one woman to grow sorghum and children. He laughed at the play of light in his hand, picturing his woman carrying one child strapped to her back while carrying another within.

It was then that the Boer cast his shadow across the Bantu's present and future.

The Bantu closed his hand over the pebble, but it was too late. Turning his head, he knew the Boer had seen the pebble; the pebble's glitter was now in the Boer's eyes.

The Boer, also out hunting, had come upon him while he

31

squatted dreaming. The Boer could stand beyond reach of the assegai's iron tip and speak death from the mouth of his gun.

The Bantu looked at the Boer, knowing the man without ever having seen him before. The elders had a saying: "If you refuse to be made straight when you are green, you will not be made straight when you are dry."

The Boer's mouth had the twist of old meanness. And now it spoke soft words that did not hide the crookedness behind them. "Good day, kaffir. Show me the *mooi klip*."

Unwillingly the Bantu's hand opened to show the Boer the pretty pebble.

The glitter grew in the Boer's eyes. The Bantu's hand closed on the pebble but the light did not go out. The Boer smiled.

"That pebble would make a nice plaything for my child. I will give you my hunting knife for the pebble." The Boer unsheathed his knife to show how it flashed.

The Bantu wrinkled his face in thought, pretending to weigh the offer, then slowly straightened. In pushing himself to his feet he palmed another pebble, a commonplace pebble, and held it in his fist along with the first.

The Boer extended the knife toward the Bantu. "So we see eye to eye. The pebble for the knife."

The Bantu shook his head. "It is a good knife, but I do not wish to trade the pebble."

The Boer slid the knife home in its sheath. "Then it is an even better bargain. I will have the pebble for nothing. Hand it over, kaffir." The Boer raised the gun so that the mouth looked at the Bantu.

The Bantu gestured around at the veldt with his closed tilt. "The pebble belongs to the earth."

The Boer's mouth tightened and the gun's mouth grew

perfectly round. "The pebble belongs to me."

The Bantu half opened his fist as though to give in. Then, while his two smallest fingers held the *mooi klip* fast, the other fingers flung the commonplace pebble spinning far. He made his voice shake with rage rather than fear. "If it is yours find it, as I found it."

The Boer's gaze followed the false flight and the gun's mouth dropped.

The Bantu whirled and ran. He remembered a dip in the earth along the back trail. But before the Bantu reached the dip and sank out of sight the Boer had seen through the trick.

The gun spoke.

So swift was the gun's word that it seemed to the Bantu his flesh heard the gun before his ears. A blow as from a flinty fist struck fire in his side.

Then he was slipping and sliding over the lip of the hollow. He lost his footing and rolled over roughness to the bottom, where dry grass grew and here and there a sizable boulder sunned itself.

He lay half-stunned, half catching his breath. Plucking at his breath's raggedness only raveled it more. He did not want to look at the hole in his side but he looked. He was losing much blood.

To have any time at all, the Bantu knew he must haul himself behind a boulder before the Boer appeared at the rim of the Bantu's barren little world. He heard the Boer's shout of rage as he found strength to plug the hole with grass to leave no trail of blood and found will to make for the nearest boulder, the pebble digging into his palm as he thrust himself along.

Rounding the boulder, the Bantu began to stretch his own length and the assegai's in the boulder's grudging wedge of shadow, then saw he shared the shade with a snake.

The snake's tongue flickered.

The Bantu's mouth pulled against pain in a smile. "Snake, do not waste your poison. I am already dead."

But the snake did not listen. It coiled to strike.

The Bantu struck first. The assegai spitted the snake and the snake writhed and died.

The Boer's voice broke into the Bantu's world. "Kaffir, I know you are down there. You cannot hide from me or outrun my gun. Show yourself and give me the pebble and I will let you go."

The Bantu tightened his hold on the pebble and smiled at the hurt. The Boer did not have the pebble yet.

But neither was there anywhere to hide the pebble from the Boer. If the Bantu scrabbled a hole, the Boer would spot the digging. If the Bantu cast the pebble away, the Boer would never leave this cup of earth till he had found it.

The Bantu eyed the snake. "Where, oh, snake?"

And the dead snake answered silently.

The Bantu laughed. "Thank you, oh, snake."

He weighed the pebble on his palm. It looked too big to go down but the Bantu made one last scan of it, put it in his mouth, and swallowed.

The pebble started down, then stuck in his windpipe, blocking all air. The Bantu's eyes bulged and his throat convulsed. Then the pebble worked its way and went down.

Sooner or later the Boer would know the Bantu had swallowed the pebble and would slit his belly and writhe searching fingers through his slippery guts. The Bantu put his hands over the grass plug. For this plan of the snake's to work, the Bantu had to hold himself together and hang on to life till the Boer found him.

To hasten the Boer's coming, the Bantu twisted so that his feet left the boulder's shade. The Boer would see the movement.

Drumbeat of death, the Boer's boots trampled dry grass.

Carefully the Boer rounded the boulder. In a sweep the Boer's glance took in the Bantu and the spitted snake.

The Bantu looked up at the shimmer of heat that was the Boer. He let his hands fall from the wound.

The Boer looked down. The Bantu's hands lay open and empty. Fresh blood loosened the grass plug from blood that had crusted around the wound and the Boer saw the Bantu had not stuffed the pebble in the wound. The ground ringing the boulder showed no smoothing over. With his foot the Boer rolled the Bantu wound side down. The Bantu's body had not been hiding anything. The Boer rolled the Bantu back with his foot.

He prodded the Bantu with the mouth of the gun. "Where is the *mooi klip*? If you have swallowed it and cannot cough it up I will take my hunting knife and slit your belly."

The Bantu pointed to the snake. Trying to hide the rawness of his throat, he spoke. "What you seek is in the snake's mouth."

The Boer narrowed his eyes. "Kaffir, if you are lying, you are just putting off your belly-slitting a little and adding to my anger a lot."

The Bantu only steadied his pointing finger. "What you seek is in the snake's mouth."

The Boer hesitated but a moment. After all, the kaffir lay helpless, eyes glazing, and the snake lay dead. The Boer leaned his gun against the boulder and knelt to probe the snake's mouth.

Reptiles have lasting reflexes. Even dead, a freshly killed snake will sink its fangs into probing flesh.

The Boer cried out.

After a time all was stillness.

And all is stillness still, but for the wind through the bones.

EXPERIMENT

Paul Snider unlocked the door and Ernest Pusey lugged the suitcase inside. Snider closed and bolted the door but did not switch on the light. Enough illumination came in through the uncurtained window from the street lamps to let them see what they were doing once their eyes grew used to the dimness.

Pusey unlatched the suitcase and assembled the components that lay neatly fitted in foam plastic molded to their shapes. The bare apartment had not even an orange box or someone's old ironing board, much less table and chairs, so Pusey stood the sturdy suitcase up on end against the window and rested the assembly on that and on the window sill. The device had its own power pack, so there was no necessity to plug into an outlet. All that remained was to pick their target for tonight.

They gazed across at the apartment complex that had yielded them subjects every night this past week. It was the darkened windows, not the scattered bright few, that drew their eyes.

"All right, Pusey, let's get cracking." With heavy humor Snider gestured broadly. "You do the honors. Pick another subject at random."

Pusey felt his face twitch and was glad for the comparative dark. He put his cheek to the stock of the device and sighted through the night scope. He pointed to the leftmost tower. "I'm choosing Block A."

"Okay. Narrow it down."

Pusey scanned a row of bedroom windows. He passed over a couple—hadn't they heard of blinds?—and a woman who sat sleeping against the headboard of her bed, facing the pattern of a channel that had gone off the air.

They needed a subject who was alone and the woman would have served, but Pusey decided against her. She seemed his mother's age. Maybe he was getting soft. He tightened his mouth and would have swung back to the woman, but again he decided no. Snider would have held that momentary indecision against him. Snider and Pusey could have no doubts or second thoughts.

His scope pulled in a man alone in bed. Warm night, no blanket, no pajama top. Shaggy male. No doubts, no second thoughts.

"This is the one. Twelve up, six across—" Pusey felt a sense of power, yet mounting misgivings made him awkward. He pressed the trigger and locked it in place. There was a hum and a small red dot appeared in the man's bedroom. "See it?"

Snider snorted. "Of course I see it. Zero in."

Pusey sought to pin the dot to the man's head. He could feel Snider's disdain and displeasure as the dot wavered. That only made it harder to hold the dot on target. It didn't help that the subject picked these moments to turn, and toss in response to some unpleasant inner vision.

Snider lost patience. "If you have qualms about this, Pusey, you're in the wrong line. The company doesn't like softies. I'm telling you right now I've been evaluating you, and the hesitancy I've noticed doesn't help you one bit. You seemed gung ho as long as you were shuffling the papers setting this project up. Okay, theorizing is fine, it's what gets projects like Mindbend off the ground, but in the end it all comes down to seeing whether or not it works. This is one experiment it's no good using mice and rats for. The proper study of mankind is man."

Pusey blinked hard to wash the sting of sweat from his eyes. He stifled the fatal urge to tell Snider that some people are rats—Paul Snider, for example. Look at how Snider stood poised to hog the credit for success or weasel out of the blame for failure. Pusey set his jaw and tightened all his muscles to make himself part of the device. The dot held steady near the subject's ear.

"Here we are."

"That's more like it, Pusey. Now see if you can manage to hold it there while I work on the subject."

Snider picked up the mike that patched into the light gun. This was the part Snider loved. He pitched his voice in a sepulchral whisper.

His whisper rode the laser beam to the sleeping man.

"Listen. Listen to your inner voices. There's evil abroad in the land, a global conspiracy of ungodly forces. Why else is the world in such sad shape, with injustice triumphant? On every hand, sinister influences. These people are doing the devil's work. Beware! One of your neighbors, one even of your fellow workers, one of your best friends, one even of your dearest and closest relatives may be in league with the devil's brood. You never know who you can trust. Listen. Listen to your inner voices."

The dot slid off as the man sat up in bed and stared around. Pusey got it back on target. Snider whispered a repeat of his spiel. The man swung out of bed and stood swaying dizzily and shaking his head. Then he strode to the window and glared out at the night.

Though Pusey knew the man could not see him, he drew back in spite of himself. Snider thumbed the mike off and laughed.

"Don't be afraid, Pusey. He doesn't know what hit him. Now get back on target. We'll show him he's not dreaming."

The dot found the man's head again. The whisper reached the man's mind again.

Pusey managed to hold on the man as the man moved around and switched his television set first on and then off. No, the voice did not come from there. The man picked up a glass from the night table and held the mouth of the glass to the bedroom wall he shared with a neighbor and pressed his ear to the bottom of the glass. No, the voice did not come from there.

Snider thumbed himself off to say, "Beautiful, beautiful." He eyed his digital watch. "We'll give him a breathing spell, let him think it's over, and when he's convinced himself he's imagined the whole thing we'll hit him again."

The man seemed to feel the feverish warmth of the infrared beam. Invisible to him, the dot rode the back of his hand as he palmed his forehead, testing. The dot couldn't follow him when he took the glass to the bathroom but it picked him up again when he came back with water in the glass and pills in his hand. He swallowed the tablets and washed them down, then sat slumped on the edge of his bed. Finally, he shrugged heavily and made ready to lie down.

Snider switched the mike on and whispered his message once more. The man pressed his palms to his ears, but he could not keep the whisper out.

Snider switched the mike off, seeming smug and yet sorry it was over. "That winds up this phase." He stretched and yawned. "I'll be glad to get back on daylight schedule—this has played hell with my biological rhythms, to say nothing of my social life." He hurried to set the record straight. "Of course, no sacrifice is too great to make for the company."

Pusey chimed in automatically. "Of course." He unlocked the trigger of the light gun. The dot vanished. He watched the subject. The man still sat slumped on the edge of the bed, his head jerking around from time to time suspiciously as if to catch the echoes in his mind. "How do we follow up?"

Snider was at his most condescending. "Simplicity itself. No need to waste precious man-hours studying the subsequent behavior of individual subjects. The scientific way to establish the effectiveness of this technique is to make a statistical comparison. We'll check with the local precinct house—without telling the police what we're looking for, of course. All they have to know is that a government agency is interested in variations in the incidence of crime over, say, the past six months—a recent jump in unprovoked attacks on strangers, on neighbors, on fellow workers, on friends, on relatives. A sudden increase in paranoiac reports to the police about conspiracies. That's what we're really looking for. Because that will prove the technique works."

He laughed. "I don't imagine you'll mind poring over the statistics. That's more your line anyway. Paperwork's so much easier on the nerves, isn't it, Pusey?" He grew brisk. "We'll pack up now. Here's the door key. I'll go down and bring the car around front. Save some time. You police the room and make sure we've left nothing to show anyone from the company's ever been here, then lock up. I'll be waiting."

Pusey had started to disassemble the light gun. He paused to nod. "Right."

Snider left. Pusey held still, listening to Snider's footsteps whisper away. His face tightened and he screwed the light gun together again. He found the bedroom across the way and pinned the dot to the subject once more. He spoke softly into the mike.

"Listen," he said. "Listen to your inner voices. You will know no peace till you strike down your enemy. Your enemy has a name. The name is Paul Snider. His address is—"

A WREATH FOR JUSTICE

Last year's leftover tinsel icicles did for this year's Christmas tree. Thomas Orth's hands hung the strips on the boughs. He watched the hands as though they belonged to someone else. Strange how you still went through the motions long after the meaning had gone. The few gift packages under the tree flaunted their false gaiety.

The doorbell rang.

An icicle of fear stabbed into his chest, freezing him through and through. Who, at this hour . . . ? Then he hurried, dripping tinsel, to answer before the doorbell rang again and wakened Lucy. He gaped on seeing who stood there— Kenneth Mathwick, Sr. himself.

Mathwick leaned forward, pushing his imposing presence at Orth. "Quick, let me in."

Still gaping, Orth gave way. As Mathwick stepped in and swung around to shut the door Orth saw he carried a briefcase in one gloved hand. He had brought the night chill in with him as well, and Orth shivered.

Mathwick looked past Orth. His eyes darted left and right. His voice came out a harsh whisper. "Your wife?"

"Lucy?" Orth felt stupid. After all, he had only one wife and her name was Lucy. "She's upstairs. Asleep."

"No one else here?"

"No." Orth spoke mechanically, his mind trying to unwhirl.

"Ah." He wasted a moment, drumming on his briefcase. Then he cleared his throat and put on the well-known Mathwick getting-down-to-business expression. "You know Judith Hillerin, of course?"

Of course, Orth reflected. She was the typist with the in-
dolent look-how-I'm-put-together shape and the insolent I-
dare-you-to-slap-me face.

Mathwick was waiting for him to answer. Now it was
Orth's turn to clear his throat. "She's one of the typists, isn't
she? Why do you ask?"

For some reason the worn star on the top of the tree held
Mathwick's gaze. He spoke to Orth at last but kept his eyes on
the star. "The office Christmas party—you were there this
evening, weren't you?"

Orth's mouth slid slightly to the left. He was only a lowly
slave and Mathwick Senior was Mathwick Senior, but had his
presence at the party made so little impression? Mathwick's
glance had passed over him several times, together with a
fixed smile, and one of those times Mathwick had even raised
a paper cup to him. Now it would seem that the boardroom
had been, for once in the year, loud and crowded enough to
joggle him out of Mathwick's sight and mind.

"I was there, but I stayed for only a drink or two. I
would've liked to have stayed longer, but I felt I'd better leave
early to be with Lucy."

"Yes, I can see how you would feel that way, especially on
this night." Mathwick's voice went sentimental, almost
mushily so, but his eyes sharpened. "How is your wife these
days? I understand she hasn't been well for some time."

Orth still had enough courage in him from his drink or two
at the party to draw himself up and try to stare Mathwick
down. This was his castle and no outsider had the right to
peer behind the arras—but Mathwick wasn't stare-downable.

"Well, the doctors haven't been able to find anything
physically wrong with her, but she does have to take medica-
tion for her nerves."

The fire in Mathwick's eyes could have come from his

mentally rubbing his hands. "Sad. Dismal for her and hard on you. Yes, that's what I had heard, that she's in this drugged state much of the time." Mathwick's eyes probed Orth's. "Then your wife would not be able to testify—I mean, say for sure—that you in fact left the party early and came straight home?"

Orth blinked. He opened his mouth, without having yet formed in his mind what he meant to say, but in any case Mathwick gave him no chance to speak.

"No, hear me out. You could say you stayed on at the office party till almost an hour or so ago, when it ended, and your story would hold up."

Orth spoke slowly, dragging it out of himself. "I suppose I could. But why should I?"

"Because something happened after you left." Mathwick's brow glistened. "I remember—and no doubt others remember—that the Hillerin girl was still full of life toward the party's end, when she dropped out of sight and I took it she had gone home or wherever. Junior and I were alone there at the finish. No one—aside from Junior and me, and now you—knows about it yet." He paused.

Orth had to force himself to ask. "Knows what?"

Mathwick's face twitched. "Junior tells me he was too drunk to remember actually doing it. All he knows is, when he came out of his haze he was alone with Judith in his private office and she was dead, with his letter opener thrust in her." Mathwick shuddered. "Awful. I didn't believe him till I went in and saw with my own eyes, and I still can't believe it." He shuddered again. "The blood on the carpet."

Orth had always felt a dull hate for Junior ever since Junior had come into the firm, starting above Orth and rising from there. Grim pleasure overrode shock, then honest wonderment overrode grim pleasure. He stared at Mathwick and tried to read between the lines of his face. "Why come here and tell me? Why not go to the police?"

Mathwick drew in a lot of air, as though more for size than for speech. "Because I can't let Junior go to jail. That would end everything for me. Junior has too much to live for to let one mad moment jeopardize his whole future. I built the firm to last after my time." His gaze fixed on the star again. "I know everyone thinks I'm cold and hard. Maybe I am. But if I am it isn't because I'm selfish. All I've ever done I've done for Junior."

Orth couldn't help making the thrust. "Why don't you take the blame for him, then?"

Mathwick waved that away. "Everyone would know I couldn't have done it. For one thing, I had no opportunity. Too many employees hovered around me every minute of the evening." His gaze fixed on Orth. "So I need someone else. I need someone who would not have drawn notice if he slipped away to the inner office with the Hillerin tramp. I need you."

"Me?" It came out a high-alto *mi*.

"It was an act of passion, a moment of madness. Too much to drink, and you're unused to drinking. Too much frustration at home, and you're faced with this temptation at hand. Perfectly understandable. Everyone knows the Hillerin girl was a teaser. Everyone knows you've always been a quiet person, a dutiful employee, a solid citizen. You'll get off lightly, especially if you come forward of your own free will. You're childless, you have a sick wife to care for. You have little to lose, a lot to gain. I'll give you—"

"You're out of your mind." There went his job, but Orth didn't care. He stared at Mathwick and anger surged. The man really thought that he should be willing to sacrifice himself for Junior, of all people. "Why should I—"

Mathwick cut him off with a gesture. "A million reasons."

He opened the briefcase, playing it close to his chest, and withdrew a sheaf of bonds. "I had these in my office safe. One million dollars in negotiable securities. Bearer bonds. See for yourself."

He placed the bonds on Orth's palm, which found itself coming up to receive them. Orth studied the bonds. They were the real thing and they would add up to a million, maybe more in a rising market.

Mathwick drew out of the briefcase a stiffly rolled handkerchief which he unfolded to lay bare a letter opener with a three-inch-deep dark red stain on the dagger-like blade. "What do you say? Your prints on the handle in exchange for a million dollars."

There was a long silence and a long stillness, then slowly, slowly, Orth's other palm rose.

Mathwick breathed out an invisible heaviness, then his voice grew brisk. "No, your other hand. You're right-handed, aren't you?"

Orth nodded numbly and switched the bonds to his left hand. Mathwick placed the letter opener on Orth's right palm. Orth held bonds and opener as though weighing them in the balance, then closed his hand over the hilt.

Mathwick sandwiched Orth's hand between his and pressed it hard to the hilt as though molding clay. After making sure each finger had good contact, Mathwick freed Orth's hand. Orth opened his hand. Mathwick's waiting handkerchief swallowed the letter opener carefully and the briefcase swallowed both—with finality. "I'm really deeply grateful to you, Thomas, and I'll see that you get the best counsel around. All you have to do now is give me an hour to take care of replacing the letter opener, then turn yourself in."

Mathwick strode to the window, parted the curtains, and

looked out. "I parked my car around the corner to make sure no one would see it in front of your house. And I made sure no one saw me come in. Now I'm making sure no one sees me leave."

He nodded farewell at Orth and put his hand on the doorknob.

Suddenly a suspicion seized Orth, convulsing his grip on the bonds and screeching silently at him to snatch back the letter opener before it was too late. "Hold on, Mathwick."

Kenneth Mathwick, Sr. turned his head and lifted an eyebrow. "Eh?"

"How do I know this isn't all a frame?"

Mathwick frowned "What do you mean, all a frame?"

The words rushed out. "I mean how do I know you won't try to have your cake and eat it too? Now, that you have my prints on the letter opener, what's to keep you from bolstering the case against me and at the same time getting your million dollars back? How do I know that after you . . . replace the letter opener, and they find Judith that way, you won't discover that the bonds are missing from your safe? I'd never be able to prove that you made this visit and that we closed this deal. So how do I know you won't lead the police to believe I killed Judith, not in a mad moment—because, as you said, I'm the quiet type—but more believably in desperation when she caught me robbing your safe?"

Mathwick shook his head. "The thought never entered my mind. I give you my word." He turned the knob.

"Not so fast, Mathwick. Whether or not it was there before, or would've come to you on your way back to the office, the thought's there now. So we'll settle it now."

Mathwick almost hissed with impatience. "I've no time to sit down and reason with you. I need to get back before one of the night people stumbles on the body. There's always that chance though I locked the door to the office. You'll just have to trust me, Orth." With an air of finality he made to go.

"Mathwick, I said to hold on." Was that his own voice, so suddenly hard and menacing? It had stopped Mathwick. "I can phone the cops and have them at the office before you get back to it."

Mathwick looked at Orth and for the first time gave him a nod of respect. "What do you suggest, then?" He frowned, but not angrily. "How can I satisfy you that I won't double-cross you?"

Orth found himself ready with the answer. "Write me out a note saying you're giving me the bonds of your own free will in payment for services rendered. If you're leveling with me I'll never have to show the note."

Mathwick's frown deepened. Then he erased it, sighed and let his shoulders droop. Though he had wiped his frown, suddenly he looked his age and more.

Yet he had control of himself—Orth had to give him that. Mathwick's hand did not tremble noticeably as he wrote. There was nothing more to say, except with their eyes, and they parted silently.

A wind had risen, and it took Orth a good solid slam to close the door after Mathwick. Orth's heart thumped an echo. Sure enough, in answer to his listening he heard the springs of Lucy's bed and her drugged footsteps moving to the door of her room.

"Who was that you were talking to?" she asked.

"Santa Claus."

One thing Lucy lacked was a sense of humor. He hadn't expected her to laugh, and she didn't; he had expected her to go on talking, and she did. Her tone was querulous; he wasn't listening to her words.

His free hand still held the feel of the hilt; he rubbed it

against his thigh. He had to find a safe place for the bonds—and the note before the police came for him or he turned himself in. The sheaf grew heavy in his hand, but its heaviness took a weight off his mind. *A million dollars.*

A million dollars could buy Lucy the best medical care. A million dollars could buy him a new life after he served his time.

Thomas Orth looked at the star on the tree without seeing it. He saw himself touching Judith Hillerin's look-how-I'm-put-together shape, saw himself trying to kiss Judith Hillerin's I-dare-you-to-slap-me face, heard Judith Hillerin's mocking voice, saw red, then saw blood, and lastly saw his hand drawing away from the letter opener in Judith Hillerin's body.

A million dollars could even buy the truth.

WASWOLF

(WITH THANKS TO CHARLES G. WAUGH)

Bain melted the dimes and quarters in a crucible, then ladled the molten metal . . . saw flow from form to morph in a smoothly twisting stream . . . into bullet molds. While the bullets cooled, Bain packed a good charge of powder into cartridges and cleaned and oiled his service .38. When he could handle the bullets, he fitted them into the cartridges and crimped them in place, then loaded the rounds into the chambers of the .38's cylinder. It was only when the wolf jumped the six foot-high cyclone fence to get at the bitch in heat that Bain, stepping between and leveling his gun, remembered the silver content of the clad coins of these days was next to nil.

Sticky with sweat, Bain awoke from the same nightmare to the same real world. What he could see of the sky through his window seemed bright enough, but he had the sense of thunderheads lurking just beyond the fleecy shape-shifting clouds.

He took his time getting out of bed. No sudden moves. He was aging and had learned that rising too quickly left the blood behind, made him black out.

He listened to the radio that had wakened him. The announcer, giving a cold reading of hot news, stumbled over foreign place-names. Made no difference; when it came to human-made and human-suffered catastrophes, countries were interchangeable.

Bain shoved slowly to his feet. Straightened up, stooped. Bain tried to smile, but his face felt stiff. Nothing to laugh at as long as the task he had set himself stayed unfinished.

He had solved the case years ago, but never resolved it—and now his flesh, his bones, his very soul, were telling him not all that much time remained to him if he were to bring the culprit to justice.

Time. The thought passed over him like the shadow of a bird.

High hysterics on the part of the radio, a voice announcing the sale of appliances at unbelievable prices, brought Bain into the here and now with a shiver. Bain snapped off the sound and smiled sourly. He believed the voice when the voice said unbelievable.

Lots of things, maybe even most things, were unbelievable. Even Bain's own inner voice could be unbelievable.

After eighteen unrewarding years of watching the Lupescus and their dog, eighteen fruitless years of spying on them from just across the fence, eighteen wasted years of looking for some telltale sign, some giveaway slip, some momentary lapse, Bain could no longer swear to what he believed.

He put himself on the stand—had his personality started to split along the grain?—and examined himself crossly. *Do you mean to tell this court that after all these years, you can be sure you saw what you say you saw? Remember, you're under oath.*

Bain remembered the suddenly ravaged faces of the Lupescus. He could look back and see them age a decade in the ten minutes it took him to convince them he wanted their son for rape and murder. And yet he had read something more than, or something other than, fear in their eyes. He had read a sorrowful yet prideful look of complicity. That shared look said plainly that they felt sure their son was safe from harm.

Holding their heads high, they let him search their house

from attic to cellar without a warrant. They had nothing to hide, they said, and they stood passively and quietly by, petting and soothing their dog that snarled and would have snapped at the intruders, while Bain and his partner all but tore the house apart for hiding places and ransacked the rooms for clues. True, the Lupescus seemed shaken when Bain showed them the murder weapon came from their carving set, and their faces went stony when he turned up bloodstained shirt and semen-stiffened pants in a hamper. But they clung to one another—and to their stubborn and almost gloating certainty about their son's immunity from prosecution, even if they no longer asserted his guiltlessness.

There was no question in Bain's mind he had found, or at least followed, the perp. The patrol car had surprised the rapist finishing off his victim with a knife, frozen him in the spotlight for an instant, then given hot pursuit when he took off down the alley. Bain, lighter and quicker back then, chased him on foot, over fences and through hedges, crookedly straight to the Lupescus' house. And there the perp vanished. Bain saw the youth drop the knife to climb the oak in the backyard, watched him leap through an open window into what turned out to be Val Lupsecu's bedroom. At that very instant, Bain's partner, clued by Bain's walkie-talkie, pulled up in front. Almost immediately other cars and officers responding to the broadcast squeal surrounded the block and sealed off the area. So where Val vanished to puzzled Bain.

The Lupescus stood with their bristling dog and watched the search substantiate Val Lupescu's disappearance into pale moonbeamish air. To Bain's eye, the animal looked more wolf than dog.

Bain remembered the shock when he first glimpsed the malevolent intelligence in the topaz eyes. He remembered putting his sweaty hand on the grip of the service .38 in his holster, his fingers itching for the beast to go from fangy growl to flowing leap, remembered raising his chin, his bared throat inviting the beast to spring.

But the dog smiled, though Bain made out red hunger back of its jaws, and held itself tightly still. Not till later, once the impossible thought lodged in Bain's mind, did Bain think to check with the neighbor on the right—the house on the left was vacant and up for sale—whether the Lupescus *had* a dog. The woman seemed half-blind and half-deaf and would have been wholly useless on the witness stand, but she did say she couldn't say as she'd ever seen or heard a dog on the Lupescus' premises. By the time a few days later when Bain asked the Lupescus where was the dog's collar and its leash and where was its license, the dog sported a collar and a tag that said its name was Fire—although the Lupescus pronounced it Fear-a—and the Lupescus produced the receipt for a paid-up license.

That left Bain with a crazy theory he didn't dare voice. Didn't mean he didn't dare follow it up. But he had to follow it up on his own time and in secret.

Secret at least from his bosses, who seemed satisfied the department had done its duty by putting out an all-points bulletin on Val Lupescu—age fifteen, height five feet ten inches, weight 150, pale complexion, dark hair, topaz eyes—and by following up with wanted posters. As soon as the story died in the media, the department seemed content to let the case folder gather dust, and crumble to the same, in the inactive files. Bain's chief, the one time Bain tried to convince him to keep it open, shrugged and said the Lupescu kid was bound to come to a bad end in the world of runaways; one way or another, Val would get what he had coming to him.

Not secret from the Lupescus; Bain *wished them to know* he

was still and always after Val, for only by rattling them or wearing them down could he prove his crazy theory.

Bain felt so strongly about it, so driven to show himself he hadn't gone wacko, so determined to make Val pay for the crime, that he took early retirement and moved not to the Gulf-fishing Florida of his dreams but to the house to the left of the Lupescus. Bain had lived alone ever since his wife walked out on him and got the divorce he never fully understood her reasons for wanting, and he had no one but himself to answer to.

In the radio's silence, Bain heard the Lupescus' car start up and pull out of their gravel drive. He padded to the window to see who-all was aboard. Sometimes they took Fire, sometimes they didn't. When they did, Bain would tail them in his own jalopy; when they left Fire home, Bain, too would stay home and use the absence of the supportive parents to torment Fire to the utmost.

This morning the parents went alone. Sometimes they were cute and seemed to be alone, but Fire crouched on the floor in the back. This morning, though, Bain caught sight of Fire stretched up to stare out the parlor window at the car shaking the gravel from its tires and vanishing down the street. Dust hung in the air; no breeze and another hot one.

Bain rubbed his facial bristle but decided against shaving even though he'd feel cooler without it. Used to be, while he was on the force, he had to shave twice a day and yet still powder to mask the bluish look. Now his beard had grayed so he could get by with shaving every other day.

He put on pants that had long since lost their permanent press, and let his shirt hang over his waistline to hide the zipper-exposing give of seams at the top of the fly. From the dresser top he picked up and distributed in his pockets his key chain with the dog whistle fastened to it, a few sheets of facial tissue, his billfold and handful of change, and the police shield and service revolver he had hung on to. He went to the kitchen for a six-pack of beer from the refrigerator and carried the six-pack out onto the front porch.

Everything about him seemed heavy—heavy features, heavy build, heavy walk. He made for the fraying wicker chair and seated himself heavily, as though tired. Then he faced the Lupescus' house and came to life, at least in the eyes. He switched on the portable fan to waft his scent toward the Lupescus' house.

Fire must've had warning before that, must surely have heard the screen door squeak and the floorboards groan, but stayed stretched and immobile, as though posing for a portrait of man's best friend awaiting man's return home. Now he slowly turned his head to meet Bain's gaze.

Bain popped a top and chugalugged, crushed the empty in his hand, and made suddenly to hurl it at the window Fire looked out of.

Fire didn't twist away. Stayed put and just kept looking straight at Bain.

Not that Bain had expected anything else. Damn monster knew Bain knew better than to lay himself open to a charge of malicious mischief. Bain had taken care all these years to stay within the law—or at least to restrict breaches of the law to measures only Fire could testify to only if Fire transformed back to Val. Measures such as blowing the dog whistle with its sounds above human range.

Bain let the empty fall to the porch floor. He drew out the dog whistle on his key chain, made a swipe at his mouth with the back of his hand, and put the whistle to his lips.

Now Fire twisted away from the window and dropped out of sight. This Bain had expected. Bain was never sure exactly where the sound drove Fire, under a bed or deep into a closet, but he felt sure it did drive Fire mad. The howling told him so.

If Bain had not been the cause of it, the howling would have been enough to drive Bain mad. But he was in control of it and could make it keep up long past what otherwise would have been his own limit of endurance.

The howling had been bad enough for the half-deaf woman who lived on the other side of the Lupescus to complain to the cops and the S.P.C.A. about, blaming the Lupescus for neglecting or mistreating their newly acquired pet; nobody but Bain and Fire—and maybe the Lupescus— knew of Bain's hand in it, Bain laying off whenever anyone came next door to investigate. But that was in the beginning; the neighbor woman had died ten years ago, and the couple who bought her house were away at work during the hours Bain blew the whistle and Fire howled.

These days, as right now, Bain blew it more out of habit than in hope. Give the son of a bitch credit, Fire had never let the torment drive him out of his shape—force him from dog form and dog hearing—at least so far as Bain knew. A few more blasts now, then Bain let up for the time being.

He had worked the six-pack down to zero by the time the newsboy rode by sailing papers onto the lawns. Bain waited for the next part of the ritual. Anyone who didn't know what Bain knew would have thought only that the Lupescus had trained their dog well.

Fire exited the house through the swinging panel cut into the lower half of the front door. With side glances Bain's way, Fire trotted to the paper, picked it up in his jaws, and. headed back for the door.

Bain pushed to his feet and moved to the porch railing nearest the fence. "Hold it, Val. Come here to the fence. I want to talk to you."

The dog did not pause.

Bain's voice took on a hard edge. "Want me to blow the whistle some more?"

Fire veered, and stalked stiff-legged toward the fence.

"That's a *good* boy." Bain bared his teeth in a grin. "Like to go for my throat, wouldn't you?" Bain half-hoped that the dog would try just that. He knew, though, there was little likelihood. The fence stood too high for a dog—or even a wolf—to overleap. But it would have been satisfying to see Fire try. Bain's hand in his pocket was on his gun. God, to be able to say, "Nice try!" and shoot. End this the right way once and for all.

Fire stood still, but the vise of his jaws tightened on the paper.

Bain grimaced and shook his head. "When you going to give it up and change back? I have to say I never thought you'd stick it out this long. Maybe if I could've seen this far down the road, I might not've started this—what? dogging you? hounding you?" He chuckled. "Good, huh? Yeah, wolf, you can't keep me from your door." He shook his head to clear it for what he meant to say. "But what I called you over for was, don't you think it's time we had it out?" He grew earnest. "Right now, before your folks come home from shopping—aren't you sick of those cans of dog food and the flea collars? Right now, while it's just between the two of us, can't you be man enough to face up to what you did—*as a man?*"

Bain told himself that the dog looked weary and worn, had dull coat and lackluster eyes. But the dog, the animal that looked more wolf than the German Shepherd it passed as, panted quietly around the newspaper and gazed at Bain with disdain.

One last try to reason with the monster. "We can't change what's deep down. You're what you are, and I'm what I am.

Tell you right out I'll always be a cop, always be looking to nail you. But just what are you? Something that doesn't have the guts to get up on its hind legs and be the man you started out being? Or are you Val? Could you be yourself again? Or have you forgotten what your true self is?"

Fire stood unmoved.

Bain gave a sharp gesture of dismissal.

Fire raised a hind leg and took a territorial leak on the fence.

Bain's temples throbbed. This was what they called seeing red. He pulled his gun and leveled it at Fire. What could they get him for if he shot a dog? Nothing, really. At most a fine. Almost he squeezed off the shot.

But it wasn't a dog he was after, it was a man. It was as a man that Val had to get his. Bain put away his gun unfired He didn't know what a wolf-dog's peripheral vision was, didn't know if Fire had even been aware of Bain taking aim at him.

Bain watched Fire trot unhurriedly to the door opening and shove himself inside with the Lupescus' newspaper still firmly in his jaws.

Heavily, Bain negotiated the sagging steps of his porch to pick up from his scraggly lawn his own copy of the daily paper.

He plunked himself down in the wicker chair and skimmed the news. The second section featured travel and leisure. Bain grimaced at a shot of a record tarpon and the proud sportsman. He turned the page with a snap and fixed on a bevy of beauty queens lined up for a contest. What smooth flesh, what dangerous curves. Bain shot a glance toward the Lupescus' house. What was Fire making of this? Could a dog's eyes make sense of the dots? Why not? Bain knew dogs made sense of the lines on television screens. If Fire's eyes were looking at this picture, what was Val's mind thinking about it? What were his gonads doing?

Bain rolled the paper into a bat and smacked it against one palm. By God, that was the way to go.

He got to his feet too fast, swayed a second, but the wave of blackness passed away. He moved more slowly into the house and into the kitchen. The draw was the magnet-held calendar on the refrigerator door. His eyes picked out this month's phases of the moon. He smiled back at the sketched smile of a full moon. Luck was with him; fate was on his side.

Full moon tonight. Fire would be out on the Lupescus' lawn pointing his nose at the moon.

Bain stepped lightly to the bathroom, where he took his time shaving.

The third bar he hit was the right one. Just as sleazy and noisy as the other two, but it was the one where he found the girl he was looking for. Not *the* girl as such, but the *type* girl. One young enough and pretty enough and curvy enough, and one like enough to the girl Val had raped and butchered eighteen long years ago, but one dumb enough to believe the shield Bain flashed still meant what it said.

He flashed his wad first and bought the watered drinks she'd be getting her cut on. Her dress clung to her where she didn't burst out of it; her hair was piled high on her head; she clanked with junk jewelry. He gave a guy who wanted to horn in a hard look that made the guy drift. Her lips parted; her eyes shone. Bain and the girl sat alone together squeezed in a corner booth, and he led her on till he could get her for soliciting. In spite of thinning, the drinks still packed enough proof to make this Brenda—the name she claimed—look even better as the evening wore on. But he wasn't out to work up and satisfy his own lust. He had her in mind for Val, for the man in the dog, for the beast in the beast. And when the waiters started upending the chairs on the tables, Brenda said, "Thirty bucks for an all-nighter. Your place or mine?" and he had her.

She looked around and raised her eyebrows at the precautions he had taken. "Why do you have that big, high fence all around?"

He kept his eyes roving as he unchained the gate in the fence and let himself and Brenda in. Didn't spot Fire yet, but it wasn't high full moon yet either. "Not only that, I have traps you don't see and poisoned bait." That much was true, but Bain never really wished that these would do Fire in. Bain made a fine distinction: it mattered that Val die *like* a dog, if not *as* a dog. But no punishment, no death, seemed enough unless and until Val face it *as* a man, if not *like* a man. Bain rechained the gate from the inside and gestured Brenda to follow him onto the porch. "There's a mean dog next door that would just love to tear me apart."

"Brrr." She gave a delicious shiver. "Aren't there laws against keeping vicious animals?"

"Laws again soliciting, too."

She flushed. "You can go after me; why can't you go after the dog?"

"I am—in my own way." He let them into the house. He burned a bit with shame at the mess the place looked, though be felt sure Brenda had seen plenty worse. "In fact, be honest with you, that's what this is all about."

"I don't understand."

"You don't have to understand. You just have to do what I tell you to do."

She didn't understand what he had in mind, and gave him an arch look, but she went along when he told her what she had to do. Anything must've seemed better than a bust. So he didn't want to score, didn't want any specialities. All he wanted was for her to lounge on his porch in her slip. She shrugged and said okay. If that was all it took to keep him from taking her downtown and booking her, that seemed a small price to pay. Maybe her way of getting back at him was to tease him by asking him to help her unzip and by rubbing up against him while he fumbled for the tab and by letting the shoulder straps of her slip hang loose after she shimmied out of her dress.

That was all right with Bain. The more stirrings he felt, the likelier Val would feel something. Let Val get an eyeful.

It took an hour longer before Val got the eyeful, and then it was Brenda, not Bain, who spotted him first. Bain crouched hard by in the shadows but was dozing—at this point was having a sharp exchange with himself: "What do you mean, a leopard can't change his spots? If he leaps from here to there, of course he changes spots"—when Brenda's gasp snapped him to.

She cast a reproachful side-glance at Bain. "That's a fine-looking doggy. He don't look mean at all."

And indeed, Fire sat quietly and stared soulfully, not at the moon but at Brenda. He had let himself out through the swinging panel of the Lupescus front door and come right up to the chain link fence without a sound reaching Bain's ears.

Guess the old hearing was going. But Bain smiled, watching Fire sit there like that. It was going to work; suddenly he knew it was going to work.

He held his breath as Fire reared up and stretched full-length against the fence. Fire fixed his topaz gaze on Brenda. Bain couldn't tell from here whether Fire's mouth slavered, but he could see the tongue flicker and he could see Brenda begin to get the message.

She threw her words over her shoulder as though she

could not tear her eyes from Fire. "Hey, this dog looks like he's going to go for me."

Bain whispered gently but urgently. "Don't panic. I'm covering you. Just stand still so you don't step in the line of fire."

Fire dropped to all fours and backed away from the fence. For a second Bain feared that Fire had heard him and that prudence was overriding prurience and Bain cursed himself under his breath. But Fire withdrew far enough for a good running start, gathered himself, and came charging. He threw himself upward, and when he saw he couldn't clear the fence, pulled back for another try.

Brenda turned trembling to face Bain. "Stand still, hell. What kind of kinkiness you into, anyway? If that crazy dog comes over the fence, I'm running inside the house."

"He can't come over the fence. Not as a dog, he can't."

Brenda gaped at Bain. "What does that mean, not as a dog?"

Fire—Val—answered her by metamorphosing, flowing from form to form. The wolf-dog, with a painful lengthening and rearticulating of bones, a transforming of fur, became a naked man, pale and ghostly in the moonlight. The man stood tall, walked jerkily to the fence, and began to climb.

The man's eyes fixed on Brenda. From deep in the man's throat came long-unused sounds trying to shape words. "I-ee . . . lo-ove, . . . I-ee . . . ha-ate . . ."

"For God's sake!"

Brenda's cry broke the spell for Bain, though she herself seemed too stunned to move.

Going for his gun, Bain rose swiftly out of his crouch. *No sudden moves.* The blackness lapped at him.

What had he done? Spent all these years breathing down the killer's neck only to set up a poor doomed hooker for rape and disembowelment? Got to get Val before . . .

The blackness washed over him.

Maybe inside, Val felt still youthful—after all, he'd be only thirty-three years old if he'd stayed human all along. But in the measurement of wear and tear, a dog's year is the equivalent of seven human years. Seven times eighteen equals 126. No wonder Val looked kind of sheepish as his strength failed him and he stood all frail and wrinkled in the sight of the astonished girl just before falling away from his grip on the fence and collapsing into the dust.

THE TASTE OF REVENGE

I hate folks that toot sharp for you to come on out toot sweet. I was on a creeper under an Olds, replacing the muffler, and I saw this Jaguar tool onto the apron. I was about to shove myself out on the creeper, even got the casters started swinging, when the toot-toot sounded. The damn fool should've seen he was riding over the signal hose and that a bell would ring automatically.

I stayed under the Olds, tightening a clamp that was tight already. The toot-toot sounded again, longer, harder. I folded my arms over my unionall chest and tightened my mouth.

I heard the Jaguar's door open and slam and saw a man's feet coming toward the shop. They moved gracefully around the rainbow splotches on the apron, high noon glinting off the toes. The feet stopped, aligned alongside my head. Sharp tan cuffs rested lightly on the tops of brown calf wingtips.

A voice with the cutout open said, "Hey, wake up!" and I saw one shoe raise up and draw back.

Before it could kick forward, I swung out on the creeper. The hardwood frame struck his anklebone. I spilled off the platform of the creeper and in stumbling to my feet I clutched at the immaculate tan pants. This part was hard to make seem accidental, because the man was hopping around at the moment, but then I reckon the pain kept him from thinking of that.

I said, "Sorry, sir. I had no idea you were standing so near." I didn't care if he believed me or not.

The man's head was bent. He was rubbing his ankle and just becoming aware of the black fingerprints.

The air grew full of a silence that smelled like sulfur.

I still hadn't got a look at the man's face. But the carefully combed carelessness of wavy yellow hair ignited recognition.

He looked up.

"Hell!" he said. "This is some homecoming!"

I stared at his angry face.

"Gee, kid," I said, when I could speak, "I'm really sorry."

His face cleared slowly and he smiled. He always had a smile that could turn your heart over.

He started to put out his hand, hesitated when he saw my greasy paw, then bravely kept it moving.

"Wait a minute," I said. "One minute more on top of seven years."

He twisted his face up in thought and nodded reminiscently. "That's right, it's just about seven years." He looked out at the acres of bluegrass fenced in across the road. "It hasn't changed. Still the sticks."

I wiped my hands on a ball of cotton waste.

Even so, his soft smooth hand shrank in my grip and quickly slipped free. He tried to make it up with the loud voice and the big smile. "You look just fine, Ernie."

I indicated his suit, his car. "You haven't been doing bad yourself."

"I can't complain," he said. He took the silk handkerchief out of his breast pocket and touched it to his brow and his upper lip and his neck. "Hot." He smiled. "The old man and the old lady home?"

I was slow in answering him. I didn't like the way he spoke of Ma and Pa. "Yeah."

He took a step toward the doorway and turned.

"You coming?" He glanced at his gold wristwatch. "Time to break for lunch anyway."

"I bring my lunch," I said. "But I'll close for an hour. Hell, it's a holiday!"

"Fine!"

He saw me hesitating.

I said, "Gotta lock up. You go on and surprise 'em. I'll follow along real soon."

"Right. Oh, say—"

"Yeah?"

"Okay to leave my car here? You might go over her later and see if she needs tuning up."

I couldn't have missed the sweet sound of a perfectly tuned motor when he tooled her in, but I said, "I'd be glad to. I've never seen one of these babies close up. We don't get them in this neck of the woods, you know."

He smiled. "I know."

He went to the Jaguar and patted its metallic green side. He heaved a rich leather suitcase out.

I said, "I'm glad to see you're staying a while, Frank."

He hefted the suitcase. "Don't let this mislead you. My plans are still up in the air. I just want to freshen up and get into a change of clothing."

He looked down at the fingerprints on his pants legs and then gave me a forgiving smile. I felt my cheeks burn. "I really am sorry, kid."

"Nothing."

He waved and started walking. As he turned the corner he waved again.

I could've gone with him; I didn't need much time to lock up. But I was waiting for a sound. The sound of one horse-power.

I shed my unionall and scrubbed my face and hands raw. Ethel liked me better in a business suit and with reasonably clean face and hands.

I rubbed salve into the seams and cracks of my hands, for all the good it would do, wet my hair and combed it, and put on my tie. I was getting into my coat when I heard the hoofbeats, and I buttoned my coat on the run.

Ethel, bent low, looking almost like a boy in jockey cap, man's shirt, and blue jeans, was whipping the roan stallion across the pasture in high—straight at the unjumpable fence.

She pulled him up short at the last fraction of a second, making the stallion strike soundless sparks from the air with his forehoofs.

My heart was misfiring, but Ethel was laughing, and I knew it was no use telling—or begging—her not to be so reckless.

I scaled the fence and jumped down inside.

The stallion nosed at the pocket of my coat. I scooped out some lumps of cane sugar and let him rasp my palm.

Ethel looked down at me with a pout. She poked me in the belly with her riding crop and I saw that I had misbuttoned my coat. With my free hand I buttoned it right.

"Now am I fit to kiss?"

She raked me with her eyes, cocked her head on one side, and after a long still moment suddenly stirred. She tore off the jockey cap, spilling her flaming hair, and was off the stallion in a flash.

The stallion had to nose the last lump out of the blue grass.

In her lighting on the ground and in the feel of her body against mine she made lies of the man's shirt and the blue jeans.

I came up for air only when the butt of her whip jabbed me in the small of the back. Then we stood there simply looking at one another, she gravely, myself, I suppose, smiling foolishly.

Ethel all at once lifted an eyebrow and smiled. "Why're you racing your motor, Ern?"

I thought I was holding myself in, but she sensed excitement even beyond the excitement she caused. I couldn't talk right away. She looked for my lunchbox.

"Aren't we sharing your lunch today?"

"My brother's home!"

She stared at me. "Frank?"

I nodded.

Her eyes switched to lower beam for a minute. She slashed at the grass with her whip. The four hundred and fifty dollars I had saved up to buy me a wheel balancer sparkled on her engagement finger. When she spoke again, her voice was cool.

"I'm sure it will be nice to meet him again after all these years."

I looked at her in surprise. "Come on, Ethel, don't be like everybody else around here. I know they all think he's good for nothing. But he's doing fine now. Look there, see the Jaguar? That's his."

She gave it a long look. Then she turned and smiled at me. "All right, Ern. I'm impressed. I'll be very, very glad to see him again."

"Then walk home with me."

Her sudden changes of mood always baffled me. Right now she seemed almost shy.

"No. Not just yet." She flicked the roan with her crop. "I have to remind Daddy to fix the latch on this bad boy's stall. Can't allow philandering on a stud farm."

I gave her another kiss. She broke this one up more quickly. And she was on the stallion and drumming away.

I walked the three blocks home kicking pebbles. I didn't know why; it was a kid thing to do.

Frank was in snappy powder-blue. He had changed to black shoes, too. Ma was busy with the tan pants and she asked me if I minded helping myself to the veal, she wanted to work on the stains before they set. She loosened the dirt and the fine bits of metal by rubbing lard in and then sponged with carbon tet, while Frank kidded her. I silently cursed myself for giving Ma extra work.

But she seemed to be getting such pleasure out of doing for Frank. A sweet smile lit up her face. She was looking as young and alive as when I was a kid.

And Pa too was enjoying himself, taking in Frank's sharp clothes and sweet talk. Pa's chest was as big as if an air hose had just given it twenty-eight pounds. He hooked his thumbs in the armholes of his vest and winged out his elbows. *One* of his sons was in the heavy sugar.

Well, the other son had to get back to work.

I finished with the Olds and my mouth watered looking at the Jaguar, but I had tubes to patch and spark plugs to clean before I allowed myself the luxury of exploring her innards. I also gave away air for tires with three layers of fabric showing and water for a couple-three steaming radiators, and sold a buck's worth of gas.

The bell sounded as a car rolled over the signal hose.

I had just spit on a likely spot on a tube and the invisible leak was bubbling the spit. I set the tube down on the bench so's a wire buffing brush would be pointing to the hole, and went out. The sun was on a slant by this time and I shaded my eyes.

It was a black Cad, long as a hearse. It stood on one side of the pump island, the Jaguar stood on the other. It held two men. Both were in dark-blue. The driver was pale and thin, the other was dark and fat. They were looking at the Jaguar. They turned to each other. The dark fat one got out.

The pale thin one gave me a swift glance and said, "Fill up the tank." His voice was pale and thin. "High-test."

By the time I had the spout in the tank the dark fat one was at the door of the restroom. He moved fast for a man his size and I half smiled.

He stuck his right hand in the pocket of his jacket and with his left flung the door open. He stepped in. He came right out. He gave the pale thin man a shake of his head.

By now the half smile had frozen on my face.

My jaw worked stiffly when I said, after hooking the hose back on the pump, "Check the oil, sir?"

The pale thin man nodded. His eyes were flickering between me and the other man, who was looking into the shop, the Jaguar, the Olds.

Under the hood I worked my face free, thinking, That's what they are—hoods.

I checked the dipstick. They had come a long hard way. I poured in a quart of oil while the dark fat man took a stroll around the building.

I started to wipe bugs and bug juice from the windshield.

"That can wait, Philip," the pale one said.

So Philip's the dark fat one's name, I thought, and I kept on wiping.

"I said that can wait, Philip," the pale one said, and I saw he was talking to me.

I said, "My name is Ernie." I pointed. "See?"

He glanced up at the sign—ERNIE'S SERVICENTER—then turned his eyes on me again. He shook his head.

"Philip. Your name is Philip. Philip the Tank." His voice had no expression in it at all.

I almost jumped when the dark fat one spoke. I hadn't heard him come up behind me.

"Philip." His voice was deep and hoarse. "Philip the Tank." He made a choking noise way down in his throat.

I tried to smile. "That's right," I said. "My name is Philip."

"No, it isn't," the pale one said. "Your name is Ernie." He pointed to the sign. "See?" He shook his head sadly. "Now why do you lie to us?"

"We want you should tell us the truth, Ernie," the dark fat one said. His hot sickly sweet breath was close to my ear.

The pale thin one nodded at the Jaguar.

"That car belongs to a friend of ours, Ernie. We're anxious to talk to him. Tell us where he is."

I knew I couldn't be silent long. I began answering before I had my answer really thought out.

I heard myself saying, "All I know is, that there foreign heap broke down and the man driving it left it here and got a lift to Luketown."

The pale man said, "Luketown? Why Luketown, Ernie?" There was the shadow of doubt on his brow.

The dark fat man was breathing closer. He said, "Philip might lie, but not Ernie."

I heard myself saying, "Luketown's a fair-sized place, where he can get a room in a regular hotel. Ain't no place good enough for him around here. Besides, from there he can grab a train to Baltimore, where he said he had some business, if I can't get this thing running." I scratched my chin. "I dunno. I might have to send away for parts. I'm supposed to let him know when he phones tomorrow morning."

There was no sound but the dark fat man's breathing.

"Baltimore," he said after a minute.

The pale thin one nodded. "Pimlico," he said.

And I knew that somehow, without planning it, I had said the right thing.

I reckon some part of my mind had recalled that Frank had come from the direction of Louisville, where the Derby had run a week ago. And that same part of my mind had recalled that the big one at Pimlico was coming up next week.

The hot sickly sweet breathing faded away and the dark fat man got into the Cad. I was praying Frank wouldn't pick this minute to pay me a call. The pale thin man kept his eyes on me as he drew out his wallet. I told him what the gas and oil came to. He handed me a fifty. I looked at it.

"It's good, Ernie. We have them made specially for us by the U. S. mint."

"It ain't that," I said. "It's just I don't think I can change it."

"Who asked for change, Ernie? We give our friends what they deserve."

I felt the first chill of coming dusk.

The fifty trembled in the wake of the Cad. I hoped that was what made it tremble.

I waited until the Cad was around the curve on the road to Luketown. Then I put the fifty in the till.

I moved slowly to the phone on the wall outside. Maybe I was wrong. Maybe they were really friends of Frank's and he'd be mad because I had misled them. Or he might laugh. But I had to tell him.

I was almost at the phone when the red glint of the sun on glass reached the corner of my eye. I didn't turn. I sensed more than I saw a dark fat figure standing at the curve of the road studying me through binoculars.

I walked past the phone to the Jaguar. I took a look at the engine. I monkeyed with the distributor, the carburetor. I stood up, took a step back, and scratched my chin.

I moved to the car door. In the rearview mirror I saw, dim and small, the dark fat figure.

There was an auto robe folded on the seat. I shook it out and spread it over the driver's seat to keep from soiling the leopard upholstery when I sat down. I started the motor after a few coughs. I drove the Jaguar around the apron. It bucked and bolted and finally stalled. I got out and took another look at the engine. I took a step back and scratched my chin again. I moved to the car door.

The mirror showed the dark fat figure disappearing behind the curve.

I got in and started off again. This time the Jaguar jumped only a few feet before it died on me. I got out and looked at the engine. I shook my head in slow despair. I was pretty sure I had no more audience but I made out to be tinkering hit-or-miss while I readjusted the carburetor and the distributor.

For a minute I forgot the two men. Something about the car had begun to bother me. I looked more closely at the engine serial number. Someone had stamped ones into fours and threes into eights.

I got my head out, stepped back, studied the car.

And there was the paint job. It would pass casual inspection, but someone had been in a hurry to spray green over tan.

I remembered to glance in the mirror. No sign.

Even so, I spent another few minutes just standing looking at the car as if hoping she would move by herself.

Then I shrugged, both to play the part and to say to myself chances were there was no need to play it anymore. I headed for the restroom.

I slipped by it and made for home. Not directly, but by a way that screened me from a possible watcher.

When I drew near to the house, I heard music and dancing.

They didn't hear me come in.

Ethel, in her best party dress, and her hair drawn back smooth and shiny as sunset on a stream and tied in a ponytail, was whirling around with Frank. Her skirt swirled away from her calves, spun higher, showed white flesh. Ma and Pa were dancing too. The tune on the radio was "Ain't She Sweet?"

Ma and Pa broke off their dancing, winded, and stood laughing out-of-breath laughs and clapping time.

They were first to see me. They smiled and kept on clapping. I smiled back.

Ethel and Frank saw me. They didn't stop. Ethel gave me a wave and Frank gave me a wink. I wanted to cut in and tell Frank about the two men, but I held back.

It could wait a bit. No use scaring Ma and Pa half to death. Luketown was fifteen miles away. The two men would waste at least some time checking at the hotels. Frank had maybe an hour, an hour and a half at the outside. It could wait a bit—but not too long.

I was glad when the song ended and a commercial came on and Pa turned the volume down. Ma laid out coffee and cake. Pa wondered what brought me. I told him I wanted to see Frank about his car.

Frank looked over from seating Ethel. He asked Ethel to excuse him and moved to my side. He smiled. "My car? Thinking of buying her, Ernie?"

I smiled and shook my head. I said, low, "It isn't really about the car. It's something else. I think it's important."

He lifted an eyebrow and smiled. "Important, hey? Let me get a cup of java first."

He moved to the table. Ma poured him a cup. She looked at me and raised the pot. I shook my head no.

Frank's hand held on Ethel's when he passed her the cane sugar. "Sweets to the sweet," he said. And the way he said it, it sounded sophisticated. Anyway, Ethel seemed to think so.

He moved back to me. "Quite a gal you have there, Ernie."

I reckon Ma had told him. Or the diamond on her finger had made him ask Ethel herself.

"Yessir," he said louder. "Ethel's quite a gal."

Ethel caught her name and said, teasing, "You didn't think so when we were kids."

Frank teased her right back, winking at me. "Why should I think so, about a scrawny little pigtailed tomboy?" He looked at her and smiled. "But now is something else again."

He turned to me at last and asked me what was so important.

In a half whisper I told him. I described the men.

The cup rattled a bit in the saucer. He said, in the same kind of half whisper, but to himself, "I thought I had a few days' lead."

"If it's bad," I said, "I mean if they're out to—to harm you, we can call the sheriff."

By now he had absorbed the shock. He smiled as if he was tasting something sour and finding it funny. "The sheriff!"

"Then what are you going to do?"

"Only thing I can do—keep going." He gripped my shoulder and shook me a little. "I'll be down for the Jaguar in a short while."

I didn't know what it was all about, but I remembered the look of the pale thin man and the dark fat man. I nodded.

There was nothing more for me to say. I felt uneasy standing there beside him, with Ethel looking across at the two of us, her eyes shifting from one to the other.

I stirred and said, "I'll leave it to you to break it to Ma and Pa. I have to get back."

"Sure, sure," he said, thinking of something else. There was some compression of his mouth.

As I left, Ethel's lips blew out. It might've been a kiss, it might've been to cool the coffee.

Pa walked over with a heavy step. I came out of the shop, where I was doing nothing but watch the tube on the bench

74

grow smaller, to meet him. He said he just came to see the Jaguar.

He saw it and was proud. But his eyes were puzzled. "Why can't he at least stay overnight?"

"Important business, Pa, I reckon. But he'll be back."

"That's right. He'll be back."

And he walked away with a lighter tread.

Frank walked over, carrying his suitcase. He shoved it in the car and then came to where I was standing. He took me by the arm and said, "Let's go inside."

We went inside. It didn't come to me until long afterward that he had worked it so's I had my back to the doorway.

"Well, Ernie," he said, and I was wondering why he spoke so loud, "like I said before, this is a fine homecoming!" He stared past me into the evening. "Look, Ernie," he said, and I was wondering why he spoke so low, "can you let me have whatever cash you have on hand?"

I reckon I stared at him.

"Oh, I'll pay you back," he said.

"It isn't that," I said. "It's just I thought you were in the heavy sugar."

He smiled his sour-funny smile. "Tell you the truth, Ernie," he said, still keeping his voice down, "I'm broke."

I know I stared at him.

"That's true, Ernie. I did have my hands on a bundle, but it belonged to somebody else. A big wheel. He wants it back—or else. I dropped it all on the horses." He smiled a twisted smile. "Looks like it's going to be 'or else'."

I opened the cash drawer. "I'm afraid I don't have that kind of money."

He laughed. "I know you don't, Ernie. All I need is enough to put some distance between me and those friends of mine."

I handed him the fifty and the other bills. He riffled them. He made a face. "This all you got?"

He looked in the empty drawer.

I spread my hands. He shrugged, then he turned on a smile so sweet I could almost taste it.

"Well, thanks a million, Ernie. I'll send it back first chance I get." I put up a hand. "No, no, I mean it. I'll repay you soon as I'm able."

One thing I couldn't understand. "If you need money, Frank, why do you put up this big front? You could've sold the Jaguar and pawned your watch and your luggage."

"Pride, Ernie. Pride. I couldn't come home with nothing to show for seven years of being away." He snapped the fifty and smiled. I'd told him the pale thin man gave it to me. "At least it's nice to know the ones who're after me are helping foot my getaway." He pocketed the money. "Well, Ernie," he said, and again I was wondering why he spoke so loud, "I'd better say so long."

I wiped my right palm on my unionall and we shook hands. "Where you heading?" I asked.

"Down the long black road," he said. He smiled. "No, I'm taking the side road far as it goes. From there—" He stopped and shook his head. "Maybe it's best you don't know just where I'm winding up, if you know what I mean."

I thought I knew what he meant, but he seemed to be saying two things at once.

I watched him go out in the dark to his car. He fussed with the blanket on the seat and heaped it beside him, muttering to himself.

"Want a hand?"

I made to come out.

He said fast, "No."

He started her up. I reckon he got a look at the fuel gauge.

76

"Hey, Ernie, how about filling her up? I'd hate to get stalled on a lonely road, if you know what I mean."

It struck me funny he didn't come right out and say what he meant. Then I thought, well, he doesn't want to think about what would happen if those two caught up with him.

"Sure," I said. "Back her up to the pump." I hurried out. I felt bad I hadn't thought of filling her up.

He backed up and cut the motor.

I stuck the spout in the tank. I hope he makes it, I thought. I looked at the back of his head and smiled a sad smile. Fine homecoming!

Then I saw an arm steal out from under the heaped-up auto robe. A diamond sparkled as the hand wound around Frank's neck.

He shook his head sharply as if in warning and quickly shoved the arm down under the robe. He shot a look into the mirror.

My head was down, my eyes on the spout. And my heart was snapping like a cooling motor.

I shut off the flow of gas but left the spout in the tank. "Wait a minute, Frank," I said. "I just remembered my wallet."

I went inside where my coat was hanging. My fingers were numb as I felt through the pockets. I came out and handed him the few bills I found in the wallet.

"Thanks, Ernie," he said. His voice was hoarse.

I turned on the flow of gas. My mind was blank until I heard him say, "That should do it, Ernie." He sounded anxious to be on his way.

I drained the hose and replaced the cap.

He switched her on again and waved. The Jaguar should've handled like a dream, but Frank was nervous or Ethel was teasing him. He got off to a jackrabbit start.

My eyes followed the dimming taillights.

Headlights swung onto the apron. The bell sounded.

I had unhooked the air hose and was about to coil it and put it away for the night.

It was the Cad.

This time both men got out. They came toward me. They stopped.

The pale thin one stood with his feet at a slight camber, rocking on the outer edge of each sole.

"Why did you lie to us?" he said softly. "Your name isn't Philip. It's Ernie Nerf. Frank Nerf is your brother." His voice grew even softer. "Which way did he go?"

I said nothing.

He drew a pistol.

I whipped the air hose at him. He backed away fast. I started to whip it at the other, but he was already behind me and in a second I was in his clutch.

First the dark fat one held me so I couldn't dodge or block while the pale thin one swung his pistol butt right and left. Then they cross-switched. The pale thin one held me for the dark fat one.

I slumped to the ground when whoever was holding me at the end let go.

Water hit me like a slap.

The watering can clattered on the ground.

"Now Ernie'll tell us the truth."

"Which way did he go?"

I told them.

"You believe Ernie told us the truth?"

"I believe it."

"Even so, we'll never catch Nerf in that heap of his with the lead he has on us. And first chance he gets he'll ditch it and glom another."

A kick in the ribs.

"Well, we gotta try. Let's bug out."

I heard the Cad drive off.

My head was full of screeching brakes. The globe of the gas pump had taken off into the sky. Then I got my bearings. I saw it was the moon.

In my mind there was something pressing me. I had done something. Or I had to do something. Which?

I got to my feet and stumbled to the faucet and splashed water in my face. I leaned against the doorway of the shop. The inner tube on the bench caught my eye. It had shriveled. Was that the something I had to do?

Vulcanizing would keep till tomorrow. Time to knock off, if that was all.

I shed my unionall and scrubbed my face and hands raw. I rubbed salve in the seams and cracks of my hands, wet my hair and combed it, and put on my tie. I was getting into my coat when I heard the hoofbeats, and I buttoned my coat on the run.

The roan stallion was waiting at the fence.

I managed to scale the fence and let myself down inside. I held onto the fence, exhausted, hurting.

The stallion nosed at my pocket.

I put my hand in. It came out empty. Both of us looked at the empty hand.

Now I knew what I had done.

"Sorry, boy," I said. And whether I was talking to the horse or to Frank I don't know.

The sugar was in the tank of the Jaguar. Gumming up the engine. Stalling it on the lonely road.

BORN VICTIMS

Detective Third Grade Andrew Flint took the topmost complaint card from the waiting stack of fresh forms and made ready to fill in the blanks.

Complaints. He had his own complaints, but could do nothing about them. An already overwhelming caseload, and here came one more. A sweltering day, the air-conditioning still on the blink, yet because the precinct commander had a thing about his people's appearance—anyone who met the public had to look buttoned-down neat—no shirtsleeves.

He looked at the young woman in the chair beside his desk and lost some of his resentment. Someone that pretty shouldn't look that worried. The chair she sat in, the desk she rested her hand on, the air about her, all vibrated to her nervousness. But he had to remain the cool professional.

Complainant. "Your name?"

"Analisa Sanders. One 'n' in Analisa. My problem is—"

Marital status. "Miss or Mrs.?" Hardly any insisted on Ms.

"Miss. I—"

Address. "Where do you live?"

"Four twenty-three Montvale Avenue. Apartment 5 C. What I—"

Crime. "All right, Miss Sanders, what's the complaint?"

"A man is following me around and threatening me."

He eyed her sharply. She looked much too young and pretty and undried-up to be one of those wackos. "Do you know the man? Can you describe him?"

She gave a small ironic laugh. "I know the man. I can see him with my eyes closed."

"Do you know his name?"

"Sam Locke."

"Description?"

She ran a vaguely measuring gaze over Flint. "He's a bit taller and heavier than you, with dirty-blond hair and hazel eyes. He has a pleasant face that can turn mean in an instant." Though it was hot, she shivered.

Flint put down "6' 1", 190 lbs., medium-blond hair, brown eyes."

Distinguishing characteristics. "Any scars? A limp? Anything like that?"

She shook her head. "Nothing to make him stand out in a crowd." But her haunted eyes said they could always pick him out.

Flint nodded. "How long has he been following you?"

It was as though his question had pricked a balloon. She let out air and sagged. "One year."

He stared. "And you're only now reporting it?"

She shook her head wearily and managed a tired smile. "I reported it back home a year ago."

Flint tried not to show his relief. He had it figured now, saw how to get out of this one. If in one full year they had been unable to resolve the case back home—wherever back home was—then the job was clearly one for Detective Cann: the wastebasket. This was simply a lovers' quarrel and she and Locke would have to work it out themselves. Still, he had to hear her out.

"How did it start?"

She looked back through him. "This was up in Ridgeway, where we both come from. I met Sam at a party. We got to talking and he seemed nice so I dated him a few times. But he soon showed his other side—his mean, jealous, egotistical nature, his explosive temper."

Miss Sanders kept watching Flint to see how he reacted to what she said. He kept nodding but maintained a noncommittal expression.

"Once he knocked out a waiter who spilled a drink on him. Another time he slugged a man he said was staring at me. These things frightened me and I decided to have nothing more to do with him. But it proved impossible to let him down gently. He seemed to think the few times I went out with him made him my steady.

"I told him I wasn't ready to go steady with anyone just yet, but he said I was his and he wasn't about to share me with anyone else. He hung around and scared off any other men that showed interest. That's when I went to the Ridgeway police. But they said Sam hadn't actually. done anything they could book him for and they suggested I see the district attorney about a restraining order.

"I went to the district attorney, but he said I hadn't told him anything he could get a restraining order on and he suggested I see the police."

She looked at Flint, but he was busy doodling on a sheet of scrap paper.

"I couldn't take it any more. I packed up one night and left town without telling anyone. I didn't know myself where I was going. I just took the first bus out. It brought me here." She smiled. "I really thought I lost him." Then the smile faded and she spoke dully. "But somehow he tracked me down and followed me here. I had a few good months here before he showed up. I not only found a good job but got to know and like a man at the office, George—a kind, compassionate widower who says he loves me. He asked me to go out with him, and I agreed."

Her eyes pooled. "But that very day, I spotted him—Sam. And I had to tell George I was sorry but I wasn't in love with him and it wouldn't be fair to lead him on. I couldn't bring myself to tell him the real reason."

Flint looked up. "The real reason being that you believe Sam would threaten this George?"

She leaned forward. "Not just threaten, kill. He'd kill another man rather than let him have me."

Flint shifted uncomfortably. "Look, Miss Sanders, this is all conjecture. We can't proceed against Sam until he actually does something."

She herself seemed ready to explode. "All I want is to live a normal life! Is that too much to ask?"

Flint thought it was, but didn't say so. Normal life, as he saw it, was full of harassment and fear. "Why not take a positive attitude? Confront Sam. Reason with him."

"That's what all you law-enforcement people seem to think: that it's always the victim's fault, that in some perverse way victims like myself goad the victimizers on. Well, I never led Sam on. I told him when I tried to break up with him that time wouldn't change my mind. I've kept away from him, but he won't keep away from me. He has this sick idea that because he loves me—whether or not I love him back—he owns me. That if he can't have me, nobody will. Try and reason with that."

Flint sat mute.

She sighed. "I see it's no use. I could plead myself hoarse and you'll say the same thing: there's nothing you can do."

"That's right. Because it's the truth. You don't know how sorry I am, but that's the way it is." He put his hand on top of the pile of file folders on his desk. "Lady, look at my case load. We don't have enough personnel. We can't spare the people to guard you and this man around the clock against somebody who may or may not be a nut."

She eyed the folders. "I get the message. If Sam kills

George, *then* you can take action against Sam."

Flint flushed. He drew a long sigh.

She spoke more to herself than to him. "I slipped out the back way to come here. Sam will be waiting in front of my office building, watching for me to leave for lunch so he can follow and see who I have lunch with." She stood and gathered herself to go.

Flint watched her. He had told her the truth, but he felt uneasy. And in some measure, as part of a society that lets bad things happen, guilty. But what could he do? This Analisa Sanders had to live out her fate. Some people were born victims. He stood as they said goodbye and watched her go, no starch in her back, no lift in her shoulders, no snap in her walk.

Then, as she reached the doorway, she straightened and though he could no longer see her face he felt it had lost its beaten look. He stared after her for a wondering moment, then picked up the complaint card, tore it in four, and fed it to Detective Cann. He looked at the clock and a wry smile surfaced. It was about time to eat.

He nearly choked on a sparerib. Somehow Analisa Sanders had found out where he ate lunch and was sashaying straight to where he sat alone at a table for two.

Her eyes seemed unnaturally bright, fueled by some fever of excitement. She kissed him on the cheek before taking the seat opposite his and picking up the menu.

"Hey, what—"

"I'm glad you went ahead without me. I'm sorry to be late, but you must be getting used to it by now," she chattered gaily as her eyes roved the menu.

She made up her mind, looked around, and a waiter appeared. She smiled up at him. "A tunafish sandwich and a cup of coffee, please."

The waiter nodded and left.

Flint was in a daze. What the hell was this? *Was* she wacko, after all? The best thing for him to do was hurry through his meal and get out of here.

He tried to do just that, but she kept putting her hand on his arm and chattering as though the two of them were intimate friends. He wanted to tell her to shut up and leave him alone, but he was too polite and finally he saw it wasn't going to go on forever. She glanced at her wristwatch, took a last bite of her sandwich and a quick sip of coffee, wiped her mouth with her napkin, and said with a laugh that she had better get back to the office before they realized they didn't really need her.

And at least she wasn't going to stick him with her lunch. She placed a five-dollar bill under her plate, then she was on her feet, her hand on his shoulder as she leaned toward him and whispered in his ear. "I know one thing: the police go all out to catch a cop killer."

"What are you talking about?"

She gave him a dazzling smile. "You don't know how sorry I am, but it's my only chance." Her hand pressed on his shoulder as she bent to kiss him soundly.

As he sat in frozen disbelief, she slipped gracefully between the tables and left the restaurant. Outside, through the window, she stopped briefly and blew him a kiss.

With a thrill of fear, he grew aware of a nondescript man who had been watching her from the sidewalk register his presence, take a long look after her as she disappeared from sight, and then reach for the door and enter the restaurant.

SANITY CLAUSE

Ho ho ho.

They said he used to come down the chimney. But of course these days there were no more chimneys. They said he used to travel in an eight-reindeer-power sleigh. But of course these days there were no reindeer.

The fact was that he traveled in an ordinary aircar and came through the ordinary iris door.

But he did have on a red suit with white furry trim, and he did carry a bundle of toys, the way they said he did in the old days. And here he came.

His aircar parked itself on the roof of the Winterdream apartment block, and he worked his way down through the housing complex. The Winterdream block's 400 extended families, according to his list, had an allotment of nine children under seven.

The first eight were all 'sanes' and did not take up more than two minutes of his time apiece. The ninth would be Cathy Lesser, three years old.

Like the others, the Clements and the Lessers had been awaiting his visit in fearful hope. The door of the Clement-Lesser apartment irised open before he had a chance to establish his presence. He bounced in.

He read in its eyes how the family huddle saw him. His eyes, how they twinkled! His dimples, how merry! His cheeks were like roses, his nose like a cherry! His droll little mouth was drawn up like a bow, and the beard of his chin was as white as the snow. The stump of a pipe he held tight in his teeth, and the smoke it encircled his head like a wreath. He had a broad face and a little round belly that shook when he

86

laughed, like a bowlful of jelly.

"Ho ho ho."

He looked around for Cathy. The child was hanging back, hiding behind her mother's legs.

"And where is Cathy?"

Her mother twisted around and pushed Cathy forward. Slowly Cathy looked up. She laughed when she saw him, in spite of herself. A wink of his eye and a twist of his head soon gave her to know she had nothing to dread.

"Ho ho ho. And how is Cathy?"

He knew as soon as he saw her eyes. He vaguely remembered them from last year, but in the meanwhile something in them had deepened.

Cathy stuck her thumb in her mouth, but her gaze locked wonderingly and hopefully on the bulging sack over his shoulder.

"Cat got Cathy's tongue?"

"She's just shy," her mother said.

"Cathy doesn't have to be shy with me." He looked at the mother and spoke softly. "Have you noticed anything . . . special about the child?"

The child's mother paled and clamped her mouth tight. But a grandmother quickly said, "No, nothing. As normal a little girl as you'd want to see."

"Yes, well, we'll see." It never paid to waste time with the relatives; he had a lot of homes to visit yet. Kindly but firmly he eased the Lessers and the Clements out of the room and into the corridor, where other irises were peeping.

Now that she was alone with him Cathy looked longingly at the closed door. Quickly he unslung his bundle of toys and set it down. Cathy's eyes fixed on the bulging sack.

"Have you been a good little girl, Cathy?"

Cathy stared at him and her lower lip trembled.

"It's all right, Cathy. I know you've been as good as any normal little girl can be, and I've brought you a nice present. Can you guess what it is?"

He visualized the beautiful doll in the lower left corner of the bag. He watched the little girl's eyes. She did not glance at the lower left corner of the bag. He visualized the swirly huge lollipop in the upper right corner of the bag. She did not glance at the upper right corner of the bag. So far so good. Cathy could not read his mind.

"No? Well, here it is."

He opened the bag and took out the doll. A realistic likeness of a girl with Cathy's colouring, it might have been the child's sibling.

"Ooo," with mouth and eyes to match.

"Yes, isn't she pretty, Cathy? Almost as pretty as you. Would you like to hold her?"

Cathy nodded.

"Well, let's see first what she can do. What do you think she can do? Any idea?"

Cathy shook her head.

Still all right. Cathy could not see ahead.

He cleared a space on the table and stood the doll facing him on the far edge. It began walking as soon as he set it down. He lifted Cathy up so she could watch. The doll walked towards them and stopped on the brink of the near edge. It looked at the girl and held out its arms and said, "Take me."

He lowered Cathy to the floor, and the doll's eyes followed her pleadingly. Cathy gazed up at the doll. It stood within her sight but out of her reach. The girl's eyes lit up. The doll trembled back to pseudo-life and jerkily stepped over the edge of the table.

He caught it before it hit the floor, though his eyes had

been on Cathy. He had got to Cathy too in the nick of time. Strong telekinesis for a three-year-old.

"Here, Cathy, hold the doll."

While she cradled the doll he reached into a pocket and palmed his microchip injector.

"Oh, what lovely curls. Just like the dolly's." He raised the curls at the nape of Cathy's neck, baring the skin. "Do you mind if I touch them?" For some reason he always steeled himself when he planted the metallic seed under the skin, though he knew the insertion didn't hurt. At most, a slight pulling sensation, no more than if he had tugged playfully at her curls. Then a quick forgetting of the sensation. He patted the curls back in place and pocketed the injector.

"Let's play that game again, shall we, sugar plum?"

Gently he pried the doll from her and once more put it on the far edge of the table. This time it did not walk when he set it down. With one arm he lifted Cathy up and held her so she could see the doll. The fingers of his free hand hovered over studs on his broad black belt. The doll looked at the girl and held out its arms and said, "Take me."

The girl's eyes yearned across the vastness of the table. The doll suddenly trembled into pseudo-life and began to walk towards them, jerkily at first, then more and more smoothly. He fingered a stud. The doll slowed. It moved sluggishly, as if bucking a high wind, but it kept coming. He fingered another stud. The doll slowed even more. In smiling agony it lifted one foot and swung it forward and set it down, tore the other free of enormous g's and swung it forward, and so kept coming. He fingered a third stud.

He sweated. He had never had to use this highest setting before. If this failed, it meant the child was incurably insane. Earth had room only for the sane. The doll had stopped. It fought to move, shuddered and stood still.

The girl stared at the doll. It remained where it was, out of reach. A tear fattened and glistened, then rolled down each cheek. It seemed to him a little something washed out of the child's eyes with the tears.

He reached out and picked up the doll and handed it to Cathy.

"She's yours to keep, Cathy, for always and always."

Automatically cradling the doll, Cathy smiled at him. He wiped away her tears and set her down. He irised the door open. "It's all right now. You can come in."

The Lessers and Clements timidly flooded back into the room.

"Is she—?"

"Cathy's as normal as any little girl around."

The worried faces regained permanent-press smoothness. "Thank you, thank you. Say thank you, Cathy."

Cathy shook her head.

"Cathy!"

"That's quite all right. I'll settle for a kiss."

He brought his face close to Cathy's. Cathy hesitated, then gave his rosy cheek a peck.

"Thank *you,* Cathy." He shouldered his toys and straightened up. "And to all a good night."

And laying a finger aside of his nose, and giving a nod, through the iris he bounded. The Clement-Lesser apartment was on the ground floor, and the corridor let him out on to a patch of lawn. He gave his aircar a whistle. It zoomed from the roof to his feet.

As he rode through the night to his next stop, an image flashed into his mind. For an instant he saw, real as real, a weeping doll. It was just this side of subliminal. For a moment he knew fear. Had he failed after all with Cathy? Had she put that weeping doll in his mind?

Impossible. It came from within. Such aberrations were the aftermath of letdown. Sometimes, as now after a trying case, he got these weird flashes, these near-experiences of a wild frighteningly free vision, but always something in his mind mercifully cut them short.

As if on cue, to take him out of himself, the horn of his aircar sounded its *Ho ho ho* as it neared the Summerdaze apartment block. He looked down upon the chimneyless roofs. Most likely the chimney in the Sanity Clause legend grew out of folk etymology, the word chimney in this context coming from a misunderstanding of an ancient chant of peace on Earth: *Ho . . . Ho . . . Ho chi minh.* His eyes twinkled, his dimples deepened. There was always the comfort of logic to explain the mysteries of life.

The aircar parked itself on the roof of the Summerdaze block, and he shouldered his bundle of toys and worked his way down through the housing complex.

Ho ho ho.

THE PERFECT ROTTER

I've never kippled, but I know a character straight out of Kipling when I see one. The ruddy beefeater complexion, the stiff upper lip that mustered a military brush, the whole bearing of an officer and a gentleman, all bespoke long service in Her Majesty's Army of the old days.

Our encounter came when we took hold of chairs at the same time and stood staring across the empty table at each other. He leaped to the attack.

"My table, I believe."

I believed otherwise, this being my usual table at the West End establishment I favored whenever I came up to town. But before I could splutter to this effect he had dismissed all argument with a disarming wave of the hand.

"Not to worry. We'll share it, shall we?" He thrust out his hand. "Colonel Sir Robert Fredericks, late of the Fusiliers."

I gave my name in return, and a wince. We seated ourselves and Colonel Fredericks frowned roundabout.

"Where's the waiter? Never around when you want them." He winked at me, then gave a parade ground shout—"Service here!"

A waiter quickly appeared and snapped to. Colonel Fredericks grimaced disparagingly at the bill of fare but ordered heartily. I don't have that ruddiness to maintain, yet I could not but respond to the challenge by making my side of the board equally groan.

He turned out to be a pleasant chap as well as a good trencherman and, as we dug in, a good conversationalist. Anyone who draws me out about myself is a good conversationalist. I have a lot to be modest about; it grew embarrassing to expand on my few accomplishments.

"But what about yourself, Colonel? I can tell you've led a full life. You must have many fond memories of the service, for example."

He gazed back across the years and smiled. "Fond ones and, well, not so fond." He frowned suddenly, then cleared his brow.

"Something has come to mind?"

"Matter of fact, yes." He fetched up a sigh from the deep well of his being. "This happened long ago, and I'll name no names, so I think it's all right if I tell you."

I leaned forward. "It will go no further, sir."

His eyes were suddenly shrewd. "I'm sure of that, sir. I pride myself on being a good judge of character." He beckoned the waiter over and obtained a cheroot to his liking and got up a good head of smoke. "Well, sir, this took place in one of the, shall we say, *crucial* states bordering the Persian Gulf or Arabian Gulf—depending on who you side with. Anyway, it was a dusty outpost of Empire, a port town that was the flyspeck capital of an oil-rich stretch of sand. I don't care to pin it down any closer because of the circumstances."

He lifted an eyebrow, I nodded, and he went on to tell me the circumstances.

"There was this dashing young officer bloke, a subaltern, who served as regimental paymaster. He had just taken over from the regular paymaster, who departed on home leave thanks to fever. Three days before his first go at payday, the subaltern dashed in to see his superior officer. All in a flap, he reported that the lock on the pay chest showed signs of tampering with.

"Together they opened the pay chest. It was empty.

"Absolutely shattering. First time in the long and honorable history of the regiment anything of the sort had happened: one of its own robbing the till. For it could only have been an inside job.

"The commanding officer pulled himself together. The hair of his flesh settled down and he did first things first. No pay—even with the pay small and little to spend it on—meant muttering if not mutiny. The regiment's morale would sink even more if the men went payless. He got off a cable and the War Office flew in another pay chest.

"The same plane brought in an Intelligence sergeant. For a full day—after looking the empty chest over and politely questioning the subaltern—he nosed about town. He prowled the cafes, the bank, the jetty. The only thing he seemed to get was a sunburnt nose.

"But by the time he returned to regimental headquarters he had got more than that. He had forearmed himself with a list of the serial numbers of the currency stolen from the first pay chest. And he had traced a fresh five-pound note from the mutton butcher who had deposited it to the man who had bought fat sheep of him for a feast. The man who had bought the sheep ran a gambling den in a back room of the rug bazaar. The gambler, washing his own hands of theft, had named the British officer who had paid gambling debts with the stolen currency. The British officer he named was the subaltern who was serving as regimental paymaster.

"The subaltern at first denied his guilt. He stood ready to swear on a tower of Bibles—or Korans—that he had not stolen the cash. But the five-pound note alone damned him. It bore not only mutton grease but the fingerprints of those who had handled it, including an unmistakable thumbprint of the subaltern's.

"When he saw there was no way of getting round the evidence, the subaltern tried to take the attack. He put the blame on the Army for sticking him in that hellhole and placing temptation in his path.

"That turned even the few willing to make allowances for him against him. They said the rotter lacked the decency to own up to his misdeeds and face the consequences. He had let down the regiment.

"They locked him in the orderly room while they set about deciding what to do about him. The senior and junior officers gathered in the mess hall, cleared all the servants away, and talked it over. The concensus was that it would be best not to hold a court martial. That would lay the regiment's disgrace open to the world. There was only one honorable way out of the whole unpleasant affair for all concerned.

"The subaltern's best friend loaded one bullet into a revolver, unlocked the orderly room door, put the revolver on the desk, then went out, leaving the subaltern once more alone in the room. There had been not a word between them during that poignant interlude, but there had been a world of understanding.

"Waiting outside in the hallway, the officers listened while trying to seem not to be. An agonizing minute passed. Then the shot sounded.

"After a decent interval, they tried to open the door. It would not give. While they were busy battering down the door, which the subaltern had propped shut with desks and file cabinets, the subaltern had popped out the window and dashed down to the waterfront and got under way in a dhow.

"The dhow quickly lost itself among the many vessels on the Gulf—Persian or Arabian, as you please." Colonel Sir Robert Fredericks smiled sadly. "That was long ago as time flies. From time to time one or another of his old messmates runs across him here and there around the world. But if they see him they don't *see* him, if you get my meaning."

I blinked. "But the shot?"

"Ah, yes, the shot." The Colonel dealt with the heeltap in his stinger glass. "The subaltern used it to blast the padlock off the second pay chest. Made off with the replacement payroll." Silence for a while made me aware of the surrounding clatter and chatter. He looked past me thoughtfully, then stirred himself. "Pardon me for a moment, old man, but duty calls. Be back straightaway."

"Of course, Colonel."

His "straightaway" stretched out. Just as I began to tire of waiting the waiter came and presented me with the discreet reverse of the bill. I turned the bill over and stared at the bottom line.

"What's this?"

"The gent what left said you was taking care of the bill."

I was fit to kipple.

THE POSTMASTER & THE SLAVE

The young fellow looked, dressed and spoke more like a frontiersman than a townsman. For sure, he behaved less like a responsible postmaster, by appointment of President Andrew Jackson, and more like a lackadaisical dreamer, by appointment of Mother Nature.

He sauntered into Tom Bourse's general store and hunkered down with the other loungers around the cracker barrel and swapped tall tales and local gossip with them till he remembered—a good hour late—why he had come calling.

He unfolded to his full ungainly length and stretched. Then he took off his hat and drew a letter from its tucking place.

"Dropped by to fetch you this letter, Tom. From your cousin Jarvis upstate in Libertyville." He glanced at the postage fee inked on the outside of the folded and sealed letter sheets. "That'll be 37½ cents."

Tom made a show of scrutinizing the red wax seal's integrity, then opened the cash drawer and slowly counted out the fee into the patient palm.

The hand's owner pocketed the coins and clapped his hat back on. "Wa-al, hate to rush off, fellers, but it's high time I streaked back to my duties." He got his laugh. He gave a grave-faced, so-long nod all around, and sauntered out.

Once outside, he paused, not to eavesdrop, but to remove his hat again and hand-comb particles of red wax from his mop of hair. But it was the same as if he had lingered to see whether his cronies had anything to say about him. They had.

"I tell you this, boys, as a postmaster he's no model for others to pattern after. For one thing, he's a sight too careless

97

about leaving his office unlocked during the day. Why, half the time I go in and help myself to my own mail with no one there at all."

"That's so. I can't rightly decide if he's found his niche in life. I hain't saying he aimed too high, but I do allow as how he ought to take pains to do the job proper if he hopes to keep it. Nice enough feller, though most likely he'll never amount to much."

The nice enough feller tipped his hat in their direction and went on his way with a rueful grin.

His grin grew cheerful, lighting up his gaunt face, as he howdied the folks he passed. And even the solid citizens among them could not help responding in kind; still, he was aware of headshakes once they parted.

But he did not put on a show of going briskly about his business. He ambled officewards, his mind full of thoughts having nothing to do with his post.

The door hung half open and yawned wider at his touch. He swept the place with his gaze. Have to sweep it with a broom one of these days. But at least no one had walked away with the rickety chair or the swaybacked bench or the flyspecked portrait of Andrew Jackson. As for the pigeon-holed mail, he trusted folks to take only their own if he stepped out.

Shucking his hat and coat, he entered, closed the door, and let himself through the partition to the other side of the counter. As he hung the coat and hat he sensed a stir behind him.

Otherwise motionless, he twisted for a glance at the empty mailbags in the corner. The heap of bags was indeed astir, though so slightly that if he had not been looking for it he would have missed it.

A mouse? His first thought was to reopen the door, scare

the critter from hiding, and let it skitter out to find a more festive banquet hall. Small nourishment in paper, wax, and ink. On second thought, it likely did well on paste.

But the stirring seemed too regular, too large-scale. Under the mailbags had to be a good-sized human trying to breathe shallowly.

Who would be playing 'possum under a pile of mailbags? A thief? A friend planning to pull a prank? He grinned. Either deserved a good scare. Moving about, he made to be thinking out-loud.

"Well, now, if it hain't clouding up. Be dark directly. Better fire up the oil lamp." He made a scratching sound, a fingernail along the counter. "Consarn the no-account match. Have to strike another." Another scratch. "That's more like it. Now I'll just turn the wick up a bit. That's the ticket. Whoops! If I hain't the clumsy one, tripping over my own big feet. Spilled the flaming oil and set the mailbags afire. Stamp it out, if I can; if I can't, have to fetch water from the horse trough. Whole town's tinder dry. Only fair to holler fire so's folks can wet down their homes. But I'm wasting time . . ."

The mailbags heaved, erupting a well-built young black man clutching a broomstick and looking wildly around.

He found a tall, rawboned white man blocking the way. The two stared at one another, the black holding the broom at the ready, the white primed for a wrestling match. Then the white smiled and stood easier, though still blocking the way.

"Well, now. Be you ordinary mail or something important?"

Despite the white's friendly tone, the black eyed him warily. " 'Scuse me, master?"

"I'm not your master. But let that pass. I meant to express

my surprise. You see, my friend, I'm the postmaster and this splendiferous edifice is my office. Now how about you? What do you call yourself and what are you doing here?"

"Please, sir, my name is Coffey." He looked as if he might try to bull past the postmaster or dash for the counter and vault over it.

"Pleased to make your acquaintance, Coffey. Mind telling me where you hail from?"

Coffey hesitated. "Tennessee, please, sir."

A slave state.

The postmaster's rough-hewn features formed a slight frown. "You escaped?"

Again Coffey hesitated. "No, sir."

The postmaster felt a burden lift. But not all the way. Why the defeated, almost hopeless, tone? Did Coffey think no white, let alone a government official, would believe him?

"Then why are you hiding?"

Once more Coffey hung fire. Just as he finally made to speak the doorknob rattled. Coffey faced the door in desperate defiance.

The postmaster gestured swiftly, all indolence gone. "Back under the bags."

Coffey quickly searched the white man's face. Then, with a beseeching look that seemed to hang after him in the air, he lowered the broom and dove for cover.

The postmaster fell back into his negligent stance as the door opened. A fussy-faced woman stepped in with a great flourish and swish of sateen.

He shaped his features into a look of pleased surprise. "Afternoon, Mrs. Sears. Tol'able nice day, don't you find?"

"Humph. Weather's so changeable a body don't hardly know what to put on to go out."

"That can be trying." He turned to the pigeonholes.

"Maybe there's something to brighten your day." His long index finger pointed him to the S's. "Thought so." He plucked forth a letter. "Here you be, Mrs. Sears. Letter from your sister Sally. Hope it's good news."

"Humph. Good or bad, it's going to cost me."

"True, ma'am. Goes for everything in life. Nothing people can do but pay up and be philosophical about it."

"Humph. Well, how much is it going to cost me?"

"The post office reckons postage rates by sheets of paper and distance. Single sheet needs 6 cents postage for up to 30 miles, 10 cents up to 80 miles, 12½ cents for 150 miles, 18¾ cents for 150 to 400 miles, and 25 cents for over 400 miles. Two sheets call for double postage, three sheets triple postage, and so on."

She bit off words as though biting off thread. "Skip the details, young man. Just calculate and be done. Tell me straight out how much I owe, and I'll pay up."

"Sorry, ma'am. Took a spell to get all that by heart, and it helps to spout it every once in a while so's I don't get rusty. Your letter traveled over 400 miles and must have three sheets, because the amount written on the outside is 75 cents."

"Bless my soul! 75 cents! What's the world coming to? Sally writes much too extravagant a hand. Surely she could squeeze all she has worth saying onto one sheet. Probably nothing but a passel of empty gossip, anyway."

"Do I take it, ma'am, you want to return it 'Refused'?" He made to dispose of the letter.

"Not so fast, young man. I'll pay the 75 cents. Though I surely will give Sally a good piece of my mind in my next letter." She froze in the act of taking the letter. "What was that?"

"That" had been an unmistakable sneeze. Coffey must

have stirred up the dust in taking cover; the sneeze he had been fighting back had its way at long last.

"What was what, Mrs. Sears?"

" 'Peared to come from that corner."

He beamed his honest face at her. "Well, now, ma'am, 'twouldn't surprise me none if it turned out to be a nest of mice."

"Mice!" Mrs. Sears almost dropped the letter in her haste to raise her skirt and petticoats. "Lord ha' mercy! Let me out this instant!"

"Good day, Mrs. Sears." But he spoke to a vanishing swirl of sateen.

He grinned, then grimaced and smote his brow. "Consarn it, I was a mite previous. Scairt her away before I collected the 75 cents. Have to remember next time I see her. By then she'll swear she already paid, and believe it too." He sighed. "Have to be philosophical, I reckon." He recollected Coffey and grew brisk.

"You can poke your head out now, Coffey. Best stay put otherwise, though. Might have us more callers."

Coffey stuck his head out from under.

The postmaster studied his face. "You look uneasy, Coffey. Don't tell me there's really a mouse!"

"Don't rightly know, Mr. Postmaster. But it's something."

"To think I had company all this while and didn't know. Can you share the corner with whatever it is till dark?"

Coffey's eyes shone. "Sure can, Mr. Postmaster. I'm willing if it is."

"Good. Now, before Mrs. Sears cut us short you were telling me why you're hiding."

Coffey drew breath. "Please, sir, if you don't mind, I have to go back a ways."

"By all means, Coffey. Let's stipulate, though, that Adam and Eve left the Garden of Eden and that in the course of events our forefathers came to this continent, and had children who begat us. So commence somewhat nearer us."

Coffey blinked.

The postmaster made a wiping-away gesture. "Sorry, Coffey. Just say it your own way."

"Yessir. Whenever I asked my mammy about how I come to be, she told me to hush and never mind. She never said, but I'm lighter-skinned than her and during my raising up years I heard some talk, folks saying I looked the spit of old master. He never treated me like his other slaves, that I know. Sometimes easier on me than he was on the rest, sometimes harder. Reckon it had a lot to do with how he and old missus got along—or didn't get along, 'cause she purely can get mean whenever her grain hits her—"

"Her grain?"

"Yessir. Ever once in a while she says 'My grain is killing me,' and that's when you better look out."

"Ah, yes. Migraine."

Coffey looked alarmed. "You got it too, sir?"

"No, Coffey. It's just that I understand what it is."

Coffey's alarm faded. "But it were something more than her grain at work when it come to me. She always had a heavier hand for me than for the others. Anyway, time came, a month back, when old master knowed he was dying. He writ me a paper saying he set me free."

"A letter of manumission?"

"I know there was a man in it and a mission. Cudjoe—he's a house slave—read it all out for me when I showed it to him to find out if old master was joking me."

"Would you care to show me the paper?"

Coffey's face displayed anguish and despair. "I had the

paper on me when I set out, bound for up North, following the Drinking Gourd stars. The paper and 20 silver dollars old master handed me to start me out. But then last night, in the woods just outside of this here town, I run into two riders."

Coffey's voice went dull. "They pointed guns at me. They told me they was slave catchers and that I matched the description of a runaway slave. I said I weren't their runaway. I said I was free. I told them about the paper old master give me. They read it by the light of a match and then they looked at each other and said it would take more study."

His face twitched. "They held on to the paper while they got down off the horses and untied their bedrolls and started a campfire. They read the paper again, then laughed and tossed it into the fire. I singed my hand trying to catch holt of it, but they grabbed me and it burned to ashes. Then they started to hog-tie me. That's when they found the 20 silver dollars on me. After they turned me inside out to make sure they had it all, they finished hog-tieing me. They sat up late around the fire, talking big and drinking hard and laughing fit to kill 'bout how they was going to spend the 20 silver dollars and how they was going to take me back down into Tennessee and sell me back into slavery."

The postmaster grunted, something fierce as a mule kick striking him in the pit of his stomach. "Sorry, Coffey; go on."

"Yessir. Soon as they fell asleep and started snoring, I begun to work out of the ropes. After a while—time it took the moon to slide half acrost the sky—I got a knot untied and wiggled loose. Then I crept past the white men, holding my breath and trying not to snap a stick or crunch a leaf. When I got by, I raised up and made tracks out of the wood. I kept to the backs of houses, looking for a place to rest. I found a back porch to hide under where there wasn't no dog in the yard. I stayed till first light, when the house begun to stir. Then I moved on. I picked up a wore out stub of broom somebody had throwed away and I made out to be sweeping the walks. That's how I moved along through town without anybody paying me any mind."

The postmaster chuckled. Coffey joined in. Both chuckles tailed off into a sad silence that commented on Coffey's attainment of invisibility. Then Coffey went on.

"I kept my eyes open for something to eat or for somebody that looked like they might spare me a scrap. I noticed an old black lady toting a market basket. She put me in mind of my ma. Just as I was stepping up to her, I spotted one of the white men that had took me. He was way at the end of the street and it didn't look like he had spied me yet. I saw the door to this here place half open and so I swept right up to it—fast as I could without running—and slipped inside. And here I been since."

The postmaster reached into a pocket of his coat. "Here's an apple I've been saving. Catch."

A hand thrust up out of the heap and caught the apple. "Thank you kindly, Mr. Postmaster." Coffey gave the apple a token polish on a mailbag, took a big bite, then minded his manners and took daintier bites.

The postmaster lounged thoughtfully. "We can't write your old master for a new letter of manumission. The post office has no arrangements for communicating with heaven or hell."

Coffey ventured a sad smile. "Nossir, I didn't think so." He appeared to be looking for what to do with the core.

"Just leave it for our friend," the postmaster said absently.

The door burst open.

Gesturing Coffey down out of sight, the postmaster turned slowly to find a rifle thrusting through. A loutish stranger followed the rifle.

The stranger, after a heavy-browed sizing-up, widened his probe to cover the room. He kept the rifle in line with the postmaster. He gave a jerk of his head and advanced. A second rifle-toting lout stepped inside.

The postmaster smiled at the two. "Good day, friends. How can I help you?"

The first stranger nodded with a wolfish grin. His eyes remained restless. "Was you talking to somebody just now?"

The postmaster cast his gaze back in time. "Was I? I often talk to myself. And I like to think I'm somebody. So you may very well be right."

The man blinked, then scowled. He spoke over his shoulder. "Would you call that a straight answer, Jed?"

Jed gave a barking sort of laugh. "Any crookeder, Harl, and it would go right back down his throat."

Harl nodded. "What I thought." He came near enough for the muzzle to touch the postmaster's chest. "Mister, I don't believe you'll mind if we look around back in there."

The postmaster didn't give the fraction of an inch. "Friend, you believe wrong. This is government property, and you two are trespassing."

Harl swelled up. "Mister, we hain't asking, we're telling. We're slave catchers after a runaway slave, and we got just as much gov'ment on our side." He gestured with his rifle to call attention to it. "Maybe a sight more. Feller over yonder in the saloon says he spied a big black buck slip into this here post office. Feller says he didn't notice him come out again."

The postmaster looked out. He made out a nose pressed to the saloon's window. He smiled. "If your informant's who I think it is, he's known to see lots stranger things."

Harl blinked. "Maybe so. Still, long as we're here, best make sure. You wouldn't want no desperate runaway slave to jump out at you when you was alone. If he's here, we'll take him off your hands. Law-abiding man like you wouldn't want aiding a runaway on your conscience."

"Thanks." The postmaster spoke dryly. "On the other hand, law-abiding man like me wouldn't want condoning trespass on his conscience. Looks like a standoff, don't it?"

A heavy stillness filled the office. Then Harl spoke again over his shoulder. "You thinking what I'm thinking, Jed?"

"Yair. I think he's running a bluff on us."

Two flint-lock rifle hammers came back as one.

The postmaster straightened to his full height. "Better get me with the first shot, boys." He spoke almost offhandedly. He loosened his broad shoulders to give his heavily muscled arms play. "And better get me in the vitals."

Harl and Jed remained frozen. They exchanged sideglances. Then Harl lowered his rifle and forced a laugh. "Hell, we can wait, can't we, Jed?"

Jed lowered his rifle in turn. "That's right, Harl. No back way to this here place. Nobody's going nowhere without we know. We can set over yonder and keep watch."

"Now you bring it up, Jed, I do feel dry in the mouth. Could use a drink." Harl shoved a hand in his pocket and clinked coins. "Maybe more than one, seeing as how we're mighty flush."

Jed smirked. "Now you're talking, Harl." He clinked his share. "We'll treat each other," they guffawed.

Without a glance at the postmaster, they clapped each other on the shoulder, turned, and strode out.

The postmaster waited till the echo of their boots died out in the room, waited till they entered the saloon, waited till Coffey stirred behind him.

"What we going to do, sir? I can't leave, and I can't stay forever. And I don't want you to have to risk your hide over me."

"Thanks, Coffey. I've grown attached to this hide. But I hardly think it's in danger from the likes of Harl and Jed."

" 'Scuse me, sir, but don't you be too sure 'bout that."

"You're right, Coffey. I oughtn't to make light of any human's capacity for good or evil. Wouldn't put it past that pair to take me from behind if they saw their chance."

The postmaster stared across the way. Then his gaze lit on a portly figure striding importantly up the street.

"Stay hid, Coffey, but don't be alarmed. I see somebody I want to call in. Might be the answer to our prayers."

He reached the doorway in two strides, leaned out, and gave a holler.

"Judge! Judge Thornton!"

Judge Thornton came to a halt and looked across.

"Would you step over a minute, Judge? Got something for you."

The judge gave a nod and crossed without looking to either side, perfectly sure traffic would rein in for him. Once inside, he looked from the postmaster's grave face to the postmaster's empty hands and back again.

"Thought you had something for me."

"Didn't say it was mail, Judge, and didn't say under oath."

The judge's eyebrows flocked together. "Just why did you call me over?"

"Judge, without prejudicing in any way the outcome of the case, hold yourself in readiness to rule on a pair of scoundrelly strangers liquoring up in the saloon. I'm going to stop in there shortly for a peaceable dram. If somehow those fellers and myself have a run-in, if words come to blows, we'll be up before you for breaching the peace. Should you find it necessary to fine them I have a suspicion they're good for some 20 silver dollars."

When a gleam appeared in the judge's eyes he went on.

"And a night in the cooler would do them small harm and someone else good a-plenty."

The judge kept a noncommittal face. "Hmmm." He pulled his waistcoat smooth. "Thanks for the forewarning. I myself was about to stop in for a wee potion. Now I believe I'll turn around and go home so I don't witness what transpires. That way I can keep an open mind in court. Good day." He gave the postmaster a nod and a wink as he left.

"Coast's clear, Coffey. I take it you heard what passed between Judge Thornton and me?"

"Yessir."

"Then you know what I aim to do. I'll give the scoundrels time to befuddle themselves, then I'll go in and stir them up. When you hear the ruckus and see the town constable haul the three of us away, light out. If Harl and Jed are cooling their heels, and the rest of their anatomies, in a jail cell, they won't be on your trail tonight. You'll have a good head start, and I know you'll make the most of it."

"Yessir. Thank you, sir."

The postmaster sauntered behind the partition. He emptied his pockets of change and handed the sum to Coffey. "Sorry this is all I have to start you out with anew. But a man like you should find friends and work in short order."

"Thank you kindly, sir. I'll surely try to repay you."

"All right, call it a loan. But we'll be square when you hand it on to someone else in need." Coffey nodded. The postmaster cleared his throat. "Before we part, let's write your ma you're well on your way to freedom."

Coffey's eyes yearned, but his mouth drooped. "Ole missus won't pay for no letter to my ma—lessen out of pure curiosity. And then out of pure meanness, or out of what her grain makes her do, old missus would rip it up or worse yet lie about what's writ."

"Must be a way of getting word to your ma."

"Cudjoe, sir. Just before I left, Cudjoe say he hear ole missus tell a woman friend Cudjoe done got too uppity to suit her, and now she was free to, she would sell Cudjoe off to the neighboring plantation. Was I to write Cudjoe there, he can find way to let my ma know I'm well." He hesitated. "Trouble is, sir, Cudjoe won't have money to pay for the letter, and I can't pay you ahead of time, lessen you take back what you loaned me, 'cause other than that I don't have cent one."

The gaunt face drew even tighter in a grin. "Frankly, neither have I. No problem, though." The lanky young fellow reached out a long arm and put pen to paper.

FREE, A. LINCOLN, p.m.,

NEW SALEM, ILL; SEPT. 22, 1835.

Then he turned the sheet over and made ready to take down what Coffey had to say.

THE WHISPER OF GOLD

Tom Chaudis weighed his one loaded shell in his hand. Weighing it, he weighed also his choices, his chances. With a sigh more like a groan he shoved the shell into the shotgun.

By the light of the lantern hanging from a timber he gazed around at the false glints in the mine face. He had put a river of sweat into this hole, the whisper of gold leading him on. But what gold there was had plain pinched up and played out after the first burst of richness. And almost all that gold he had long since spent celebrating in town, believing—and leading everyone to believe—the gold had no end. The way he saw it, he had no out now but the load in his shotgun.

He knew that—so why was he putting it off?

As he slowly raised the shotgun he thought he heard the hurry of his heart. He stilled himself to listen harder and heard the hurry of hooves. Now that was a crazy sound to be coming from the ground outside with all its cracks and chuckholes. He lowered the shotgun and rounded the tunnel bend to the mouth of the mine and the blaze of day.

He gaped at the mad ride—and at the mad rider, a woman streaming yellow hair. Then he saw that the woman had lost hold of the reins and was hanging onto the saddlehorn. Something—a rattler, maybe—had spooked the mare into running wild, white-eyeballed.

As Tom watched, the mare plunged into a hole, dropped to her knees, and flung the rider from the saddle. The woman landed forked end up, then folded and lay still. Tucking his shotgun under his arm, Tom ran to her.

He knelt beside the woman and looked for broken bones. Coming quickly out of her daze, she stopped his fumbling.

111

"I'm all right. See to my mare."

Tom wasn't so sure the woman was all right, but he moved to the mare, ran his hand along her left foreleg, and found the break. He turned to the woman and shook his head.

The young woman, her bright hair tangled, had shoved herself upright. She stood swaying slightly—wobbly, but on her own two feet—smudges and all, a pretty woman. High-grade, but kind of ornery to be out this way all by her lonesome. Wilful, used to getting her way—which would stay respectable, though off the beaten track. Right now, with grief for the mare twisting her face, she seemed not so sure of herself. And not so sure she liked her present company. The way she eyed him sidelong, he must pan out mean, look like a man searching for a dog to kick.

He rubbed his face, throwing himself back to the last time he had shaved. That had been in town, and the woman he had been with had hardly assayed out to the purity of this kind of woman. This kind of woman he had always dreamed of but never aspired to. Now that she was suddenly real and at hand he felt strange, as though in a dream. Standing there with her yellow hair stirring gently in the hot slow breath of noon, she seemed like a whisper of gold come to life to lead him on.

Maybe things could work out so that . . .

Hell with it. He had no time for such thoughts. What he had was to get shut of her so he could do what he set out to do when she came along. He tried to think how he might speed her on her way. He had lost his own burro to a rattler or he would have given it to her for the ride home.

The mare's humble nickering gave him a guilty start, but he made no move to put the mare away. Averting her gaze from the mare and frowning in surprise and impatience at Tom's inaction, the woman gestured toward his shotgun.

"Aren't you going to—?"

Automatically he raised the shotgun to his shoulder, took aim, and actually had his finger on the pull. Then he lowered the shotgun without firing. Stonily, feeling a fool, he stood that way.

The woman stared, then raised her voice, more in wonder than in outrage. "What are you waiting for?"

Then her face changed and he could almost see her think he lacked the nerve. She reached out toward the shotgun.

"If you want, I—"

He felt even more a fool—a shameful fool. "It isn't that. I'm sorry, ma'am, but I need the shell. I'll put her away though."

He leaned the shotgun against a boulder, took up a length of weathered two-by-four, and, stretching himself into savagery, brought the wood down hard. With a sick sound the wood connected. He heard the woman's breath. The blow stung his palms, but the mare only lay stunned. He threw the timber aside, drew his sheath knife, and sawed her throat, all too aware of the woman watching in horror with the edge of an eye, and only just jumped away from the bloody gush. He stabbed the gritty soil to cleanse the blade before sheathing the knife, then picked up his shotgun before facing the woman.

Her cheeks flamed through trail powder and he could see her think, Butcher!

He gestured an apology. "I have just the one shell, and I'm saving it."

"I see," she said, clearly not seeing. Still, she seemed inclined to give him the benefit of the doubt. She looked away from the mare and brought a surface smile into being. "I don't want to saddle you with my troubles, but I have to think about getting back." She waited. When he came up with silence her smile slipped away and she went on. "I guess I'll just dust myself off and head on home."

He wanted to say yes and no—to keep her here and get rid of her. He found himself saying, "No. Wait here a spell, till an hour past noon. The banker's coming from town to look over my claim."

Her smile came back. She found a smooth rock, dusted it and herself off, and sat. "You're Tom Chaudis, aren't you? I heard about you and your mine. In fact, someone pointed you out to me in town."

His face burned and he felt glad for the growth of beard. He wondered how and where he had been when she had seen him. He hoped it hadn't been in the company of a dance-hall girl and a bottle.

Suddenly he had a terrible thought, a joyously unworthy thought. Could it be he had touched a chord of jealousy and desire in this high-grade girl? Then he had an even more terrible thought, a bitterly malicious thought. Could it be this whisper-of-gold girl was herself subject to the pull of riches?

Sure funny that she had chosen to ride out this desolate way, reach this particular claim. Was she after all within reach, within grasp, buyable?

The shotgun came back into his awareness. He didn't have much time. The sun had begun to lose its high.

His mind fevered, trying to figure what color he could give his going back into the mine and what judgment she would make when she heard the shot.

He gathered himself to make the move, then froze.

The woman, mistaking his stiffness and trying to keep the one-sided conversation going, gave a self-conscious little laugh. "But I haven't minded my manners. I'm Margie Lawrence."

"Don't move."

But he had spoken his harsh whisper too late. Margie,

awaking to the realization that he was staring past her, was already rising to turn and see what had caught his eye.

She saw the rattler.

The diamondback, set in an S to strike; was close enough for Tom to see the deep pit between eye and nostril on each side of the questing head. Margie's start drew the rattler's stare.

A rattler usually struck one-third its length away, but it could strike its full length away. Margie stood two feet from this six-footer.

Tom drew some hope from the rattler's silence, though he knew truth often gave the lie to the myth of a sportsmanlike shake of the rattle. The silence gave Tom mulish strength to do nothing, though Margie's eyes begged him to blast the diamondback with his precious shell.

Why couldn't Margie have come an hour earlier or an hour later? Why now? Why here? Why him?

Margie swayed. The snake would see any sudden movement as a threat. To fall in a faint would be fatal. Damn the woman!

In controlled fury Tom raised the shotgun, took snap aim, and fired.

The shot tore into the rattler and retwisted it flat and still. The shot bespattered the diamond pattern with golden glints. It brought Margie back to life.

Her gaze fixed on the gold-flecked remains. Her eyes narrowed, then widened. Tom, empty of feeling, watched her face change to mask her understanding.

"Thanks," she whispered hoarsely.

He answered with a curt nod.

She would know now why he had been so unwilling to spend the shot, even in need. He had loaded the shell with the last of his gold, meaning to salt the mine, hoping to dazzle the banker into believing the mine was a bonanza.

It was with near-relief that Tom welcomed the sight of the banker's buggy sedately trailing dust. Quickly he used the shotgun barrel to lift-toss the mortal coil into the brush. He glanced at Margie. Her face was blank.

While they waited in heavy silence, the buggy grew out of distance, bringing the banker and his son, the son at the reins. Seeing them, the son gave a touch of the whip for a dashing pull-up. He looped the reins around the buggy whip in its socket and leaped out. "Margie! What in tarnation are you doing way out here?" His gaze, coldly accusing, whipped across Tom's face. "Are you all right?"

"Yes, William."

"What happened?" He offered her a fresh handkerchief and a water flask.

She took them with gratitude and dabbed her face partway clean. "Lady Fancy spooked, ran away with me, and broke her leg."

The banker and his son followed her gesture toward the corpse of the mare, then quickly away. "That would account for the shot we heard," the banker said.

Margie cocked her head to one side and threw a glance Tom's way. "Yes, it would." Her eyes darted toward the brush where the dead snake lay and she drew a shuddering breath. "Would you take me back to town?"

The banker said, "Surely." He eyed the mine opening and swiftly veiled his gold-hungry look. "Just allow us a few minutes to do our business here, my dear, and we'll be on our way." He turned to Tom.

Tom cut him off before he started. "Sorry you had to ride out here for nothing. When I sent word in, I was sure I'd found a lode, but I guess I was wrong. Ain't no mine worth selling or buying. Ain't nothing here for nobody."

The son handed Margie into the buggy. "Lucky we went on a wild-goose chase in this case."

The father looked sour, but said nothing.

Margie looked at Tom and, after a flicker of some feeling Tom could lay no name to, nodded farewell. And then it was as if Tom had never been.

The son took up the reins, gave a touch of the whip, and said something to Margie. Her laugh drifted back, streaming with her yellow hair.

Tom stood watching them ride away till they pinched up and played out.

He rubbed his beard thoughtfully, then hunted the dead rattler in the brush, taking care—he didn't want to run across the rattler's mate or kin. He found the riddled skin and used the shotgun barrel to pick it up. It hung limp, but as it twisted slightly with breeze-given false life, it glinted.

That glint was worth saving. He would build a fire and reduce the snake to ashes. Reducing the snake to ashes and panning the ashes—that seemed the best way to reclaim the gold he had meant to salt the mine with.

Later he would make up his mind whether to blow the gold on dancehall girls and redeye or to buy stagecoach passage back to the family farm.

Either way, it looked like it was his hard lot to be honest, in spite of himself.

DEATH AND TAXES

Two old guys sitting on a nursing-home porch, staring blankly across at window reflections of the setting sun. Two old guys warding off the fall chill by warming themselves at the still-glowing embers of past glories.

First old guy, call him Death, said, "Young and old, good and bad, rich and poor, high and low, unknown and famous, all ended up the same place: where I worked. I was an undertaker. Funeral directors, they call themselves these days." Death's eyes brightened. "The deceased I remember best was Stella Lastel."

Second old guy, call him Taxes, stirred. "Stella Lastel?"

Death looked ready to be miffed. "Don't tell me you never heard of Stella Lastel."

Taxes said, "Of cause I heard of Stella Lastel. Why, once I—"

Death said, "Of course you heard of Stella Lastel. Everybody heard of her. Most beautiful movie star of her time. Made the headlines and the covers every time she married or divorced—and in-between hit the gossip columns almost daily with rumors about who she was seeing and about trouble she was giving her directors on the sets and on location. Didn't end with her passing, either. They're still writing articles and books about the mystery of her dying. 'Did she really take her own life, on purpose or accidentally, by overdosing on pills and liquor—or did someone poison her?' 'Did the FBI or the CIA do her in to keep her quiet about the affair she had with the President?' All kinds of wild speculation. At the time, though, all that was the farthest thing from my mind. All I knew or cared about was that I got to see Stella

118

Lastel close up. I remember she needed only a few touches of makeup. Even in repose, she still was the loveliest and sexiest woman I ever saw. I know I felt awful about it, thought what a terrible waste." Death sighed. "She was so young yet, had a long way to go." Then he shrugged. "But she had no more worries now, no more of the hang-ups that drove her to pills and liquor, no more anxieties to push her over the edge."

Taxes said, "I remember well when that happened. I worked for the Internal Revenue Service in those days. I know it hit me hard. Back then I was a real movie fan. Not the kind that hangs around theaters or restaurants with an autograph book, but I did want to meet my favorites in the flesh." He smiled slyly. "So what I did was, I would initiate audits of stars, even though there was nothing wrong with the return, just so I could get to meet them."

Death narrowed his eyes. "Did you ever meet Stella Lastel?"

Taxes shook his head regretfully. "Can't say as I did."

Death grinned, one up on Taxes.

Taxes was going on, though. "Funny coincidence. She knocked herself off the very day I was supposed to have a meeting with her about her return."

SPUR THE NIGHTMARE

From his catercornered hiding place in the areaway across the street, he watched her come out of her apartment house. Fighting his love and his hate and his need, he just barely held himself back from jumping her, from taking her right there in the street and frightening the horses, if there had been horses. Even at this distance he could tell she had grown haunted-eyed, hollow-cheeked, twitchy-mouthed. She stared jerkily around, then stepped onto the sidewalk as though testing the concrete, warily ready to spring back indoors.

Failing to spot him, she breathed deep and committed herself to the open. She walked rapidly eastward, unbobbed hair bobbing. Watching with jealous pride of possession, he saw heads turn as she passed. Naicar Bowtri was one of those blondes who looks terrific in lemon blouse and lime slacks; for that matter, in anything, in nothing.

He forced himself to wait in the areaway shadows till she had gone, and a bit longer. Her point of no return would be the bus stop three blocks east. When he felt sure she would not be turning back to get something she had forgotten—her billfold, her eyeglasses for reading—he left his hiding place and crossed the street. He let himself in with his duplicate key to the front door of the building. He took the elevator to the sixth floor.

So far, so good. He had not run into the super or any nosy neighbors. He turned right when he got off the elevator and strode swiftly—blurringly, if an eye happened to be at a peep-hole along the way—to the end of the corridor. But his duplicate key to the door of her apartment suddenly proved useless.

She had changed the lock since yesterday.

He grimaced. How had he missed out on that? Either the super had done it for her or the locksmith had come in a car with no advertising on its flanks. Well, either way, it was done.

He smiled. Did she suspect his visits despite his having hurled the keys back at her in parting—after copying them—and despite his pains to leave no traces? Or did she merely mean to make assurance doubly sure? She ought to know him well enough to know that frustrating him only egged him on.

It was done, but it could be undone. When you had a consuming passion even inanimate objects showed themselves to be enthusiastically with you or bitterly against you. His MasterCard seemed to leap into his hand in its eagerness to prove itself a master key. He slid it into the crack between door and jamb and forced it past the bolt. With some weight and muscle helping, the plastic gained him entry. Once again love had given locksmiths the raspberry. He stepped inside quickly and shut the door gently. He slipped out of his loafers and trod lightly in his stockinged feet so that old but not doddering Mrs. Parker in the apartment below would not hear walking about during an hour she knew to be a work hour of Naicar's.

Before he forgot, before he would let himself enjoy invading Naicar's intimacies, he made straight for the kitchenette. He opened the refrigerator. Inhaling its frosty breath seemed to sharpen his senses, to concentrate his mind into an icy dagger. His gaze shot to the quart container of skim milk. The waxy shadow of its contents, even before he took it out and hefted it, showed it half-empty since yesterday. He took three amphetamine pills from his pocket, crushed them between the counter and the bottom of a glass, scraped up the powder with a knife blade and sprinkled it into the milk she would warm to put herself to sleep. He blew away what dust remained on the counter and wiped the bottom of the glass and the blade of the knife. He reclosed the milk container and as though mixing a cocktail shook it to dissolve the powder, then replaced the container in the refrigerator.

A half-eaten tuna-fish-salad sandwich caught his eye. His smile locked in place. Losing her appetite, poor thing? Take, eat; this is my body. But hold the mayo. He loosened the clear plastic wrapping enough to take a bite, to nibble what she had nibbled, then rewrapped the sandwich and put it back. He closed the door softly. The refrigerator motor switched on to make up for the coldness he had spilled.

Now he released himself to roam her rooms. His heart beat faster, harder, louder, as he saw, smelled, felt Naicar's ghostly presence, her imprint on the place. He rummaged through drawers and poked into closets. He touched what she had touched, and in a sense that made them one again. Even to its being in the last analysis as unsatisfying; for, however close they had been, she had always kept some part of herself, however small, to herself, beyond his knowing in the unbiblical sense.

Today he made two discoveries.

The first, that she had been writing a letter to her older sister. He did not find the letter itself; that, she either had finished and taken for mailing or had given up on. He found a pair of false starts in the wastebasket. He smoothed out the crumples, read both drafts, and each time came across his own name with a shock. In what he took to be the later draft she let herself go, permitted herself to be more open about him, about their relationship.

. . . *His name is Tom Ehrsruef and he won't let me be. You of all people know why I left home. I have to keep some part of me for myself; he wants to be my everything. I'm supposed to live and breathe only him. He's obsessed with having me obsessed with him. He was my live-in lover for six months, till he got so violent I threw him out. Not exactly threw—it took a lot of doing, a lot of threatening to call the cops and whatnot. He still keeps phoning and hanging around. I'm afraid. If you saw him, you'd believe I'm the crazy one, making false accusations. Even I sometimes, even now, doubt myself. Tom a menace? You'd never think it to look at him. He has such a nice smile . . .*

Tom smiled. He knew he had a nice smile. People had told him so from the time he had been yea high. He had a memory—real or false; at this point in his life did the distinction matter?—of his mother drilling a dimple in his cheek with her fingertip. "Oh what a nice baby; oh, what a sunny smile!"

. . . But behind that smile is a warped mind. He says he loves me. That's love? I'm telling you this now so that if anything happens to me you'll have something to go to the police with. Because I'm convinced he'll stop at nothing to get me back or to get even. Oh, I know, Sis, you're laughing right now as you read this and I can hear you saying there goes Naicar again, being melodramatic!!! But I swear it's all so. He means to run my life or ruin my life. I've gone to the police myself, but—though they don't say so in so many words—they think I'm paranoid, or at the very least fanciful, over-imaginative, because he's made no overt move. But I can feel his eyes on me. I know he follows me, spies on me . . .

Fiercely, he recrumpled the draft letters, faintly feeling crinkly protest of ignored memory of original crumpling, and hurled than back into the wastebasket.

His second find was something in the morning paper. Rather, something not in it.

She had refolded it neatly, though jam smears and orange juice stains blazed a trail through the once-timber when he opened it and fanned the pages. She had filled out the current-affairs quiz and done the crossword puzzle; she had this drive to better herself, to build her vocabulary, to speak knowledgeably, cultivatedly.

The paper told him nothing more, except that juice stains, like a parked car's oil drippings, showed she had lingered over a Lord & Taylor ad; it would be the crew-neck sweater that caught and held her eye. Told him nothing new, that is, till he reached the classifieds.

There he discovered a hole. She had snipped out an inch-high ad, razored it out, rather, with the tool she used for cents-off coupons.

His heart went erratic. What was she up to now? Hunting an out-of-town job, looking to get away from him? He heard the blood pound. She ought to know better than to think that she would ever get away from him.

Hold on, it wasn't that; the pigeonholing wasn't among the Help Wanteds; the placement had been under the heading Personals. His temples throbbed. Personal? The word turned red. He would show her personal. Unless—

Swiftly, he turned the page. No, there was no ad missing on this other side. On this other page the hole appeared in the middle of a display ad for an auto dealer giving away Cadillacs if you could beat his price. Tom turned back to the original page. Personal it was.

He started to tear the whole page from the paper, stopped himself, and instead familiarized himself with the ads surrounding the hole. He refolded the paper as neatly as Naicar had, then put it back where he had found it. He looked around, regained his terrible calm. No sign Tom Ehrsruef had ever been here. Still, maybe Naicar would sense the electricity of his emotional storms, breathe ionized air charged with his presence, and start at shadows and shiver. He slipped into his loafers and left as softly as he had entered.

★ ★ ★ ★ ★

He stopped at a newsstand. The thick-lensed newsy still had copies of the morning paper. Tom, in his impatience, in his need to know, wanted to rip right through all the layers to the gold of his Troy, but disciplined, sado-masochized himself to walk around the corner—a Troy wait, he told himself with his nice smile—before opening the paper and riffling through to the classifieds, to Personal. He got his bearing, located the ad to fit his mental template.

WANTED: NIGHTMARE-SUFFERERS TO TAKE PART IN SCIENTIFIC SLEEP STUDY. ONLY THOSE WITH FREQUENT AND INTENSE NIGHTMARES NEED APPLY. PHONE FOR INTERVIEW.

The ad gave no name or address, but the exchange of the phone number it did give belonged to the University area, so it was probably on the up-and-up.

During the time he had been with Naicar she had never once mentioned having nightmares. Nightmares were not a thing you could hold back from your bedmate, keep under cover. So the nightmares had started only since his leaving her. He smiled his nice smile, pleased to have come across this sign that her suffering went soul-deep and had to do with him.

His smile turning to one of wonder, he stared far into the realm of possibility. A flash of circuitry; a whole new line of thinking and planning had opened up for him.

What kind of nightmares did she have?

Was he in them?

He looked around for a pay phone, spotted one on the next corner. Fingering the change in his pocket to see if he had the necessary dimes and nickels, he made briskly for the phone.

He dialed the number, got a busy signal.

Herds of nightmares on the gallop, he guessed, lots of hagridden riders of the mind's nag. He held on.

At last the busyness ended. A woman's voice came on the line. "Are you responding to the ad?"

"That's right."

The woman rattled off a rote speech. "If you volunteer, and if you're one of those we pick, you'll have to spend several nights in the sleep lab here at the University. Are you free to do so?"

"I am."

"There's no real pay involved, just expenses." The voice hurried on, overriding itself. "Though the primary purpose of the study isn't therapy, it's possible you may get some relief."

"I understand."

"Good." Firm and brisk, though the no-nonsense voice strove to sound friendly. "I'll take your name and set up an appointment."

"Bill Dewey."

"Fine, Mr. Dewey, I'm putting you down for six a.m. Thursday the twentieth. Is that convenient for you? Can you make it?"

"Sure. Thursday the twentieth at six."

"Just ask for the Sleep Clinic in Montague Hall."

"Right."

He hung up, knowing he would not keep the appointment even under the phony name he had given. While it was tempting to visualize surprising Naicar at Montague Hall and letting her see he knew how badly he troubled her mind, he had no intention of spending this golden opportunity so unthriftily, of frightening her away. He wanted her in the program, he needed to know her nightmares.

★ ★ ★ ★ ★

He made certain Naicar followed up on the ad. He tailed her to the Sleep Clinic twice and proved to his satisfaction, to his grim delight, that she had passed the interview and had signed on.

Then he phoned the public relations department of the University and found himself speaking to a Ms. Joy Larkin.

"My name's Jack Neilsen. I do free-lance articles on scientific subjects for the popular magazines. My editor at *Pop Psych* suggested I do a piece on the nightmare research your Sleep Clinic is carrying out."

"It's not my Sleep Clinic, it's Dr. Zareh's." Ms. Larkin's voice seemed a bit querulous. "I'm not sure Dr. Zareh would welcome any publicity at this early stage."

"Then that's the very stage I want to be in on. I don't care to settle for the handouts everyone gets after the thing is over. If that was all I got I'd pass it up altogether. What I'm after is an exclusive. I promise not to publish till Dr. Zareh gives the okay, but I would like to be in at the start and follow the progress of the research. You think he'd go for that?"

"She. Dr. Em Zareh. Woman. Female. Opposite sex." The tone was mockingly reproving.

"Oh."

"Yes, oh. That, with a cross under it, is the symbol."

"You do have a cross to bear." He put his smile into voice and she laughed. He pressed his success. "Well, do you think she'd go for that?"

"I can ask. I'll get back to you. Where can I reach you?"

"I'm out in the field most of the time. How about if I phone you tomorrow, say at this same hour?"

"You'll have your answer. I hope it's affirmative, for your sake and mine, but Dr. Zareh's a funny gal and I never know how she'll take it whenever I urge her to cooperate with the press. She seems to think cooperating with means pandering to."

"Tell her I've heard of nightmare research on the West Coast and that I'd just as soon cover that, what with winter in the offing."

"Is there nightmare research on the West Coast?"

Tom put a shrug in his voice. "I don't know. Anything's possible, isn't it?"

Ms. Larkin laughed. "Winter sure is. I'll be waiting for your call."

"The answer's a reluctant yes. I think you got to her with the hint somebody in her field may beat her out. Can you make it here this afternoon at four?"

"Wait while I look through my appointments . . . I believe I can fit her in."

"I'll tell her to expect you. Maybe if you're through playing hard to get you'll find time to stop in and see me either before or after."

"I will that. Thanks much. Be seeing you, Joy."

In the few horns before his appointment with Dr. Zareh he did some quick research on her at the public library. He looked her up in *Who's Who* and *Encyclopedia of Associations*, skimmed through her book *Traum & Trauma* and her latest articles in professional journals, and read reviews of the book. Her portrait on the dust jacket of *Traum & Trauma* showed a serenely assured woman looking younger than the forty of her bio, with regular features and smooth, almost lacquered, skin over fine bones, a severe hairdo her only sign of or concession to pedantry or punditry.

Her appearance in person matched the portrait except that she was smaller than it and her voice had led him to expect. And on closer look a frown had wedged its way between her eyebrows since the picture taking or had been retouched out of the portrait. Then, too, her hairdo had changed and had broken training since the sitting, stray wisps and loose curls softening the portrait's image of total control.

She gave him a brief but firm, firm but brief, handshake. After the token amenities, she beat him to the first question. "Who on the West Coast is doing nightmare research?"

"Not West Coast; Gulf Coast."

"Trust Larkin to get it wrong. Well, who on the Gulf Coast?"

"Fellow at U. of Louisiana."

"Oh, Louisiana." She gave a slight and slightly scornful toss of the head. "What line is he taking? If you know."

"Correlating nightmares and biorhythms."

"Oh, biorhythms." She gave a slight and slightly more scornful smile.

He nodded earnestly. "I feel the same way. In your *Traum & Trauma* you pretty much demolish any such tie-in. At least you convinced me."

A curve of her mouth said she took that with a grain of salt but still found it sweet. "I see you've done your homework." She looked thoughtful and shook her head. "Maybe I convinced you, but I'm afraid biorhythms, like astrology, will always be with us." She threw off her resignation and grew brisk. "All right. You have my permission to observe our progress." She gave him a hard stare. "I want no premature publicity. I won't have myself looking like one of those oddball faddists."

"I understand."

Her frown wedged suddenly deeper. "Have we ever met before? I have this feeling . . ."

Only over the phone, when I used a phony name. The

gone and forgotten whosit—Bill Dewey? Ought to keep a little black book to check them off in. Better remember who he was now—Jack Neilsen. "A definite no. I certainly would have remembered meeting you."

She ignored his try at soft-soaping. "Then it must be déjà-vu experience. Freud, you know, sums all such experience trace back to the mother's womb and environs—we've all been there before. If I had the time, I'd stop to analyze why the thought surfaced just now."

Because you suddenly recalled my voice and my words over the phone, and mom comes into it because the phone is umbilical, that's why. Better get her going about her project, keep her mind on that and off who Jack Nielsen reminded her of. "Speaking of time, when do your nightmarers start nightmaring?"

"They've been at it for six months." She cracked a wise smile at the jolt she gave him. "My early subjects have been University students. I'm widening it out now to sample nightmare-sufferers among the general public." Her frowning smile surprised him by turning impish. "Frankly, I'm weary of the sameness, of nightmares expressing fear of exams. There's variety out there, and it's true that variety is the spice of life." Her smile grew serious again. "And of course generalizing the sample will make our findings more valid, more universal. But, as I say, we're fairly well along." She even made a small joke. "I think I can see the tunnel at the end of the light."

"Have you reached any preliminary conclusions?"

"None that I'm ready to talk about. What I am willing to talk about is our procedure."

"Fine. I'm ready and willing to listen."

"Then it's show-and-tell time."

She gestured toward a door stenciled MONITORING,

led him through it to what looked like a control room, what with all the screens and dials and all the computers and peripherals. She seated him before a video monitor and switched it on to pull in an empty cot strewn with wiring. For an eerie instant he had the crazy impression a ghost was getting an EKG.

He let his disappointment show. "I hope you'll let me observe something more than an empty bed."

Dr. Zareh made a face. "Don't panic. This is only to ground you in our technique. As you can see, and will see, we wire the subject up. That's not as bad as it sounds. We merely tape electrodes to record brain rhythms, patterns of blood pressure, pulse, respiration, body temperature, skin resistance, muscle tone, and eye movements. We record everything, and we videotape the subject, printing real time right on the tape—à la Abscam—so that we can match what's going on on the outside of the subject with what's going on inside. We let the subject fall asleep naturally. No drugs to induce sleep or alter normal thinking patterns." She looked thoughtful, almost dreamy. "That may come later." She shook herself. "But we're keeping this stage clean and simple, with minimal variables, elegant, not open to question." She looked to see if he was with her, and went on after he nodded. "We let the subject sleep till the subject wakes by him- or herself. If the subject reports a nightmare, the person monitoring from this station will interview the subject through an intercom system."

All this talk of a subject made the subject seem an object. Tom nodded. "Gotcha. What then?"

"Let me back up a bit. While the subject sleeps the various sensors determine the onset of a nightmare." She hesitated an instant, hovering in mid-decision, then went on. "At that point, a computerized visualizer projects the nightmare on a screen."

It took a beat or two for that to sink in. Then the violence of Tom's reaction, his grabbing her arm and thrusting his face eagerly into hers, gave Dr. Zareh a scare.

He spoke obliviously. "You mean you can actually see someone's nightmare?"

"You're hurting my arm."

"Oh. Sorry." He let go.

She rubbed her arm with her other hand ruefully. "That's the sort of reaction I'm afraid of, the press media's tendency to sensationalize the more dramatic aspects of our work." She took in his sheepish nice smile and strove to be fair. "A certain amount of the right kind of publicity makes for easier funding, but too much of the wrong kind makes reputable backers shy away, to say nothing of lowering one's standing in the eyes of one's peers. That's why I stress that there must be no premature disclosures of tentative conclusions."

Tom smiled earnestly. "I promised I won't print until you give the nod, and I won't. But I have to know if you mean what you seem to say. Can you or can't you see someone's nightmare?"

Dr. Zareh sighed. Clearly, laymen tried her patience. "Remember, don't quote me yet, but I believe we can. I said it's a computerized visualization, but the computer interpretation is based on thousands of correlations of brain wave jiggles with previously verbalized nightmares. It appears to hold up better and better as we go along, as we enter more and more data. After the subject awakes and is debriefed, we determine how closely the computer came to matching the electronic signals with the scenes and events of the projected nightmare."

"And how close do you come?" He leaned toward her in his eagerness to know.

She eyed him a moment before trusting him with the answer. "Off the record for now, I feel I can say we know more, or at least more than the subject remembers, about the subject's nightmare than the subject does."

"Fabulous." He meant that. "I can't wait to see."

"You'll have to wait." She held a poker face for a long moment before dealing him the card he was looking for. "Till nine tonight, anyway."

He forgave her and rewarded her for that with his nice smile.

He touched base with Joy Larkin on his way out. A toothsome dish, and he played up to her, and she proved a willing player.

"So you're Jack Neilsen. I'd like to see some of your work."

"You will. Remind me to show you some time."

"I will. How'd it go with you and the good doctor?"

"She's letting me observe, starting tonight at nine. I owe you a drink."

She shot a glance at the wall clock. "I'll remind you of that right now." She swept things off her desk into her bag and got up and stood close with no wasted motion.

He smiled his nice smile. It couldn't be his own place or a bar in his neighborhood, where she would find out he was not Jack Neilsen but Tom Ehrsruef.

"Do you know a good watering hole around here?"

She did indeed. And after more than one, passing up the water chasers, she was more than willing for him to see her home.

It might or might not go further, but it would go no deeper than his smile. He didn't have to remind himself he was a one-woman man and the woman was Naicar. Joy was merely something to use till he regained full mastery over Naicar.

Till he regained full mastery of Naicar he would know no joy.

Luck was with him—though when you came right down to it hadn't he made his own luck?—and Naicar and her nightmare lay open to him that very night.

The sleep lab proved to be pretty much a one-woman operation. A colorless student assistant prepped the subjects for wired slumber, three subjects a night in individual cubicles, then retired to an alcove and either pored or dozed over his books for the rest of the night. Dr. Zareh juggled the three nightmarers without missing a nuance; when nightmares surfaced simultaneously, she took one by voice and the other one or two by taped responses—encouraging sounds, mainly—to provide supportive feedback. Tom felt it would have been this way even had a retrenching government not cut this year's grant.

Dr. Zareh—he made a mind bet that before the night ended she would tell him to call her Em—sat beside him at the screen. Feeling her glance, he tried to damp down his responses, his vital signs, at the sight of Naicar. Despite the concealing eyeshades and the blocking wires, he knew by the golden hair it was Naicar. Dr. Zareh sounded somewhat amused. "You'd never know from the snaky Medusa appearance the wiring-up gives her, but that's one lovely girl. I imagine that's the kind of lead you use in your pieces, isn't it?"

He smiled bravely over the hurt. "Please, Dr. Zareh. Don't prejudge me."

"You're right. I'm sorry."

"That's okay:" Then he smiled winningly. "Do you mind if I steal that lead?"

She laughed, and he saw she had warmed toward him. Yep, her melting point wasn't all that high.

Watching Naicar sleep brought memories of watching Naicar sleep, of whispering in her ear, "Dream of me, dream of Tom." Damn; he was getting worked up. Dr. Zareh would notice and start wondering about his professionalism, his reportorial objectivity. He took refuge in taking notes. "What's her name?"

"Subject N.B. I won't tell you her full name. We promise all our subjects strict confidentiality."

He shrugged. "Okay with me."

"Some history, some background. Three months ago her violent, jealous, paranoid boyfriend choked her unconscious. From then on, according to the subject, she's had nightmares of a man with a noose in his hand standing at the foot of her bed."

Tom found his voice. "Sounds scary."

Dr. Zareh glanced at worksheets on her clipboard. "In her first dream as a volunteer here she dreamed she was trying to climb her way out of a glass bowl." Dr. Zareh gave a deprecating toss of her head. "That's not a nightmare yet, just an anxiety dream. She feels trapped; she's sorry she signed up for this experiment. But she's settling down and I'm hoping for the real thing tonight."

"So'm I, Dr. Zareh."

"Call me Em." She eyed him curiously. "Do you have nightmares?"

He had won his bet but he felt uncomfortable. "Not anymore, Em."

She pounced on that. "But you've had them. When, and what were they about?"

"As a kid I had a run of bad dreams. I guess you could call them nightmares. I'd wake up screaming, sweating, shaking, because I saw a witch in a tall hat menacing me. The witch, I mean; though the hat, too, looked menacing with its sharp point." He had given away too much; he made himself make light of it. "Easy enough to explain. At the time, my mother was going to have another baby soon, and she was rough with me for behaving possessively, crankily, for filling the air with bad vibes that could affect the baby. As it turned out, my mother had a miscarriage."

"I'd call them night terrors rather than nightmares. There's a big difference, as I thought I explained in my *Traum & Trauma*."

He had missed that in skimming through the book. "That's right, you did. But that's as close as I can recall coming to genuine nightmares."

Pursuing another line of thought, she ignored his last words. "And so you remained an only child?"

"How did you know that?"

Dr. Zareh nodded. "Ah. The miscarriage would have been traumatic all around. It would have filled you with guilt—and at the same time have given you a sense of power. And it would have made your mother cling to you all the more—and at the same time have filled her with hostile feelings. Of course she and the witch looked alike, were one and the same."

He blinked. "You hit it." He smiled, but spoke vengefully. "You know, Em, you remind me of my mother."

Her turn to blink, but she smiled understandingly. "And of the witch as well, Tom?"

He didn't answer. Saved by the indicator light. The little red flashing snared Dr. Zareh's attention.

"What's up, Em?"

She waved him to silence, hit several keys and RETURN on the keyboard.

A monitor came to life and showed strange shape-shifting images that gradually pulled into focus. They lost abstractness and became anthropomorphic.

Over Em's tensely hunched shoulder he watched a sleeping beauty in bed, but in a bed that rode the rapids, that bobbed and swirled and plummeted with the furious rush of white water deep in the gloom between high and almost over-arching palisades. The blond princess—so that was the way Naicar saw herself?!—awoke and sat up in frozen fear as the bed headed for a rock dead ahead in the center of the narrow stream. A tree had somehow taken root in the stone. It had only two limbs, and these hung out over the swift narrow water on either side, each dangling a nooselike vine. "Phallic," Em murmured to herself, "androgynously so," and scribbled a note without taking her eyes from the screen. The screen showed the perilous obstruction from Naicar's view-point, distorted by fear, in what amounted to a zoom shot as the flash flood swept the bed headlong—rather, footlong—in an excruciatingly prolonged moment of suspense toward the treetopped rock. At the last possible instant, Naicar threw her weight to one side, tilting and swerving the bed, so that it scraped past the rock on the rock's right. But before she could twist or duck, the vine on that side lassoed her, dropped un-erringly over her head, tightened around her neck, and lifted her from the bed as the bed rode on. The screen went blank, and in the monitor Naicar sat up screaming soundlessly, her hands clutching her throat.

Em switched on her intercom and spoke briskly but reas-suringly into it. "You're quite safe, Ms. B. Quickly, before it fades, tell me all you remember about the nightmare. That's what it was, a nightmare. Go right ahead."

Naicar stared around at the neutral gray of the walls, looked down at the nonflowing floor, and slowly loosened her hands and let them fall, first to her breasts, then to her lap. She spoke in a draggy, almost drugged voice. "I was in bed—

137

not a bed like this one, but a big four-poster. I guess there had been a big flood, because the bed was afloat. There was a big wind, too, that helped move the bed faster downstream. The wind, in fact, was strong enough to tear the bed's curtains to shreds."

Em made a face and shook her head; the simulator hadn't picked up on those details. "Good. Go on."

"The wind died down after a while, but the current strengthened as the stream narrowed. The bed sped even more rapidly toward a mangrove tree growing smack in midstream. Then I saw the mangrove was a man. He had taken root, had grown a hide of bark and moss. He stood arms wide; each arm ended in a hangman's knot. Somehow I had time for a good look at his face, a face carved out of the living wood, and the shape of the outline of the face was a carved heart. It was the face of Tom—I told you about him—and the face was alive. I felt fear, and yet a kind of pity, when I saw a red gum or a red sap drip from the eyes. I don't know if mangroves have sap, or sap that color, but this mangrove wept red. Up to now I had the feeling that in spite of everything I still had a measure of control. Somehow I knew I could steer the bed with my mind. I only had to think 'Go right' and it would veer to the right or 'Go left' and it would steer left. But the tree's face held me frozen with its bleeding eyes, with its terrible stare, and I had a hard time finding the strength, the will, to break free and pick which way to go. Either way, I would head into a loop, a hangman's noose. At the very last second, when the face in the trunk opened its mouth wide in a smiling hollow big enough to swallow the bed, and me with it, and when I had the sinking sensation, the drowning feeling, that I had waited too long, that no time remained to swerve, I thought desperately 'Go right' and the bed swung right. I was so pleased with myself at escaping the smile that I forgot about the loop. Next thing I knew, the noose was around my neck and tightening. And that's when I woke up."

Tom found himself in a sweat of mixed pleasure and alarm; pleasure that he played the key part in Naicar's nightmare, alarm that Em would prematurely identify her Jack as Naicar's Tom. So far, his luck held; the visualizer hadn't picked up any details of the mangrove's face, of his face. If his face had shown on the screen, clear enough for Em to recognize, Em's latent suspicions would have surfaced, the coincidence of his resemblance to N.B.'s image of her ex-lover would have been too much, Em would belatedly have demanded to see his credentials, and his imposture would have ended right then and there.

As it was, Em frowned. But her frown proved not for him. She spoke into the intercom with preoccupied kindliness. "Thank you, N.B. That was very helpful. Now put your sleepshade back on and try to go back to sleep." She switched off the intercom. She remembered Jack Neilsen and turned with a quizzical look. "Well, what do you think of our little demonstration?"

Tom swallowed hard before answering. "Remarkable: I seemed to be right there."

Em shook her head. "Close, but no cigar." She looked suddenly inward. "Why 'cigar'? What's the association? . . . Ah: pipe dream." She turned outward again. "Okay. The visualizer missed several significant details: bleeding eyes, cavernous mouth. Still have a job ahead of us, much refining to do."

The details they did have fascinated Tom. With a shiver of pleasure he retasted the knowledge that he was implanted— even if all too literally, as a tree—in Naicar's nightmare. He wanted to understand the details, penetrate Naicar's web of associations. Why a mangrove? Why the four-poster? Why the flood? Maybe Em could tell him. Start with the two nooses. "What do you make of there being two nooses?"

Em frowned. "A bit early to dissect the nightmare. I'll want to rerun it a couple-three times, I'll want to study the debriefing, I'll want to look at the sensor printouts. All these things intertwine, interrelate. But okay. Off the top of my head I'd say two nooses reflect one of the dream mechanisms—overdetermination."

He pretended to take notes. "How would you define overdetermination?"

She eyed him rebukingly. "I don't like definitions—as you should know from *Traum & Trauma*. I'll give you a for-instance instead. Take the name 'Fanny Assingham' in Henry James's *The Golden Bowl*. Not two, but three, of the same thing. Now there's overdetermination!"

She stretched and sighed. "Take off your jacket and tie and settle yourself, Jack. It's going to be a long night. They're all long nights." But her sigh and the words had a satisfied tone; long nights belonged to the work she loved doing.

Tom needed no second invitation to make himself at home. Her stretching and sighing had done things to her body that had done things to his, but he reminded himself he was a one-woman man. He gave Em his smile of fellowship. He shared her devotion to the task at hand. Tonight and the nights that would follow could never be too long.

Em wondered aloud why Tom stuck with N.B. and N.B.'s essentially drab nightmare. Em said openly, in so many words, that for her own part she found subject C.Q.'s case history much more interesting biographically and infinitely more rewarding psychologically. And C.Q.'s nightmares! The richly symbolic images stemming from the time she was eight years old and her pillar-of-the-community churchgoing father sexually molested her! Talk about trauma! At eight she knew what Daddy did was wrong, unspeakably wrong, but at eight she couldn't give up the image of the all-wise, always-right father. Just look at the suppressed volcano, all the pressure building up deep down from the inability to talk about society's most powerful taboo: fearful word even to speak in. a hissing whisper, *incest!* You could see at the root of C.Q.'s nightmares the thought, "Since it's too dirty even to talk about, what a filthy creature I must be!"

Tom was immune to Em's enthusiasm. He did not want to say that Em surprised and shocked him. On a gut level, he found her love of C.Q.'s sick case sickening. As a supposedly hardened journalist he should be able to take C.Q.'s problem, and the cloacal imagery it evoked, in stride. He could not let Em see his almost prudish distaste, his outraged righteousness. He found an out for the perfunctory attentiveness he showed whenever C.Q. performed her nightmare. "You yourself said at the outset that you're agin sensationalistic journalism. I know my editor, and she won't go for an in-depth study of kinky nightmares harking back to a horny father. Seems to me N.B.'s case strikes the right note."

"I know, Jack, but . . ." But then Em shrugged and swallowed the, for her, sour note. "You're the expert in your field." She left unspoken the corollary that she was the expert in her field, left unsaid that if he wanted to ignore her advice she questioned his judgment but he was free to play the fool.

Another night, another nightmare. A good one. He needed no visualizer to picture the wild eyes behind Naicar's eyeshades. He felt charged but shaky, shaky but charged; weak with hunger but wildly in touch with the secrets of the universe, like a mystic fasting to see visions. When it had come time for the hooded garroter to remove his hood, Tom had been sweatily certain that the visualizer would reveal the face of Jack Neilsen.

Instead, the hood had lifted away to show a headless executioner.

To his own surprise, in a switching of dreads, he found himself masking a scowl of disappointment at his nightmare image's sudden facelessness. Could Naicar be working her way out of her obsession, freeing herself of his hold, driving him from her mind?

"Why did—" He stopped himself in time from saying "Naicar." "Why did N. B. rise from the dead and kiss the empty air where her executioner's head should've been and then spit out a string of snakes?"

Em made a face. "You persist in asking nightmare logic to make daylight sense. Okay, I'll take a stab. Ever catch yourself humming a rock tune you hate? Consciously, it arouses sophisticated distaste for its maudlin lyrics, its childish sentiment, its defective rhymes, its nagging beat, to say nothing of its scruffy performer; unconsciously, it satisfies some primitive need."

He thought that over, and nodded. He eyed Em with sudden curiosity. "What sort of nightmares do you have—if you have nightmares?"

Was he wrong, or did her eyes jerk for the space of a lightning flash toward the locked cabinet in the corner?

"Oh, I have them." She would have let it go at that, dropping her pen as a way of not meeting his gaze and of dropping the subject.

"Well?"

She picked up the pen, straightened, and gave him a none-of-your-business stare.

He pressed on. "Are your nightmares connected with your

work? You'll admit it's a legitimate point for me to pursue. Are your nightmares the very reason why you're into nightmares?"

She smiled. "Is that the kind of pap psych—sorry, slip of the tongue—pop psych"—she was not sorry and it was not a slip of the tongue—"you feed your readers? You really think it's a case of 'Physician, heal thyself'? Okay, I can tell you it's not. Like all analysts, I've been through analysis, so I know my own hang-ups and I can say my getting into this field has nothing to do with my own nightmares. As a matter of fact, my nightmares started afterwards, after I conceived and programmed the visualizer and the . . . other research tools. Okay. So I guess you can say they are connected with my work." She bit her lip, as though she had said too much, then shot him a look to see if he had caught that giveaway of remorse.

He had. "How so?"

She hesitated, but he sincere-ed and pleasant-ed her helpless with his nice smile and his look of earnest inquiry. She caved in, though she gave him a hard stare. "This is all off the record, understood?"

"Understood." He reinforced it with a nod.

"Okay. I have a recurring nightmare that someone will misuse my electrochemical technique for getting into the nightmare. So I've shelved it. That's it in a nutshell."

He snatched at that. "Getting into the nightmare? You mean literally plugging into the nightmare?"

She nodded. "I mean getting right inside and sharing it as it plays in the nightmarer's mind. I call the instrument an impathizer. Okay. You and the sleeper wear linked headphones—though of course they're more than just headphones—and you find yourself inside the subject's head, sharing the subject's nightmare."

He spoke accusingly, almost hotly. "You have that and you don't use it? Why don't you?"

She gave him a bittersweet half-smile. "For one thing, it's scary. I know. I've tried it. But the real reason is ethics."

"You're already invading the subject's inmost privacy, digging out the subject's deepest secrets. At this point, where does ethics come in? What's really holding you back from using the whatchacallit, impathizer?"

" 'Whatchacallit.' Interesting. The usual locution is 'whatchamacallit'; you suppressed 'ma.' Most interesting." She grinned mischievously. "Okay, I'm not trying to side-track you. You asked what's holding me back from using the impathizer. I'll answer. Not so much what I, Em Zareh, might do with it. I trust myself, go with my instincts—that may not sound scientific, but then science isn't all that imper-sonal and I'm sure I wouldn't misuse it. And in any case my subjects are volunteers who know up front what they're in for. Okay. What worries me is what others, with fewer scruples and headier ambitions, would do if they had it. Rulers have a way of beating plowshares into swords—look what happened with nuclear research, what's happening with the space race. Wouldn't authoritarians just love to lay their hands on the impathizer, wouldn't the power-greedy do anything to get hold of it! It's the key to mind control."

"If it really works the way you say it does."

She saw his hook, yet rose smilingly to the bait. "I'll tell you, in a general way, how it works. In the wakeful state, vi-sual messages that reach the hippocampus are transmitted to the hypothalamus. Okay. Normally, the brain's nerve cells translate what the eyes see—patterns of light, darkness, and color—into a coherent picture for the brain. Nightmares work the other way around. They originate, or localize, in the hypothalamus and are transmitted to the hippocampus. Call the hippocampus a projection screen, a cathode ray tube. Okay. You plug the subject and yourself into the impathizer, which puts your serotonin receptors in phase with the subject's. Okay. Neurotransmitters in the sleeper's brain carry the nightmare's sound-and-light show to the subject's serotonin receptors, and these, in effect, broadcast the same signals to your serotonin receptors. And there you are—inside the subject's nightmare."

Yes, there I am, inside Naicar's nightmare, springing out of hidden recesses of her mind to show her she can't escape my love, taking her in my all-powerful embrace to teach her she's safe from me nowhere, absolutely nowhere.

Tom smiled, then awakened to awareness that his smile was working something other than charm; Em looked positively frightened at having told him of the impathizer.

Knowing he would get nothing more out of her about it in the way of description, much less demonstration, he rushed to reassure her.

"It's all off the record, Em. A crying shame I can't use it, but I gave you my word." He heaved a heavy sigh, then lightened the mood with his best smile and shoved up out of his chair. "I could use a cup of coffee about now. How about you?"

Em nodded. She seemed thankful for, badly in need of, a break. The wedge of frown split the forced brightness of her countenance. He knew he had pushed her to the limit. He would get nothing more out of her. He'd be lucky if she didn't soon find some excuse to cancel their arrangement and boot him from the sleep lab.

Still smiling, he stepped out into the corridor. The door hissed shut behind him. He stood a moment, thinking. Yes, this had to be the time. Now or never—at least never with less difficulty. He made for the bank of dispensing machines, slotted the right change, and drew two cups of coffee. Looking around to make sure he was alone and unobserved, he laced one coffee with sleeping powder. He pinched a crinkle in the lip of that cup to tell it from the other; now he would not mix them up when he juggled them in opening the door.

He entered slowly, careful to keep from spilling drop one. He handed Em the cup with the crinkle. "Here you go."

Weary eyes lit with gratitude. "Thanks." The wedge had driven deeper, though, and he knew he had chosen—in time—the right time.

He gazed at Naicar in the monitor. She stirred, almost as though she sensed his stare. She tossed, moaned.

Em shot a glance at the readouts. For a second, Tom was afraid she would put the coffee down untasted. But she took a quick sip, made a slight face, gave a slight shrug of resignation, and chug-a-lugged to drown the taste, get it over with.

The stuff worked fast. Just before the weary eyes closed, they flickered in alarm and fought to open wide and fix on Tom. Then Em slumped. Tom dispassionately cushioned the fall as her head bent to meet the desk.

He paid no further mind to arranging her comfortably, but made rapidly for the locked cabinet in the far corner of the room. She had given it a give-away glance; this had to be the first place to look for the impathizer.

The lock would be nothing much if you had the right tool. His credit card was not the right tool. He rearranged Em so he could get at the desk drawers. He scrounged for something, anything that would give him leverage. He found a steel ruler, but it would not slip into the crack. He found a pair of compasses. The ruler hammered the steel point of the compasses into the crack, the compasses worked a space for the ruler to pry the cabinet door open.

Two linked sets of headphones rested on the top shelf. The impathizers?

It looked like merely two linked sets of headphones. The impathizer. Had to be.

He forced himself to snatch it slowly, grasp its operation carefully. You hook it up like so, pressed this switch, turned this dial. He glanced at the delicately snoring Em. Okay.

He found a spare white smock and put it on, a tight fit but it would do. Through this door, carrying the impathizer, then briskly past the alcove where the student assistant pored or dozed, and past C.Q.'s cubicle and O.P.'s to N.B.'s.

Naicar lay enmeshed in sleep and wiring. She stirred but did not wake as he fitted one of the headpieces over her skull. He found a stool, seated himself slightly behind Naicar, and fitted the other headpiece over his own skull.

He took a deep breath, pressed the switch, and slowly turned the dial. Things happened inside his head.

At first, only a buzzing light, a flickering sound. Then he found himself walking down a corridor remarkably like the one leading to Em's sleep lab—only the door at the end bore no legend. When its malevolent blankness failed to faze Tom and he reached the knob, the door's surface rippled, froze into evil wrinkles into which you could read a face, a face with a stern gaze and a wedge of frown.

The door suddenly boomed, in a viragoish version of Em's voice. "Danger! Unauthorized persons keep out."

Tom felt doubt, knew puzzlement. This couldn't be Naicar's nightmare. This had to be his. But he wasn't sleeping, wasn't dreaming. Something, someone, was putting it into his mind. That someone was not Naicar, though he had linked himself to her mind. Em. Em must've programmed a warning into the impathizer.

He narrowed his eyes, tightened his mouth. He opened

the door and stepped inside. With a sorrowfully satisfied sigh the door hissed shut behind him. He whirled to look back. The door had disappeared.

But that did not matter. Now he was in Naicar's nightmare. He recognized the touches that made this uniquely Naicar dreamscape, Naicar unreal estate, Naicar nightmare territory.

The pervasive off-indigo of the sky, the slowly wheeling polar constellation in the form of the letter N, the forest—not so much a forest as a tangled web of shadows—the muddy swirl of the river in flood.

The river. She had returned to the time and place of the first nightmare he had witnessed. There she went, flood-carried on her bed. Now, however, his vantagepoint had changed. The river swirled around him, swept past him on either hand. He looked around, stiffly, finding it hard to turn, wondering where the mangrove was. Further upstream? Further down?

Before he could figure that out, the dreamscape trembled in a mindquake. Even the constellation wobbled in its course. The sky could not contain the terror; it yawned in a scream, showed behind the darkness a deeper darkness.

Naicar knew he was there.

The mindquake rippled up the scale, but it failed to dislodge him. He felt all-wise, all-powerful. She could not drive him out. The mindquake subsided, the dreamscape looked faded, spent.

Then a voice entered his mind, spoke to him in the tones of Em.

You ignored the warning, went ahead, used the impathizer without authorization. Okay. Now you pay the penalty. There's a built-in booby trop. I programmed the impathizer to stimulate delta-endorphins in the blood. These create a lower-brain block, cutting off the reticular formation and the hypothalamus, pre-venting them from relaying messages to the brain. Sorry, but you're stuck in the subject's nightmare for good. When I get around to unhooking you—or, if not me, whoever comes along— you will still be locked in the subject's nightmare, your body a zom-bie-like shell.

Fleetingly, he saw his Witch plain. Then, as the voice faded even from echo, so vanished the Witch even from memory, and he had the flickering awareness that not even his own nightmare remained to him, he was implanted in Naicar's, and would be forever although she herself in time forgot it.

And now he knew why he could not see the mangrove.

He was the mangrove.

Groaningly, gnarlingly, he twisted his trunk to see Naicar, to follow her. Through a moist red film he watched her ride the rapids in her bed, which, even as he looked, subtly shifted shape and became a prowed barque with a golden sail spread smooth and shining as it left the narrow river and headed out upon the wide waters of a bright blue lake.

FAIR EXCHANGE

Philip Atley went over his client's itemized deductions once more, scrutinizing them in light of the latest tax court rulings, checked the figures again, then signed his name in the proper space on the form. He had taken advantage of every loophole, but he had not ventured into illegality. Whether or not his client or the tax examiner would rhapsodize over the result Atley could not care less. He had done his best for his client and at the same time had not done the United States out of what the laws said rightfully belonged to the government.

A good morning's work. He had earned his lunch. He shoved back from his desk, rose, looked out at the sullen sky and rubbed his hands, anticipating the balanced meal in his habitual restaurant and the brisk march there in the brisk March air. His desk clock informed him it was not yet the clasp of noon; but he had earned that slight indulgence.

He put on his overcoat and homburg, drew on his gloves, and emerged. The sound and sight of his secretary typing away efficiently in his outer office burst comfortingly on his ears and eyes.

"I'm going out to lunch, Miss Quimby."

Martha Quimby barely paused. "Yes, Mr. Atley."

Good girl, that. Though why they called themselves girls when they were well into their fifties was beyond him. Though, to be fair about it, men also called themselves boys—"one of the boys," "night out with the boys"—when well advanced in years. To be even fairer, take himself: he knew himself to be a mature man, yet he knew equally well that boyish traits, ways, and feelings still carried on in him.

In his musing he did not notice that the door to the hall

was already opening. And on her part Kay Newcomb, the bubbly young secretary from L. Baxter's law office down the hall, did not notice that Atley was preparing to stride forth as she bounced in, a double armload of old clothing blocking her view.

She caromed off Atley, teetered to keep from spilling her burden, and giggled her apology. Atley murmured in return, steered safely around her into the hall, and paused outside his office suite to smooth such of his attire as, the encounter had disarranged.

He heard Miss Quimby's typing slow slightly. "Kay, you know better than to barge in right now. I told you to wait till lunch-time."

"Oh, don't be stuffy, Martha. It's in a good cause, isn't it? Why should he mind?"

"Mr. Atley's nice enough to let us store the clothing here in his office till we collect enough to make it worthwhile sending it off to the mission. But that doesn't mean he's paying me to be a Good Samaritan. Neither is Mr. Baxter paying you to be one. The least we girls can do is attend to it on our own time."

"Really, Martha, you're carrying conscientiousness too far. What's a few minutes?"

"I'm surprised at you, Kay. But maybe I shouldn't be. You're so young. Still, youth is no excuse for flightiness. As far back as I can remember I've made it a rule to give my employer full value."

Atley nodded to himself approvingly. As he strode away he heard the last exchange diminish.

"Does that mean you're going to let me stand here holding this till the last stroke of twelve?"

"Oh, all right." The typing stopped. "Here, I'll hold the flaps of the box open for you."

"Ah."

He heard the rustling fall of old clothes. Then the typing resumed and he knew it would continue a fraction past twelve to make up for the interruption. He smiled. He held the smile as he passed the open door of Baxter's suite. Baxter, who had evidently been lying in wait for him, called and beckoned him in. "Got something to show you. Come all the way in and close the door."

Atley did so, wondering at Baxter's unusual mysteriousness. He'd heard his own stomach rumble faintly at the delay, but he maintained his smile. Baxter was a pleasant enough fellow tenant, and they had traded professional insights— legal know-how for tax expertise—for some years now.

"What've you got, Baxter?"

"Atley, you'll never guess."

"Then I won't try. I see no point in wasting energy on some thing useless. If you want me to know you'll have to tell me."

Whatever it was, Baxter had it in a locked attaché case in a locked file cabinet. When it came to opening the attaché case, Baxter paused as though having second thoughts. Then he gave himself a quick shake of the head and unlocked the case. With reverent care he displayed a block of four postage stamps in a glassine envelope.

"Did you ever see the like in your life?"

Atley stared. He could not find voice to answer. Even his stomach stilled.

But Baxter did not expect or at least did not wait for an answer. "I just bought this block at a private sale from the estate of the previous owner. The widow might've got more by holding a public auction—indeed, I'm certain she would've got more, much more—but that would've meant waiting and she needs spot cash. An hour ago I handed over a cashier's check for I'm ashamed to say how much. In a few minutes I'll be putting this block in a bank vault."

Atley found his voice and it sounded strange in his own ears. "I didn't know you collected stamps, Baxter."

"We big-time enthusiasts tend to keep our passion secret. We shy away from publicity so that the underworld—or other enthusiasts—won't rip us off. But this acquisition is too great a prize. I just couldn't keep it to myself. Saw you pass by and knew I could trust you. Well, Atley, what do you think of my prize? It's a beauty, isn't it?"

Atley reached for the glassine envelope but Baxter pulled it back.

"Don't be offended, Atley, but I'd rather you didn't handle it. So easily damaged, you know. Ruin the value. Condition is almost everything."

"Quite right, Baxter. I can see it well enough from here." He studied the colors—red frame and black center—and the old-fashioned-looking design. He shook his head slightly, his eyes gimbaling to stay on the block. "It's valuable, is it? You wouldn't think so to look at it. What makes it so valuable?"

Baxter laughed. "Look closer. Notice anything peculiar about these stamps?"

Atley bent nearer. "Why, the plane in the center is upside-down in relation to the frame. Unless it's supposed to be making a loop-the-loop?"

Baxter laughed again. "No, Atley. It's not supposed to be making a loop-the-loop. But you've spotted the peculiarity that makes this so valuable. This is the famous 24-cent air-mail invert error. There is only one sheet in existence, and this is a corner block of four from that sheet. Well, what do you think now?"

Atley's eyes did not leave the block, but they lost focus. "Strange, the values in this world. I can imagine someone purchasing that original sheet at the post-office counter and, ignorant of the value of such an error, indignantly handing it back to the clerk and demanding a perfect sheet."

Baxter shivered at the thought. "Please." Then he mused in turn. "I suppose we enthusiasts do have an upside-down set of values and tend to lose our sense of proportion. But when you consider the span of a human life as against the vastness of infinity, and take into account the small amount of enjoyment one can hope to squeeze into this one life, who's to say our enthusiasm, whatever it might be, is out of proportion? So, to me, it's not so strange. To you, I suppose, these are mere bits of paper. But to someone like me, with a secret passion for collecting—why, there's no telling what another collector wouldn't do for these."

Atley managed a smile. "Really? Tell me, Baxter, from your enthusiasm for these—er—bits of paper, I take it you wouldn't consider selling them? Say at a ten percent profit?"

"I should say not! Never!"

Atley laughed and threw up his hands. "I give up. I can see your passion goes deep. Stick to it, by all means. But I hope for your sake you're taking precautions in carrying it to your bank."

It was Baxter's turn to laugh, scornfully. "Here's the only guard I need." He whipped out a gun.

"Careful, Baxter. Are you sure you have the safety catch on? Mind if I look at it?"

Atley took the gun, eyed it, released the safety, shot Baxter through the heart, put the gun down, picked up the glassine envelope, and pocketed it carefully. He made sure to insulate it from his body heat by interposing the letter he had been meaning to answer—the letter from his vacationing wife; he would hate to damage the glue and reduce the block's value.

That done, he eased out the suite's side door. Just in time, for he heard Kay Newcomb bounce in on her platform shoes through the suite's front door. Then, unobserved, he took the stairs down to the street.

It would be asking for detectival notice if, on this day of days, he broke his routine in the slightest. So, though he pulsed with the urge to rush his acquisition to his own bank's safety-deposit vault, he walked at his normally brisk pace to his favorite restaurant.

He forced himself to swallow the suddenly tasteless food with his usual prim gusto and to take his usual digestive leisure. Then he paid up, making his usual small talk with the owner's wife at the cash register, and returned to his office at his usual time.

Miss Quimby greeted him with unusual vivacity. "Oh, Mr. Atley, you missed all the excitement! Someone shot Mr. Baxter dead while you were out to lunch!" She remembered the proprieties. "Isn't it terrible?"

"It certainly is, Miss Quimby. Someone told me about it coming up in the elevator and I saw the policemen when I passed poor Baxter's suite. What happened?"

"The police haven't found any motive or any witness or anything. The closest to a witness seems to be Kay—his secretary, Miss Newcomb, you know. The police are waiting to question her again after she gets over the shock. Poor Kay. She must have got back to her office right after it happened. She smelled smoke, and knew Mr. Baxter doesn't—didn't—smoke, and it seemed sharper than cigarette or cigar smoke. She knocked on his door, and when Mr. Baxter didn't answer she went in."

Atley frowned. "Smoke?" Then his brow smoothed. "Ah, yes. Gunsmoke."

"That's what it must have been. Anyway, she found him on the floor with a bullet hole in his chest. She ran here screaming. I'm the one who phoned the police. They're questioning everyone in the building. I imagine they'll get around to you. They already questioned me."

"And what could you tell them?"

"Nothing, I'm afraid. But one of the detectives said they can tell who fired a gun by the powder traces it leaves."

"Is that so?" He looked thoughtful and put his hands behind his back. He worked his gloves off, gazing at the heap of old clothing in the corner behind her desk. He brought a naked hand around and pointed a finger at Martha Quimby. "I'll bet you've missed lunch, Miss Quimby. How do you plead? Guilty or not guilty?"

She blushed. "That's true. In all this I entirely forgot. And now I don't know if I feel like eating."

"Nonsense! I order you to go. And I insist that you take your full hour."

"Thank you, Mr. Atley."

As soon as he was alone, Atley buried his gloves deep under the dresses, blouses, shirts and trousers of the mission clothes. He smiled to think of some African or Polynesian village chief laying claim to the pearl-gray gloves.

Even more secure behind the closed door of his inner office, he gloated over the block of postage stamps. He studied his treasure lovingly. Beautiful. The world would never know it was in his possession. Correction—till after his death. But then it would matter as little to him as it now did to Baxter. What mattered was that while he lived he would enjoy owning the treasure.

Time passed. With a start he heard Miss Quimby's typing begin again. He looked at his clock and smiled. She had taken her hour to the second.

Her typing stopped almost as soon as he became aware of it. Someone had come in. A pair of someones. Two male voices. The police! Quickly Atley put the block in his desk drawer.

Miss Quimby used the intercom to tell him they were there and would like to see him. He picked up a tax return and rose as they came in. They introduced themselves as Detectives Tausch and Barrett and he shook their hands. Only one of them did the talking.

Maybe Mr. Atley knew a motive? They hadn't found one yet.

Atley shook his head in sorrowful bafflement. "Baxter was the mildest, most inoffensive person you'd want to meet. I don't know of any enemies he might have made. And I can't even picture anyone killing him."

"Well, someone did." Maybe Mr. Atley saw someone suspicious lurking in the corridor when he went out to lunch?

Atley weighed whether or not to say he had indeed seen some unsavory type lurking in the corridor. That would focus suspicion elsewhere but it would be a strain on him to keep his story and description consistent under determined questioning, and it would keep him too much in the company of the police.

True, if he stayed close to the investigation he would know how it was going. But straw men have a way of falling apart. Even to say he had heard loud voices when he passed Baxter's suite would involve him too deeply. No, on the whole it was better to stick as close to the truth as possible.

"No, I can't say that I did."

Well, if Mr. Atley should remember anything that might in any way throw light on the case would he please get in touch with them?

"Of course."

He saw them out. His heart broke its rhythm as Tausch— or Barrett—paused to glance at the pile of old clothing.

Miss Quimby also intercepted the man's glance and proudly explained the worthy charity.

Barret—or Tausch—lost interest. "Oh." Both detectives nodded their thanks and left.

Shortly after, Atley told Miss Quimby he was going down to consult with a client, Mr. Murphy on the eleventh floor. If anyone called, he was out for the rest of the day.

This was not too much of a break with routine. It often proved easier for him to go where the records were kept than for the client to lug bulky ledgers to him.

And since this consultation looked as if it would take a while, he wished Miss Quimby a good night; she was to go straight home and drink warm milk and not think too much about what had happened. Because he did not put on his hat and coat he gave Miss Quimby no reason to think he would do other than visit Mr. Murphy.

But what he actually did was go all the way down and slip out to the bar in the building next door. What he had done had started to hit him hard.

He had another and another—till with a start he made out it was past five a.m. With exaggerated sobriety he left the bar and returned to his now darkened office. He let himself in, locked the door again, and switched on his desk lamp.

Sight of the block of stamps would reassure him it had been worth what he had done to gain it. He opened the drawer. He stared down at three quarters, two dimes and one penny.

And a note. "Dear Mr. Atley. I ran short of postage for the mission parcel, which I am depositing in a package box on my way home—straight home as you thoughtfully suggested, rather than around to the post office—and have taken the liberty of scrounging through your desk. Luckily I found four 24¢ stamps, making a total of 96¢. I leave this exact amount in exchange."

STATE OF THE ART

Roger Ryall smoothed his lapel. Because he stood at gunpoint he moved his hand slowly. He spoke evenly but couldn't control the hand tremor. "Do you no good to rough me up."

"Do me plenty good," Sam Yoder said.

"Keep what's in my wallet. I forget how much it is—"

"Four hundred twenty-three bucks."

"Whatever. Take it and go. I won't report the stickup."

"Hell you won't, soon as you step inside. But I don't want your lousy four hundred twenty-three bucks. I want my seventy-five thousand dollars."

Ryall's eyes narrowed. "What seventy-five thousand dollars?"

"For the franchise that went down the drain."

Ryall looked sad. "Oh, were you one of my licensees?"

"Yeah, I was one. You don't remember my face, much less my name, but I went to all your inspirational meetings, and heard all your evangelical talks on making it big, and yelled myself hoarse along with all the other suckers."

"Now, wait—"

"Your phony promises made me withdraw my savings and put the house and car in hock. Lots of suckers just like me built you this mansion and your fortune—your 'pyramid empire' the papers called it—while we went bust. But I'm one sucker that's going to get his money back."

Ryall drew himself up. "That's slanderous. I worked strictly within the law. The grand jury failed to indict me, remember. That was in the papers too."

"Sure, because you're too slick."

"No sense standing out here getting overheated in the

chilly air. Let's go inside the house. But easy on the manhandling. I can't take pain. If you pistol-whip me I'll have to yell, and my wife and the help will hear, and they'll phone the police."

Yoder shook his head. "There you go, real slippery. I been watching your house. The lights don't mean a thing. Your wife's out for the evening, all dressed up for a charity ball. The chauffeur held the limousine door for her and they drove toward town. The other servants have the night off. I saw them leave right after your missus. But you're right about going inside. We got that business to take care of."

Ryall smiled ruefully, and with the gun prodding him unlocked the front door. They went inside.

Yoder caught himself stepping lightly on the thick carpeting; he gave Ryan a shove forward and followed with deliberate heaviness. "Okay, head straight for the room that has your wall safe."

Ryall half-turned, carefully. "Wall safe?"

"Maybe it's a floor safe. Don't play dumb." Yoder waved a slip of paper at Ryall. "I found this in your wallet. It has three numbers on it. That has to be a combination."

Ryall made a gesture of surrender. "You guessed right. It's a wall safe. I have a bad memory."

Yoder waggled the gun. "This'll help jog it."

With a wry smile Ryall led the way to the master bedroom. An oil painting of the woman Yoder had seen drive away swung out to reveal the wall safe.

Ryall put his hand to the knob of the dial. "I don't keep the kind of money you're talking about here."

"We'll see."

Ryall shrugged, glanced at the numbers on the slip of paper Yoder held, and twirled the dial. He pulled the safe door open.

"Step back and stand still." Yoder took his place and reached inside.

Ryall looked anxious when Yoder pawed through papers in the safe. But Yoder wasn't interested in papers. Yoder's fist closed on a wrapped bundle of currency.

He counted. "Fifty hundreds."

"Five thousand dollars. I told you I keep nothing like big money here."

Yoder pocketed the bundle of bank notes. "On account. You owe me seventy thousand more. You keep that much in your office safe?"

Ryall looked more assured, more in control of himself and maybe even of the situation. "Perhaps. But even if you could get in, I'm afraid you couldn't open the safe. I just don't remember the combination."

Yoder waved the slip of paper. "You looked at these numbers, but they ain't the ones you turned to on the dial. This has to be the combination to your office safe."

Ryall's eyes twinkled and he chuckled admiringly. "Good for you. If you're always this suspicious how'd you ever get, as you call it, taken?"

"You taught me to be suspicious."

Ryall looked rueful. "Sorry you feel that way, friend."

"Sure. And right now I got the feeling I better be extra careful. You're probably cooking up some scheme to trap me. Looks like I better tie you up before you try something."

"Now wait a minute, friend—"

"You ain't my friend and I ain't yours." Yoder looked around, then tore the velvet ropes from the velvet curtains and bound Ryall firmly to a decorator chair. "Okay, you're going to tell me how to collect the other seventy thousand bucks."

Ryall frowned. "You've been behaving like a primitive.

These are sophisticated times. Let's settle this nicely, like civilized human beings."

Yoder tightened his mouth.

Ryall pressed on. "I'm quite willing to write you out a check for the remaining seventy thousand."

Yoder seemed momentarily set to jump at the offer, then settled back. He shook his head. "You'd only stop payment."

"My word."

"Your word." Yoder gave a bitter laugh. "That's how I got into this—your words." Then his face creased in thought. "This is Friday evening. Banks don't open till Monday morning. Can't leave you tied up here—your wife and servant'll be back before too long. Could keep you tied up in the trunk of my rented car till after I cash the check first thing Monday—"

"You couldn't." Alarm flashed in Ryall's eyes. "I'd die. That would be murder. I can see you're a basically decent person. I know you draw the line at that."

"Person can be pushed just so far, then there's no telling what he'll do."

"No, no; not you."

Yoder was listening now only to his own thoughts. "You can get into your office building at any time, though, can't you? Any day, any hour?"

Ryall nodded slowly. "With the right ID."

"Thought so." Yoder began searching Ryan's person.

"What are you looking for?"

Yoder kept searching, then gave up with a muttered "Your ID card."

Ryall laughed. "Cards can get lost, cards can be stolen."

Yoder stared. "Then what ID do you use to get in?"

"The latest method. State of the art." Ryall nodded back over his shoulder at his right hand and wiggled his thumb. "I press my thumb to a sensitized plate. The computer recognizes my whorls and loops, and buzzes me through. Same for all my employees."

"Oh."

Ryall smiled. "Sure, we have enough time before my wife returns. But what are you going to do, carry me to corporate headquarters like this, just to press my thumb against the sensor? Even if you left me untied and brought me there at gunpoint, it would be obvious I'm under duress." He poured all his bland reasonableness into the suggestion he made. "So take my check and my word, or be satisfied with the five thousand and go." Smoothly, "I tell you, it's too sophisticated for you to beat."

Yoder stared at him.

Ryall's smile broadened. "You see?"

Yoder said nothing, but left the room, located the kitchen, and came back with a cleaver.

RUBOUT

Someone brushed against Alden Mortimer but Mortimer remained too intent on seeing his baggage quickly and safely aboard the cruise ship to spare more than the most fleeting glance of annoyance.

He spoke sharply to the luggage handler who was taking the bags out of the trunk of the taxi. *"Hurry! . . . Careful!"*

He knew he must seem overly fussy to anyone watching but he didn't care. Time to relax once he and his belongings were under way. "Make sure they're right side up."

Too late—the stupid handler had grounded a suitcase wrong. Mortimer feared the gritty pier floor would scratch or even destroy the elegant initials.

Small consolation to take it out of the tip. Mortimer hated this last-minute rush. It got what should be a good experience off to a bad start. The worst of it was he had allowed lots of time, yet the taxi driver, who to hear him tell it knew how to run the country if not the world, had managed to lock them into an infuriatingly long traffic tie-up and had delivered him here only minutes before sailing.

Up the gangplank. Aboard at last. Mortimer knew his stateroom's location by heart and led the way. He had picked the stateroom himself, determining from a model of the liner in the steamship line's own office the best location, taking into account the prevailing winds. The empirical British had known a thing or two about comfortable sailing—hadn't the word *posh* come into being from Port Outbound, Starboard Homeward?—and he could have done worse than follow their example. No telling but that even a modern luxury liner's air conditioning might break down in torrid zone waters, so he had chosen the cool and shady side.

With a satisfied smile, he strode toward his stateroom, heading his safari of one plus bearer through a jungle of bustle and confusion. A man who knew where he was going had the edge on the uncertain ones. He imagined a slight sway to the huge vessel but walked with the assurance of a man who had long since got his sealegs. Still, he looked forward to a bit of air conditioning right now. This last-minuteness had put him in something of a sweat.

He found his stateroom without trouble and his satisfied smile increased. The door stood half open and the smile uncreased. Someone already occupied his stateroom.

An old man, from what Mortimer could see of him. A scarf muffled him to his dark glasses. He had settled in among a smother of fruit and candy and flowers and books. A room stewardess was seeing to the old man's comfort and it was she who looked up in surprise at Mortimer and company and who spoke up in the old man's behalf.

"Good afternoon, sir. What stateroom are you looking for?"

Mortimer backed up a step for another glance at the face of the door, then stepped forward again. "This room." He winced at the bother they would have to put the old man to in resetting him wherever he belonged, but right was right.

"I'm afraid there's been a mistake. You see, this room is mine. I definitely booked for this room." His firmness proved too much for the stewardess to deal with on her own. She put in a call for the ship's purser. While they waited for the purser Mortimer nodded for the bearer to put down his bags and paid the man off—not forgetting he had promised himself to lessen the tip.

The ship's purser appeared, a harried man who carried it

well. He heard Mortimer out, then pursed his lips. "May I see your confirmation, sir?"

Smiling gladly but stiffly, mortified that he hadn't thought of it himself, Mortimer felt his pockets for the telltale bulge. "Of course." Only now, and fleetingly, did it strike him as strange that no one had asked him before for ticket or boarding pass. But no doubt that had been due to his being, and behaving like, a man who knew where he was going. All other thought, however, fled as his more and more frantic pats paced a more and more rapidly beating heart. "I seem to have lost—"

His mind flashed back to the someone who had brushed against him down on the pier. A pickpocket!

"Look, purser, someone stole my wallet and my ticket. But you should find the name J. Alden Mortimer on your passenger list."

The purser looked terribly patient. "Sir, the first thing I did when the room stewardess phoned me was examine the passenger list. The name J. Alden Mortimer does not appear on it. Shall we move along toward the gangplank? Time is short."

" 'Does not appear?' Are you sure? You must have missed it."

"Very well, sir. I'm sure, but I'll look again." He took out a typed list. "This is the final list, ready for the shipboard printer to print." He ran his eyes down the names, let Mortimer look over his shoulder. He shook his head. "Sorry, sir, but it's as I said. No Mortimer. So if you'll—"

"There must be some mistake."

"That's right, there must be. I'm afraid, sir, it's yours. You're not down on the passenger list for this stateroom or any other. This gentleman is, for this very stateroom. So—"

"You still have time to phone your steamship office. They must have a record of my booking. I know damn well they cashed my check. You can do that."

The purser looked to heaven—or toward the captain's station—for strength or forgiveness. He had an air of I-only-have-a-hundred-million last-minute-nuisances-to-take-care-of-and-now-this extra nuisance turns up!

"Yes, I suppose I can do that." He snatched up the room phone and barked through to the line's headquarters. He repeated, for his own satisfaction and Mortimer's benefit, the answer he got. "No reservation for a J. Alden Mortimer, for this sailing or any other? Thank you." He hung up.

He signaled and two stewards approached. Mortimer noted that they were burly. The purser brightened as the public address system began shooing visitors from the ship.

"Sorry, sir." He did not look sorry. "You'll have to leave. We're about to put to sea."

"But—"

The purser turned a deaf ear to Mortimer and a talking nod to the pair of stewards. The stewards walked Mortimer and his luggage along the deck and down the gangplank. They released him outside the small wooden enclosure on the pier. They returned to the head of the gangplank and stood there watchfully.

People crowding the pier and lining the rails stared at him. Did they think the ship's personnel had caught him trying to stow away? Maybe they thought the line's security force had forestalled a notorious gambler? Didn't they know he was J. Alden Mortimer?

He moved forward a few steps toward the foot of the gangplank. The stewards stiffened. He stopped. He stood unaware that he blocked the way, that the last of the departing visitors rubbed him right and left squeezing past.

The last of the last, a man in his early forties, murmured

an apology in pushing by, then hesitated, turned and came back to Mortimer's side. Mortimer watched disbelievingly as the gangplank lifted and the ship made ready to move away without him. He grew aware the man was eyeing him curiously. The man gave a half-smile.

"Are you feeling all right?"

Mortimer did not answer.

The man nodded. "I know. Partings aren't easy. I've been seeing someone off myself. Look, I'm driving back uptown. Maybe I can drop you off?"

Mortimer let the man lead him to a chauffeured limousine parked on the pier and sit him inside. Mortimer started.

"My luggage!"

"Oh?" The man followed Mortimer's finger. He looked puzzled but signed to his chauffeur, who retrieved the bags and stowed them in the trunk of the car. The man settled back beside Mortimer. "Now. Where would you like to go?"

Around the world, the way he had planned and paid for. "I don't know."

The man frowned. "I don't understand."

"Neither do I!" It all burst from Mortimer—the old man occupying *his* stateroom, the missing wallet and ticket, the lying passenger list, the ignominious walking of the gangplank.

The man listened with growing wonder. "Strange—very strange. I'm a businessman myself and I know that's no way to run a passenger line." His eyes slid toward Mortimer. "If what you say is so." He watched Mortimer swell and stopped him from bursting again. "I apologize. Of course, you're telling the truth. I know you couldn't have made it up." He looked thoughtful. "But you have to go somewhere. Where have you been staying?"

Mortimer told him the hotel.

The man reached for the mouthpiece of the speaking tube and gave the chauffeur the name. The chauffeur nodded and the limousine sat them smoothly back. The man smiled reassuringly at Mortimer.

"Maybe we'll find you left your papers at your hotel."

For a second, Mortimer sparked into life. Then, "No, I'm sure I had them on me. My wallet, my credit cards, my travelers checks, my passport, my cruise ticket. Someone picked my pocket."

"Yes, well, we still may come up with something there."

They came up with worse than nothing.

There was no record that a J. Alden Mortimer had stayed the night. The man stood by, lending moral support and physical presence as Mortimer besieged the desk. The manager reinforced the clerk.

"You can see for yourself, sir. There is no record."

Mortimer looked around wildly but found no face to grasp at to back him up. That was understandable. He had only overnighted here—even if these people denied it—after flying from the Midwest and this was a whole new day crew. But that there was no record of his stay—that was not understandable.

He found himself sitting again in the limousine. He stared at the back of the chauffeur's head. The chauffeur sat patiently awaiting orders. Mortimer realized the car's owner was speaking—speaking to *him*.

"Time we introduced ourselves, don't you think? My name's Borg." He waited as if that might mean something to Mortimer, then smiled his half-smile and shrugged slightly. "Frank Borg. I know your name's Mortimer."

"J. Alden Mortimer."

"Are you still set on the cruise, Mr. Mortimer? If we straighten this out you can catch up with the ship at an early port."

Mortimer warmed at the "we." "I'd like to, if only to tell that purser a thing or two." From looking forward he looked back. "The cruise was something I planned with my wife." He grimaced. "My ex-wife." As he plunged on his stare defied Borg to smile. "After thirty-five years of marriage, she left me for another man."

He frowned. "I can't understand that. I don't mean about *her*, though that took me by surprise too. I mean about *him*. He's much younger and, I guess, good looking—what they called in the old days a gigolo type—and he could have his pick of pretty girls with money. What he sees in Emma I'll never know." He thought Borg looked embarrassed to be hearing all this but he felt he had to open himself to the one sympathetic ear. "As for Emma, her time of life I suppose.

"But about the cruise. Right after she left, a conglomerate took over my firm. I manufactured heraldic plaques—not much volume but high-priced goods. The conglomerate paid me a surprisingly good price—I saw to it Emma heard how good—but eased me out of all responsibility. I found myself at loose ends. Didn't know what to do with myself. Then I remembered the plans we had made—dreamed of, rather—and so—"

"And so the cruise." Borg glanced at his wristwatch. It was easy to see Borg was a man of decision, modern and efficient as the digital timepiece. He picked up his carphone, called his office, and spoke to his secretary. "Cancel all my appointments for the rest of the day." He hung up, turned to Mortimer, smiled his half-smile. "Now for our next move."

Mortimer gaped at him. "Why are you doing this?"

"Oh, I'm not as unselfish as you think. If a thing such as this can happen to someone of obvious consequence, like yourself, it can happen to anyone." His jaw set. "I mean to see this through to the end. Don't worry, we'll find out what's behind this."

Mortimer felt the tears start and looked his gratitude. He left their next move up to Borg. He was certain it would be a good one.

Borg, taking up the speaking tube, was like a skipper ordering full steam ahead. "Police headquarters."

The chauffeur nodded and they got under way. Mortimer's heart lifted. He had known he could count on Borg.

Borg proved to be a man with pull. They got full and fast cooperation from the head of detectives on down. But the deeper the detectives dug, the deeper the pit Mortimer found himself in. He felt himself sink out of existence.

For a solid hour, two detectives manned phones and placed calls to the police department in Mortimer's home city, to the city and county clerks, to names Mortimer gave them. And each call, instead of bolstering his identity, turned up another blank.

There was no record of a J. Alden Mortimer. No one had ever heard of a J. Alden Mortimer.

J. Alden Mortimer told himself with great calmness, *This is only a nightmare. I'm going to wake up soon.*

Dimly, through the blurry air and the blood hammer in his veins, he saw a detective hang up with finality and take Borg aside and he heard the words. "I don't know what this guy's game is, Mr. Borg, but I wouldn't have anything more to do with him if I were you. Personally, I figure he's a nut case. I'm for sending him to Bellevue."

Borg sidewised a glance at Mortimer and gave the detective a quick hard shake of the head. "No, he's not crazy. Upset, yes. Confused, yes. But not crazy." He grew brisk. "Thanks for your help and your suggestion, but I can't abandon him now."

Tears came again to Mortimer's eyes as Borg crossed the room to his side and took his elbow.

This time the limousine pulled up at a drab apartment house.

"Here we are."

Mortimer stirred at Borg's voice, eyed the building vaguely, then remembered that Borg had said something about his needing a place to stay till this was all straightened out. He moved at Borg's touch and joined him on the sidewalk.

He stood for a moment, uncertain. Could it be that he had lost his memory of who he really was and had imagined himself a non-existent J. Alden Mortimer?

No. Borg believed in him. He turned to Borg.

"I don't know how I can ever repay you, Mr. Borg."

Borg brushed thanks aside. "This way."

He led Mortimer down into a basement apartment. The way took them past a nakedness of pipes and meters and a huge boiler that rumbled. The room itself seemed little more than a cell. The furnishings were equally Spartan. But what seized Mortimer's gaze was the heap of documents on the deal table.

He recognized his wallet, his passport, his traveler's checks, his cruise ticket, his credit cards . . .

He stared at Borg, as the room whirled and brought Borg into focus. "What have you been *doing* to me? You *knew* all along that I'm J. Alden Mortimer."

Borg gestured at the heap. "*That's* J. Alden Mortimer. Birth, school, employment records, bank, social security, tax records, marriage license, driver's license, library card. You're not J. Alden Mortimer, because there's nothing left in any file anywhere to say there ever was a J. Alden Mortimer."

He looked Mortimer up and down with an undertaker's, eyes. "I see you standing in front of me, a living, breathing man. But without those papers you're nobody—nothing!"

"But *why?*" Hollow voice, hollowness at the heart.

There was a thunderous silence as Borg looked deep into Mortimer's eyes. Then it was Borg's turn to burst forth. "My father is George Borg—the old man you found in your stateroom." He saw Mortimer mouth the name and nodded. "That's right, George Borg. Remember the name now? Thirty years ago, he was the school janitor in my hometown—and yours.

"You were on the Board of Education. It was budget time and he was cleaning up in the hall outside the meeting room. I was twelve, and I had brought him a thermos of coffee from home, and we were standing in the hall when we heard you and the cozy group of board members decide how to cut up the pie and hand out contracts. You wanted to institute the awarding of plaques.

"One of the other members reminded you the budget was tight and the janitor had been putting in for a new boiler. You said, '*Him?* What does what he wants matter? He's a *nobody!*'

"I heard the others laugh, and I couldn't look at my father. Well, the company you had stock in, and later became head of, put in the winning bid to provide plaques for athletes and good citizenship. And two months after the meeting the boiler blew up.

"It scalded and half-blinded my father. You and the others denied he had ever asked for a new boiler. You saw to it the verdict was carelessness on my father's part. Not only didn't he get just compensation, but the scars didn't make him pleasant for children to look at. He lost his job and we moved away.

"But I had made up my mind even before that to get back

at you some day. I made up my mind the night of the board meeting."

For God's sake, why? Mortimer could not voice it but he could look it, and Borg answered.

"Because that's when you scarred me for life. You had shamed him in front of me—'He's a *nobody!*'—and you had wounded my pride in him."

The chauffeur brought in Mortimer's luggage, set it down, stood by. Mortimer noted dully that the initials were gone. He felt sure all identifying marks would be missing from the contents.

Borg had control of himself once more. He even gave Mortimer a half-smile. "I suppose I should thank you. Would I have had the will to rise in the world if it weren't for my wanting to . . . rub you out? But it's been a bittersweet rise. I've had to do things I'm not proud of." Bleakness showed through for a moment. "Maybe someone hates me as much as I've hated you."

His voice went flat and drove on. "Anyway, I've been watching you through the years, rubbing you out little by little." He nodded at the heap of documents. "And now, here you are. No identity. No assets. True, my conglomerate gave you a good price for your company. But you no longer have bank deposits or brokerage accounts. You're alone in the world. No friends. No wife—I saw to that. Even your daughter is lost to you."

"You know about—?"

"Know about her taking up with a far-out religion that required her to renounce home and family? I gave generously to the sect. They were happy to indoctrinate her so that you would never hear from her again.

"And now for the end of J. Alden Mortimer." Borg nodded at the chauffeur.

The chauffeur scooped up all the documents from the table. He toted them out to the boiler and kicked open the firebox. Mortimer's eyes were fixed on the flames. He lowered his head to charge the chauffeur.

"No!"

Borg stepped unhurriedly between. He caught hold of Mortimer. They were no match. Mortimer stopped struggling and apathetically watched his identity turn to smoke.

The chauffeur closed the firebox and left the basement. Borg released J. Alden Mortimer.

Mortimer spoke emptily to the floor. "What happens now?"

"Nothing. You can stay here, rent-free, for as long as you live. You'll get a monthly allowance. But only if you answer to the name Blank. Are you *listening?* Do you *hear* me, Mr. Blank?"

Mortimer's eyes blazed, then the fire in them died. He spoke slowly, dully. "Yes. My name is Blank."

The chauffeur reappeared, toting a heavy shrouded object.

Borg gave a little start. "Oh, yes, a small present for you."

He gestured for the chauffeur to set it down. With a last look around, he followed the chauffeur out.

Mortimer stared at the closed door, then wandered around the room, casting aimless glances at his surroundings. He stopped to gaze at the "small present," bent to unveil it. He still had a glimmer of curiosity.

A blank tombstone . . .

The solid basement floor seemed suddenly to rock like the deck of a ship at sea in a storm.

TROUBLE LIGHT

The woman in the street-corner phone booth fumbled through her pocketbook, first for the scrap of newsprint she'd torn out of the morning paper and then for the right change. She heard clicking as the pay phone swallowed the coins, then humming as it waited for her to dial. Her eyes switched back and forth between the news item and the dial as she dialed the toll-free hot line.

A recording told her that calls were flooding the line and asked her to hang on, a response would come as soon as possible.

Anxiously she reread the item. It was about a household trouble light that could cause fatal shock. The insulating cover for the socket assembly doubled as a handle for the unit. But the insulating cover was made of exceptionally soft, flexible plastic that, as it turned out, created serious potential for electric shock. When the person using it grasped the handle, he—*he;* always the old male chauvinism, she thought—could touch the metal part of an electrical outlet placed in the handle for plugging in power tools.

The Consumer Product Safety Commission had investigated several fatalities reportedly caused by the product and were recalling it.

A harried but politely authoritative voice came on the line. "U.S. Consumer Product Safety Commission, Miss Hart speaking. Hello? May I help you?"

The woman in the phone booth fought down a surge of nervousness. "I hope so," she said. "It's about the trouble light. That's what they call that light bulb in, like, a wire cage with a hook on top and a long cord, isn't it?"

"That's the product. I'm glad you've seen our alert to consumers. We've ordered a recall of that particular model, but it's impossible to monitor all retail outlets, especially the smaller ones. If you run into a problem taking yours back, tell the dealer to check with this number."

"But that's just it. My husband's on the road and I don't know where he bought it. With the kids in the house, I don't want the thing around. But I don't want to throw it away unless it's the faulty model. My husband would kill me."

"I can give you the model number. Do you have a pencil handy?"

"Yes—just a second—yes, here it is."

"The manufacturer is Lite-Way Electric Corporation and the model is 124C."

The woman in the booth repeated the information aloud as she copied it down.

"Lite-Way Electric Corporation, 124C."

"That's right."

"Thank you so much, Miss Hart."

"You're welcome."

"Goodbye."

The woman hung up. She looked out at the small dusty-windowed hardware store across the street and searched through her pocketbook, first for the ten-dollar bill secreted under the lining, then for her compact.

She freshened the powder over the bruise under her right eye, then returned the compact to her bag, reviewed the information Miss Hart had given her, let herself out of the phone booth, and started across the street to the hardware store.

DEVIL'S PASS

Location had a lot to do with the success of *Anne's Diner—Last Stop*. The stretch west, especially, was rough going—narrow, twisting, steep, and more often than not slippery. Nowhere along it to pull off for a nap. It took a clear, wide-awake mind, a responsive body, and strong nerves to negotiate Devil's Pass and still make time.

But long-haul truckers stopped at Anne's Diner as much to feast their eyes on Anne as to get a good hot cup of coffee and a platter of lean bacon and eggs without runny yolks. She had a brassy personality and copper-haired good looks to match. The truckers got an earful as well as an eyeful. It had become a game, a tradition, for truckers to try and make a pass—and for Anne to put them in their place. She enjoyed it and it helped business.

Tonight was no different, though it seemed both better and worse. The barometer was way down and Anne was in top form. Everyone sat looking inward, not outward. The rivulets on the steamy windows showed wet darkness outside and the waiting lights of rigs. Those truckers who had just come through were glad to forget Devil's Pass and those who had yet to tackle it were putting off thought of it as long as they could. All were cheered by both Anne and her antagonist.

The trucker up at bat was a boastful, cocky young male animal. To tell the truth, Anne could have gone for him. He had the rough good looks she liked and it didn't matter that he seemed a bit too young for her. But she had something solid going with a contractor in town. Besides, she had to keep the game from getting serious or it would be bad for business.

She had more on her mind at the moment than the obvious passes of a passing stranger. But she kept up her end of the banter to the delight of the cheering section.

"You tell him, Anne."

She told him. "Sure I'll give you a date—753 B.C. That's when they built Rome."

"That's telling him, Anne."

The trucker flushed. "No, I mean me and you, Anne. That kind of date." He flashed a grin. "I promise you *we'll* make history."

"He's got you now, Anne."

Anne stiffened slightly. Nobody had her, now or ever. She was her own woman. She grinned back. "You're spinning your wheels, buster. As far as I'm concerned, you're already history."

"Right on, Anne."

The trucker did not yield easily; she had to hand him that. "Now, listen, Anne—"

"Sure, Your Highness."

"Highness?"

"You're King of the Road, aren't you?"

"Anytime you want some royal lovin', honey, just let me know." He shoved his sleeve up to save it from a wet spot and rested his elbow on the counter.

Anne stared at the muscular forearm. He smiled, but it was the tattoo he had bared that had caught her eye. She reached out with a finger and tapped the tattoo.

She kept her voice light. "Why the bugle?"

With a straight face he told her a few lies first—that the bugle was there to wake him in time to roll after a night of love, that it was there to sound the alarm whenever some dame spoke of marriage, that it was there to play taps when an affair ended. But then he told her, kidding on the square, that

179

it wasn't a bugle, it was a post horn, and it was there because his name was Horn. William Horn. "Bill to you, honey."

He looked around smiling when she failed to come up with a snappy comeback. He was in the driver's seat. Anne was aware that for the first time in memory she must seem at a loss to the regulars, flustered, vulnerable.

A crash in the kitchen gave her an excuse to break off.

"Don't go away, Your Highness. I'll be right back."

The door swung to behind her and she stood still, staring at Doc, who knelt picking up pieces of crockery. His gaze slid away from hers. It came slowly back as she stood there not looking at him but through him.

Doc breathed easier. "For a minute there, Anne, I thought you were going to crawl my frame over the plate I dropped."

Anne eyed the pieces impatiently. "That? Forget it."

That nerved him to go on. He stood up eagerly. "It wasn't my hands. The plate was greasy. We have to get a better pearldiver." He wiped his hands on his apron and held them out. His fingertips were blurs. "You'll see. I'll be fine. I haven't had a drop since you told me what you would need me for. I'll be over the shakes tomorrow in plenty of time to do it." He grew bolder in face of her silence, almost demanding in tone. "Of course, I'll have to go into town to get the instruments. And you'll have to give me the money. Let's see, I'll need . . ."

His voice trailed off but he tried to hold a smile in place. "Haven't you been listening to what I've been saying? Where have you gone to?" He sang a phrase in a cracked voice. " 'Annie doesn't live here any more.' That was a pop song— before your time."

Anne came back from where she had been and eyed him levelly. " 'Physician, heal thyself.' That's an old saying that means you're hanging on after your time."

Doc lost his hold on the smile. "You can be hard, Anne, and heartless."

"I can be realistic, you mean, and practical." She made a face at herself. "I'm sorry, Doc. I don't know why I'm taking it out on you, but you know what I have on my mind."

"I understand, Anne. That's all right."

She patted his narrow shoulder. "Take care of out front, will you, while I run out back?"

He nodded and she made for the rear door. She stopped herself, and him too.

"Oh, just in case. How many of those pills do I slip Jane if she goes hysterical on me again? I want it to work fast—knock her out in, say, five minutes. I can't spare the time to stay with her."

Doc frowned. "Well, if you absolutely have to. Let's see, for someone slight as Jane I'd say five should do it."

Anne nodded and went out. She crossed to her living quarters—a double-size mobile home on a concrete-block foundation. At the door she stopped in spite of the cold drizzle and looked back at the parked rigs. None of the truckers was pulling out yet. Her smile got snarled up. They were all waiting for the finish of her match with Bill Horn. She let herself in.

The night-light showed her that her kid sister lay curled up in bed. Jane had gone back to her childhood and earlier—night-light and fetal position. Jane's suitcase remained half unpacked.

"Jane."

Jane was not sleeping. Slowly she rolled her head to stare blankly at Anne. "Yes?"

"How are you feeling?"

"All right." Dull eyes, dull voice.

"That's good." While she talked Anne busied herself finishing Jane's unpacking. "Doc will take care of it tomorrow. This is a nice clean place. It'll go fine. Doc was good once, you know—one of the best. It wasn't his fault he cracked up." But Anne was already having second thoughts. Maybe she should take a day off, drive into the city, and arrange a legal abortion "for reasons of the mother's mental health." But that could wait till tomorrow. Right now she had another point to settle.

She closed the dresser drawer. "There." She stood looking down at Jane. "You say that while you were going around together he called himself Bill Harrison, but that after he ditched you and you tried to trace him, you found that wasn't his real name. Is that right?"

Slowly Jane rolled over onto her back and stared at the ceiling. "That's right."

"You mentioned that he has a tattoo on his forearm—a tattoo of a bugle. Is that right?"

Jane rested both hands on her belly. "That's right." Then, almost indifferently, "Why?"

Grief tore at Anne's insides. Janie didn't live there anymore. Not the Janie she had known. Anne knew why. It was that smiling animal in the diner. Anne had felt sure of it. But she had had to feel surer to do what she was going to do.

She gave a half-careless, half-angry laugh. "Oh, I don't know. I guess I was thinking of maybe hiring a private eye. But at this point there doesn't seem any point in it, does there?"

"No, I guess not." Empty eyes, empty voice.

Anne let pressure come out as a sigh. "Close your eyes and try to get some sleep." She touched her cold hand to Jane's hot brow.

"I'll look in on you again. Remember, baby, you're not alone."

She palmed the bottle of pills from the dresser top as she left. Once outside she locked the door as quietly as she could.

A glance at the parking area showed her all the rigs were still there. She felt the cold tears of the drizzle on her face as she hurried back to the diner. In the kitchen she picked up a clean cloth and patted her face and hair dry. Then out front.

Anne's nod answered Doc's look as they switched. She turned on her smile for the truckers—and for Horn.

Horn grinned back. "Well, Anne, you been thinking it over? Did you decide you're going to be sweet to me?"

"That's just what I decided." Anne spoke slowly, drawing it out as her hands busied themselves out of sight. Under the counter she crushed pills into a coffee cup. For Jane, five; that meant double should do the job for Horn. She lifted the cup to the spout of the coffee machine and filled it, then put in three teaspoons of sugar and set the cup in front of him with a swirling flourish. "You earned yourself one on the house with lots of sugar."

Horn scowled, then joined in the laughter. Only when he downed the coffee did Anne let out her breath.

The game had ended. The diner filled with so longs, and emptied.

Anne abandoned the cash register and stood at the open door to wave and watch. She saw Horn climb into the cab of his tractor-trailer. She waited. Why was it taking him so long to get his rig going? Had the doctored coffee hit him too soon? Then the exhaust flamed and the rig rumbled and the wheels hissed free.

Her gaze fixed on the rig as it followed the shining blackness up through Devil's Pass. She tracked the dwindling sweep of headlights and the bunching cluster of taillights as the rig climbed the night, reaching the dangerous dip.

Then it came—the sight of the sudden failure to make the

hairpin turn, the crash through the guardrail, the plunge down sheerness, and the final flaming. Now the sound of it shook her.

Had Jane heard it? No, it had been fainter than it seemed; she herself had heard it only because she was listening for it. But truckers and highway cops would shortly bring the echo back to Anne's Diner. What lies would she have to tell Jane to keep her from ever finding out who the driver had been?

She broke loose and ran around back, unlocked the door of her quarters.

"Jane . . ."

But Janie wasn't there any more. The dresser drawer stood crookedly open, empty but for a dangling stocking. The suitcase was gone. A chair rested up against the open window. Before climbing out, Jane had found a pencil stub and a scrap of paper and had weighted the note down with an ashtray.

Anne—Your questions and your locking me in made me wonder. I looked out and saw Bill's rig. He's going to find me waiting in his cab. When he learns about the baby, maybe we can make a life together . . .

FROM PARTS UNKNOWN

He stood on high, above good and evil. Forethought empowered him to seek out in the night and strike down as with a bolt the one he would destroy. Dominion was his, and wisdom as well.

Wisdom held him from losing himself in the abstract. He balanced the concrete block on the parapet of the Edgeware Street overpass lest the weight—and the wait—cause his arms to quiver. Not luck, but his will, kept anyone from crossing to witness that he stood here. The parkway's strings of lights formed a shooting-gallery frame for the rolling ducks below.

He would know the one when he saw the glowing Mark of the Beast.

Here it came. His mastery of elemental forces told him when to lead the target.

Now.

The plummeting block crashed through the windshield. The car swerved hard right and struck the abutment and came to a crumpled halt.

The parkway policeman, a county cop, went through the driver's wallet while the ambulance attendant plugged blood plasma and oxygen into the shallowly breathing form. The cop scanned the driver's license and looked up swiftly.

"Will he make it?"

The paramedic shrugged. "We'll take him to the hospital, sure, but there's no call to rush. Poor guy's too brain-damaged to be more than broccoli if he lives."

The cop pointed to the license. "See this? Let's get him there fast anyway."

They poured on the siren and got him there fast.

185

He lay on a gurney. A ventilator kept him breathing, intravenous fluids maintained his blood pressure. The doctor looked at the flat reading on the scope, nodded grimly, and made a phone call. "He's legally brain dead. All activity in brain and brain stem has stopped. He's all yours now. "

Day broke as the plane swung to land at LaGuardia. Dan Bowman edged forward to look past his seatmate—fellow in the aluminum-siding line. Bowman made out a toy water tower with the name LAPHAM. On the side of a nearby toy building an arrow of on-off light bulbs, probably showing the way to a shuttered tavern, seemed to aim at the name of the town Bowman headed for. Save a lot of time if he could parachute down.

Now the jet passed over Long Island Sound. First-light edged the silken pull of crosscurrents; Bowman's eyes drank in the weave of waves, swallowed the hundreds of small craft caught in the net of water. The air darkened as the day broke, and by the time they landed and deplaned, rain was falling. Bowman and his seatmate nodded on patting forever.

The siding man grimaced at the silver lines striking and streaking the terminal building's glass. "Rain."

Bowman nodded. "Beautiful, beautiful."

He stood alone in the center of the concourse, letting people swirl around him, creating his own crosscurrents. Here he was. He felt a surge of excitement. He put his carry-on bag down to let his right hand feel the pulse in his left wrist. Strong steady, all vital signs go. Grinning tightly, he picked up his bag. Red-eye or not, here I come.

He made for the rent-a-car counter, flashed his credit cards. He locked his carry-on bag in the trunk of the car, studied the road map of the metropolitan area, and imprinted the route numbers to the bedroom community of Lapham.

Fall foliage spread a feast for the eyes. *Smell the flowers.* The honking fools whizzing by, wasted their eyes glaring at him instead of taking in the scenery. A year ago he would have been one with the oblivious rush toward *Please omit flowers.* Now the mindlessness of it saddened him.

Lapham, the Friendly Town. So the welcoming signs said. He put on his friendlier expression and asked the first traffic cop the way to the public library. Something in Bowman's face and voice made the cop look at him hard before pointing the way. In the side mirror—lightly stenciled *Objects in the mirror are nearer than they seem*—Bowman saw the cop stare after the car. Likely couldn't make up his mind whether Bowman was an old crook or an old cop. Bowman smiled his tight smile.

The library stood in the heart of town, just past the shopping mall, as the cop had said. Bowman took note of the people streaming to and from the mall, a curious mix of the well-off and the shabby. Today's main attraction, the marquee said, was a psychic fair.

Bowman found lots of space in the library's parking lot. The library itself proved small but modern.

He stood at the information desk while the librarian gabbed with a patron about knitting. Though they had to be aware he stood there, they avoided eye contact with him and kept him waiting while they chatted. "I have an uncle who does needlepoint," the librarian said, and went on about the uncle who did needlepoint. Bowman looked around, taking in a display of schoolchildren's valentines. Flock of cupids, some cherubic, some grotesque, some a meld. But Eros is Eros is Eros.

Maybe Bowman should have got a haircut, shaved closer, worn his best suit, shined his shoes. Only a year earlier

Bowman would've exploded, roaring for all the world—or at least all the library—to hear what the librarian could do with her uncle's needlepoint. Today when he tired of gazing at the valentines and the reading lists of romantic novels and love poetry, he merely cleared his throat.

The patron hurried away, the librarian gave Bowman a tentative smile. "May I help you, sir?"

"I'm looking for a news item about a local man who died in a car crash around here just about a year ago."

The librarian found him the back-copy microfilms and showed him how to use the reading machine. He had to leave his driver's license as pledge for the microfilm.

Corey Urneg's death was more than a mere item. It was a cause celebre, the rallying point for a drive to have the county dismantle the overpass. Some ten years back, when the county constructed the parkway, which cut through right along the border between Lapham and Ranfield, the county threw a pedestrian bridge across to rejoin them—to give nearby Ranfielders access to Lapham's shopping mall and to provide Laphamites with day workers from Ranfield. Ever since, though, the Edgeware Street overpass had been a source of worry to Laphamites. Lapham was an upper-middle-class village, Ranfield, a steadily deteriorating city. Laphamites fell victim to thievery, mugging, and just plain malicious mischief, with the overpass allowing fast getaway into the warren of Ranfield. The senseless death of Urneg brought matters to a head.

A Loveday Fletcher had the original byline. She set the facts down simply and clearly.

Corey Urneg, fifty, an engineer just returned from a long stay overseas on a construction job, had died at the hands of one of the vandals from Ranfield's blighted area. Those hands had hurled a concrete block down upon Urneg's on-coming Cadillac. Since the crime seemed so motiveless and no one had witnessed it—or come forward claiming to have witnessed it—the perpetrator remained at large. A childless widower, Urneg left behind only his niece, Cora Urneg Gessler, who lived across county in Saxon Heights. Bowman jotted down the name and address and made note of the by-line.

That was all the paper had to say about the Urneg case, except as it kept turning up during the mounting controversy over the overpass. Urneg lived on because those gathering names for a petition to dismantle the bridge kept citing his death.

Laphamites split on the issue. Most homeowners looked upon the parkway as a moat that would keep undesirables out, most storeowners feared loss of trade. But only this month two holdups had taken place, the stickup-man in each case making his getaway across the bridge. Now even the holdout shopkeepers leaned toward doing away with the bridge. An editorial in the *Lapham Courier* asked, "Are we bigots?" and answered, "We think not!" True, with the over-pass gone, the long way around to Lapham's shopping center would take Ranfielders the better part of an hour as against the present ten minutes, a hardship for the elderly poor, but Lapham had itself to think of and charity began at home.

Bowman rose with a half smile and handed the microfilm in. He asked to see a map of Lapham. He photocopied the map for fifteen cents on the library's copying machine, then handed the original in and got his driver's license back.

The Edgeware Street overpass stood at the other end of town. That took him by the mall again. He parked near the overpass and stepped onto the pedestrian bridge.

At least the county learned from its mistakes. Take a catapult now to hurl a concrete block onto the highway below. A high screen of new cyclone fence stretched along either parapet, so he couldn't lean over to look straight down. But he saw enough to know how it must have happened. The concrete block balancing right about here before dropping to shatter the windshield of Cory Urneg's car. Bowman stood in perfect stillness for a solid minute, then looked across to the Ranfield side.

Blight, but in patches of raw color that made an interesting abstraction.

He looked back to the green Lapham side, to the colonial-style row of taxpayers. One of the stores was a stationer's. He retraced his steps to Lapham and went into the stationer's.

He bought a clipboard and asked for forms.

The saleswoman stared at him. "What kind of forms?"

"What kinds you got?"

She blinked, then gestured toward a section of shelves.

He pointed at random, found himself buying a sheaf of court reporter forms. "Oh, and a box of chalk."

"What color?"

"What colors you got?"

He took a rainbow assortment. Then he headed back to the overpass. He stopped at his car to drop off most of the chalk and the greater part of the forms. Make interesting notepaper to write letters on. If you had someone to write to. Then he crossed to Ranfield.

The blight was less colorful close up. He could see where landlords had walked away from their property and where they had torched for insurance. What brick buildings remained were almost visibly falling from disrepair into ruin. Graffiti helped hold them together.

He passed a young man carrying a box radio and wearing

mirrored sunglasses. Boombox and shades, audiovisual aids to communicate noncommunication.

Bowman spotted loose bricks aplenty in the littered lots. Any Ranfielder out for a bit of fun could have picked up a few to chuck at Charlie from the overpass. But someone bent on malicious mischief had lugged a heavy concrete block.

Pausing every so often to jot a meaningless note on the topmast form in the clipboard and to chalk a meaningless symbol in red on a telephone pole or in blue on a lamppost, Bowman took his survey.

Surprising how many flowerpots flourished on window-sills. Smell the flowers. People with flowerpots were likeliest to have books. Lots of folks, even if they could afford better, would jerry-build bookshelves with concrete blocks and boards. Against that, those very folks were least likely to take up concrete blocks in acts of random violence. No; loose concrete blocks, if here for the taking, reposed in some backyard.

He strode, purposefully, deeper into Ranfield. He paused at each alley to draw a firm fluorescent purple X on the side of one building or the other and ran his gaze up each garbage-strewn dead end in a vain search of loose concrete blocks. He also drew hard stares, and finally a muttered "Pig." At the "Pig" he stopped dead before a building showing better upkeep than most.

A slack-bellied fortyish man enthroned on the stoop glared at Bowman, the whites of his eyes red-streaked yellows. Two heavy women stood breast to breast just inside the open front door.

Bowman glanced at the building's number, gave a general nod, made a check mark on the form in the clipboard, and headed up the stoop. Might as well try this building. Keep putting it off, could wind up with one harder to get into and out of. Better the devil you know, his father used to say.

He smiled at the man and kept on. The man had to hump himself to one side or get stepped on. The man moved out of Bowman's way. The women stayed put.

One picked up a conversation that had frozen at Bowman's coming. "The doctor say, 'See, I can move your leg up,' and I say, '*You* moving it up ain't got nothing to do with *me* moving it up.' "

"Pardon me, ladies. Got to get in to do my job."

They took their time unblocking the doorway.

"Thank you, ladies."

He made for the stairway, looked up the stairwell into high dimness: Six stories. A year ago he would have said the hell with it.

Behind him, he heard two doors slam, then a whistle sound shrilly. He turned. The man had gone out into the middle of the street to aim his hooked-pinkies whistle up the face of the building. The women had vanished into their flats.

Bowman felt a tightness across his chest. He compressed his mouth and started climbing.

Every flight added its local color, its territorial stains and smells.

By God, he made it to the top without feeling a flutter or having to stop to get his wind.

The door to the roof stood open. He did stop to draw breath, but that was the old need of all life to swell and recharge in the face of danger. He fine-tuned his ears to the roof but heard only silence. He caught a stir of shadows, but that could have been from laundry whipping in the February breeze. He climbed the last flight and stepped out onto the roof. Three men closed in on him.

Bowman's gaze shot to a blanket spread at the base of the parapet. He nodded at the men but locked eyes with none. No sense giving them the stare direct, making this a macho thing. Still, he shifted his grip on the clipboard—held it by a bottom corner, so that if he had to swing it the metal clip would do damage. Before they could move in on him any closer he stepped briskly between two of them.

This seemed to suit them, after their initial surprise. They smiled around at one another and moved to block the doorway.

He gave no sign of alarm, he hoped. He made straight for the parapet. He leaned over and looked down. He had a good view of a half dozen backyards.

A quick scan yielded no loose concrete blocks amid the midden. The sandpaper scrape of a shoe on the rough asphalt roofing pulled him back and turned him. They had started his way.

If they meant business, he would yank the blanket and spill the first to step on it, then he would fling the blanket over the others. That and the clipboard might give him time to reach the stairs.

He gestured at the blanket. "The one who said to use the blanket is taking the other two. Blanket gives a crapshooting artist control of the roll."

All three looked startled, then two turned to the third.

That one scowled. "Honky, you unreal. You know what part of Ranfield you in? Man, you must be doing crack, flying high, to think you can come up here and give us a hard time."

The others joined in. "Yeah. Flying high. Maybe he show us how he spread his wings."

"He ain't no butterfly, neither no bee. We got to give him liftoff."

They moved in. Maybe they meant only to throw a scare into him, maybe they meant business. He gripped the clipbord tightly with one hand and got ready to snatch the blanket with the other hand the instant the man on the left set foot on the blanket.

Under the soft-shoe shuffle of their approach, he thought he caught the sound of someone wheezing up the stairs. This was their turf; whoever came would reinforce them. Likeliest candidate, the man on the stoop, the pig-baiter, the whistler. But till whoever came stepped out onto the roof, Bowman could make use of the climber.

He grinned. "Here comes my partner."

That stopped the three in their tracks. They swung their heads to listen to the labored approach.

Bowman lifted his voice. "Out here on the roof, Mike." He bulled through to the door.

A big hard belly bounced him back. A big hard man followed the belly out onto the roof.

The man mountain peeked through small eyes at Bowman and the three, took in the clipboard and the blanket.

He fixed on Bowman. "I ain't Mike. Who ain't you?"

Bowman smiled. At least he had the four of them expecting a Mike. "Just doing my job."

The man mountain became an active volcano. "Where was you when we needed you? Now we don't need you, you all over the place. We brung this building back by hard work. Fixed it up from top to bottom, inside and out. We got sweat equity in it. We don't need nobody looking for violations so he can stick out his palm for greasing."

"I'm not looking for—"

"Yeah, yeah. I know what you not looking for. What about the garbage?"

Bowman cocked his head. "What about the garbage?"

"You know what I mean. You from city hall, you damn well aware they don't make nowhere near the pickups they do in other parts of Ranfield, much less than what they do in

Lapham. Taxation without representation, that's what it is. You go back to city hall and tell them Henry Tice says that. Taxation, without representation.''

Bowman nodded gravely. "Be glad to go back and tell them, but have to finish here first." He turned and pushed past the three men, breaking up that tableau. "Excuse me." He strode to the far side of the roof, listened behind him but caught no rasp of shoe, leaned forward to peer down into another set of backyards. No loose concrete blocks. He unclipped his pen and made a few ticks on the form, then strode back. "That does it. Now, Mr. Tice, if you'll kindly unplug the doorway . . . "

Tice stared down at him, then earthquaked a laugh. "Right, man, right." Tice backed out of the doorway.

Bowman squeezed by and headed downstairs. Behind him he heard Tice step onto the roof. He heard Tice ask the three men if they didn't remember Henry Tice telling them to use some other roof for their crapshooting. He did not wait to hear the rest.

His heartbeat slowed to normal by the time he crossed to Lapham, but he sat in his car without moving for a moment before turning the key and pressing the starter. Turned *him* on, made colors brighter and the body hum, when oxygen and adrenaline fueled the system. He savored the feeling, then shook himself and got going.

The big wall calendar, featuring a field of daisies, had seen better days, had aged fast, Only February, and the pages were curl-edged from looking ahead to deadlines or days off.

A hum came from elsewhere in the narrow building, but the *Lapham Clarion*'s office held only a young woman at the editor's desk. Nameplate said Loveday Fletcher.

She stopped reading copy and looked over her Ben Franklin glasses to eye Bowman inquiringly and take his measure.

"My name's Dan Bowman."

"What brings you to Lapham, Mr. Bowman?"

A look past him out the storefront window would have shown her his rental car.

"Remember the Urneg case?"

She shook her head, but that was not a no. "His death won't die." She tilted her chin sharply higher to get him in the lenses. "What's your interest in it?"

"Just trying to make sense of a senseless death."

Her nose wrinkled as if she smelled a story. "You a relative?"

He shook his head.

"An old friend?"

"Never knew him. Let's just say I have my reasons."

She frowned. "Let's say I'm busy right now." She glanced at her wristwatch. Her eyes widened. "Damn, it's my lunch hour already." She glared left and right out the window.

"I'll buy you lunch if I can ask you about the Urneg case between bites."

She flushed nicely. "I wasn't angling for that. Matter of fact, I'm half expecting to meet someone for lunch."

"A lunch in the hand is better than half an expect."

He saw the wheels turn behind the eyes: would there be a story here?

She gave him half a smile and kept the other half for herself. "You're on. But we'll have to wait for my relief."

He moved toward a chair over in a corner. "No problem."

The wait proved hardly worth sitting down for. A mustached youth rushed in wiping his mouth with a paper napkin. Fletcher grabbed her purse, cut the youth off at the apologies, skipped introductions, and nodded for Bowman to follow her out.

She had a shape worth watching; Bowman waited till they were on the sidewalk to catch up with her. "My car—"

"We can walk. Not that far."

And her brisk pace made it not that long. She turned in at an antique store. Bowman might have passed the place by without realizing it was also a restaurant. They knew her in there; an antique waitress found them a sheltered table for two and handed them a typed menu.

Bowman's eyes lit on the special. Rabbit stew. *Granddad . . . campfire . . . pine needles . . . starry night.* "I'll have the rabbit stew."

Fletcher's glance condemned him. "The green salad, please, and the baked potato with sour cream substitute and chives."

The waitress nodded. "And decaf?"

"Check."

"No, I get the check."

The waitress twisted her wrist to point the eraser top of her pencil at him as she left.

Fletcher gazed at the door, on the lookout for the someone she was half expecting.

Bowman grimaced. Too much expecting. Too much waiting. Not enough use of now. "What kind of guy was Corey Urneg?"

She faced him with a small frown and looked back into her mind. "Like my story said. Childless widower. Construction engineer. Just back from a long stay on a big project."

Food interrupted.

Fletcher watched him dip his spoon in the bowl and waited till he had raised the laden spoon to his mouth. "How can you eat that?"

He eyed her over the spoonful of that. He was supposed to think of the Easter Bunny and Peter Rabbit, picture some floppy-eared cottontail with big soft eyes. "It's fair to eat anything that eats anything else."

That held her long enough for him to taste and swallow the stew. The rabbit meat was stringy and bland, but he didn't let the letdown show.

She stabbed her greens. "That's right, enjoy it."

"Thanks."

"By that reasoning, it's fair to kill anyone who kills." She tossed her hair back.

"You got it."

She twisted her fork in the green salad savagely. He caught himself smiling. A bleeding-heart do-gooder. Yet human enough to have blind spots and double standards. There was that "Are we bigots? We think not!" editorial.

Business with pleasure. "Is these anything you can tell me about Urneg that might not have got in the paper?"

She said, "I've kept my notes at home ever since cops started raiding newspaper offices. I'm pretty sure there's nothing I can add to the newspaper account, but you're welcome to stop by my place later. I knock off at four-thirty." She fished her pen out of her purse and scribbled her address on a scrap of paper. "Just give me time to shower and change."

He read the scribbling: 79 Middlebury Drive, 5C. The *i*'s had haloes. "Thanks. Maybe you can tell me the name of a nearby motel."

She peered past the foliage on her fork. "Planning to stay in these parts long?"

He shrugged. "How long depends on how soon I can clear up this Urneg thing. Overnight, at least."

The weighted fork pulled her hand down. " 'Clear up this

Urneg thing'? What makes you think you can come here and do in a few days or less what the local fuzz couldn't in a year?"

"I don't know that I can. But I have to give it my best shot."

"I wish you luck. The *Courier* could use the story. About a motel: Lapham zoning forbids motels. Nearest one I know of is at the other end of Ranfield, on the Post Road—the Post Road Motor Inn."

"Thanks."

She had finished eating and was looking at her watch. Okay with him; he had eaten more than enough rabbit stew to make his point. He got the waitress's attention and the tab. He paid by credit card end left a cash tip.

He matched stride with Fletcher back as far as his car. They said their so-longs. He stood by his car watching as she went into the *Courier* office. She didn't look back.

He turned the key in the ignition but sat revving up his mind.

Where to now? Urneg's niece's. Phone ahead? No. Always better to catch people off guard. Besides, setting up appointments could be as wasteful of time and effort as taking the chance of finding someone in. He unfolded the area map. Saxon Heights was *there*, Post Road Inn would be on the way. He refolded the map and got rolling.

The Post Road Motor Inn had as its sign a silhouette mailcoach-and-four, and the numbers of the individual rooms were on cutout post horns, but that was as far as the motif went. He brought his carry-on in, stayed only long enough to take a leak, brush his teeth, and freshen his shave, then got rolling again.

He located the cloverleaf that put him on the parkway. He felt a slight twinge when he found himself passing under the

Edgeware Street overpass. He drove across county to the Saxon Heights address he had jotted down in the library.

A modest house in a modest neighborhood. No curtains. A realtor's sign on the modest lawn. The house on the right had curtains and one curtain twitched.

Bowman got out of the car and shoved his hands in his pockets and studied the empty house and then strolled around to the modest backyard. Twitchy curtains followed his progress.

Vestiges of a modest garden. But what really caught his eye was a row of loosely set, unevenly spaced, frost-heaved concrete blocks that edged the property on what he took to be the Gessler side of the line. He pulled his hands out of his pocket; and knelt to upend a block and look at the bottom.

A competent lab technician could get a chemical fix on the soil that clogged the block's pores, on the leachings that stained the concrete, and on the composition of the block itself. But it would be expecting too much of the police investigators to hope that they had collected and analyzed and preserved the fragments of the concrete block that had landed on Corey Urneg's car.

Bowman knew the block that had killed Urneg would match these blocks. But knowing was not proving.

He let the block fall back into place and straightened. He gave a last look around, then made for the front walk and the house next door.

The woman who answered the doorbell had a fine head of pink rollers. "Good afternoon?"

"Good afternoon, ma'am. Would you happen to know where the folks next door moved to?"

"The Gesslers?" Her face pinched. "Can't say I'm sorry they moved. Him mostly. She was nice enough, though she changed near the end and we had nothing to do with each other, but even before that on account of him I gave up going to her for my perms." She patted her curlers. "Been doing them myself."

"He gave you trouble?"

"I never trusted him because of his eyes." She shivered. "But I tried to be a good neighbor on her account. Him, though, he not only gave me trouble—when he tried to move the property line and I licked him in court he put the evil eye on my garden so all my mums wilted—he gave her trouble."

"Oh?"

"Over the daily."

Bowman frowned in puzzlement. "The newspaper?"

"No, the *daily*. The young black woman from Ranfield who came in to clean and wash. Mrs. G. thought Mr. G. got too friendly with the woman and made him fire her." Her chin thrust forward. "I couldn't help hearing the Gesslers argue about it; they got really loud." She shook her head. "Can you imagine? Him giving her cause to be jealous over one of those people from Ranfield?"

"Was the young woman pretty?"

She eyed him hostilely. "I suppose you could call her pretty. I never really noticed."

"Not that it should make a difference, of course."

The ambiguity mollified her. "Of course." She threw the weight of her rollers to one side. "Are you thinking of buying?"

"Thinking." He smiled a neighborly smile.

She glanced at his car. "Your wife's not with you?"

"Lost my wife three years ago."

"Oh. Sorry." She patted her rollers. "I know what that is; I lost my George five—no, six—years ago last December."

"Too bad."

"Yes, but life has to go on."

"True, true."

She gave him a measuring look. "You put me in mind of George. Big like him. And rough—on the outside."

"Yes, well . . ."

"You from around here?"

"No, from out of state." He caught her eyeing the car's plate. She wasn't as sharp as Fletcher and didn't spot the rental ID. "Rented car. Staying at the Post Road Motor Inn. My name's Don Bowman . . ."

Her face cleared. "How do you do. I'm Ann Lindsay."

"Nice meeting you, Mrs. Lindsay. About the Gesslers . . ."

"Oh, the Gesslers. They moved into her uncle's house in Lapham she inherited, so they put this one on the market. But you don't need to deal with them; there's a realtor's sign on the lawn."

He looked. "So there is. Thank you."

"Don't mention it"—she cocked her head—"neighbor."

With a nod and a smile Bowman left and headed back to Lapham.

The smile hardened. He stopped once to find a pay phone with a directory, but used the directory only to look up the Gesslers' new address. Ann Lindsay was right. It was the same Lapham address he had for the late Corey Urneg.

Bowman drove past the place slowly. So this was where Corey Urneg had lived when not abroad supervising one of his firm's big construction jobs. To Bowman it looked Moorish—Morocco rococo, he'd style it, though it had to have some other name. Anyway, the Gesslers now had a lot more room indoors and outdoors than at the Saxon Heights house. This house had bright new curtains, but no cars in the driveway or any other sign of someone at home.

He wound his way out of the serpentine drives of the resi-
dential area and into the business district and stopped again
at the same traffic cop to ask the way to police headquarters.
This time the cop's gaze softened slightly, but the cop still
stared after the car.

Police headquarters was in city hall as the cop said.
Bowman identified himself at the desk and stated an interest
in the Urneg case. Tom Wilkes, the detective who had handled the case, was in and swivelled around to look at Bowman
through the open doorway, but swiveled back and pecked
away at a typewriter to finish a report or just to keep Bowman
waiting. When he was ready, he swivelled around again and
beckoned Bowman in.

He didn't offer to shake hands, but nodded Bowman to a
chair. "I have to tell you I don't much care for rent-a-cops."

Bowman spoke mildly. "I'm a private investigator. One
day, by regulation fate, or choice, you'll be off the force—and
you might find you're not ready for a rocking chair. Why not
keep your options and your mind open?"

Wilkes flushed slightly. A slight shift in position suggested
a slight change of heart. His tone softened to a finer grade of
sandpaper. "The Urneg case, hey? Does the identity of your
client have any bearing on the case?"

Bowman shook his head.

Wilkes narrowed his already-narrow eyes shrewdly. "Insurance company. I'd guess. Or lawyer for the, what's their
name, the Gesslers." He shrugged. "It's the county that's on
the hook if there's a suit for negligence. Tricky jurisdiction.
County highway running along the dividing line between
Lapham and Ranfield. The perp stood on the half of the overpass Lapham is supposed to patrol and dropped the block
from there. That's the only reason any of it lands in our lap.
Technically the case stays open for the county and for us, and

I suppose for Ranfield though Ranfield was no big help, till one of us finds the perp. Pragmatically . . ." He shrugged again. "As far as I'm concerned it ends as indeterminately as it began."

"Did you or the county save the concrete block that smashed into Mr. Urneg's car?"

"You mean the pieces. What for?"

"Evidence."

An explosive laugh came out of Wilkes's unchanged face. "You ought to know better than to expect anybody to raise fingerprints off anything like that."

"Yeah, I should." But then Bowman mentioned that such things as embedded soil, acquired organic and inorganic stains, and composition of the block itself could help tag the block and maybe match it to other blocks at the Gesslers' property in Saxon Heights.

Wilkes flushed again and his eyes bored black holes into space and his mouth tightened. He swung back around to his desk and stabbed touch-tone keys.

He spoke with a county investigator openly and Bowman listened openly, so Bowman knew as soon as Wilkes that the county had not thought to save the fragments of the concrete block.

Bowman raised a finger for Wilkes to hold the line a minute. "What about the car?"

Turned out that the car, ownership of which went to Mrs. Gessler, was fit only for the wrecker's yard.

Wilkes was again ready to hang up but Bowman again raised a finger.

"What wrecker's yard?"

They went there in Wilkes's car.

They returned with Wilkes glumly triumphant. "Told you

204

it would be stripped for parts, with nothing left to take soil particles off of or concrete fragments out of."

Bowman sat slumped. "But we had to try."

Wilkes shot a sidewise glance. "Yeah. We had to try."

He let Bowman out at police headquarters next to Bowman's car. "Best I can tell you is we'll keep the Gesslers in mind, and if we ever bust them for anything . . ." He shook Bowman's hand. "But don't set your heart on that."

Bowman smiled the tight smile. "No, I won't set my heart on that."

Bowman found a parking space near 79 Middlebury Drive. He identified himself on the intercom and Loveday Fletcher buzzed the downstairs door open.

Still toweling her hair, she let him in. She wore a robe, but it was not loose; it outlined her firmly. She raised an eyebrow and took the bottle of champagne he had stopped to buy. She did not squeal with delight but she did not gnash her teeth. " 'Candy is dandy, but liquor is quicker'? I'd better go chill this in the fridge right away." But she stood watching him look around at the macramé-hung garden that made the place an overhead obstacle course. " 'What nitwit knotted these whatnots?' " Most likely she said that to every first-time caller.

"Very nice." Most likely what every first-time caller replied.

She smiled. She left the room with the bottle and came back with a file folder. "This has my notes for the story. And shots the *Courier* bought but didn't use. A free-lance photographer took them after Urneg was out of the car and on the way to the hospital."

He found pages torn from a small spiral-bound pad; the scrawls at first skim told him no more than the news item he had read. The three Polaroids, however, made his heart leap: They were in color, front and side views of a wrecked Cadillac. The front view, through the windshield gap, was the one.

The blood spattered on the upholstery gave him a twinge but the concrete chunk on the seat showed him just what he wanted to see.

He was not jumping up and down, he felt only a glow of satisfaction, but she said, "Hey, you're excited. What is that picture telling you?" She came around to look over his shoulder.

He felt another stir at her closeness and her breath in his car, but if she read this as an excitement too, she held her tongue.

"It's the fragment of the concrete block. See the specks of soil and the stain along this edge?"

"I see. So?"

He told her about the row of concrete blocks along the property line at the Gesslers' Saxon Heights house.

"That's great!" But then she looked at his face. "You were up, now you're down. What's wrong."

"This convinces me Gessler did it, but the picture of the chunk would never hold up in court. Need the chunk itself—and the investigators failed to save it." He stared at the shot. "Even if we got the same photographer and had him use exactly the same kind of film for shots of the concrete blocks at the Gesslers' old house, that would never be admitted as evidence. Too many variables—different lot of film, different lighting conditions, different date."

"But Gessler might not know that."

"There's that. But I have to know a lot more about Gessler before I confront him." Bowman reached for the file. "What else you got in here?"

Fletcher started to pull the folder back, then handed it over.

Bowman found scrawled notes. Once again there was closeness and breathing in his ear as Fletcher had to peer through her half-glasses to translate her scrawls.

Upon moving to her uncle's house in Lapham, Cora Urneg Gessler had given up her beauty salon in Saxon Heights and leased a shop in the Lapham mall. "She changed her emphasis and her clientele. She specializes in nails. No more hairdos. Though she does sell a wrinkle cream she says she formulated for herself. And I have to say she looks much younger than the forty-nine she admits to. I've never seen such smooth skin. Karl Gessler was strange too. His eyes." Fletcher shivered. "I can't explain, but when you meet him you'll see what I mean. People claim for him that he performs surgery—in quotes—with his bare hands."

Click.

"A psychic." Bowman eyed Fletcher. "Would he be at the psychic fair in the mall?"

"One way to find out is to find out. It's on all this week. Meet you there tomorrow at 1:00 p.m.?"

"It's a date." He handed the folder back and got up to go. "Meanwhile I have a sidebar for you."

"On what?"

"Garbage."

"What?"

"Garbage collection in Ranfeld."

"This is Lapham. What has garbage collection in Ranfield to do with Lapham?"

"Everything. Wouldn't there be less friction if Ranfielders didn't see Lapham as an enclave of privilege and exclusivity? Are they bigots? We think yes!"

Fletcher looked at him over her lenses. She flushed. "You

saying the *Courier* owes Ranfield another editorial?"

"You laid Mr. Urneg's death on Ranfield and urged tearing down the overpass. How about doing one on building bridges?"

Henry Tice looked up from the carbon of the editorial Fletcher had typed before Bowman left her apartment. "You say this going to be in tomorrow's *Courier*?"

Bowman nodded. "Maybe the point about taxation without representation will shame Ranfield city hall into better garbage removal."

"Maybe, maybe not. Leastways, it's a start." Tice regarded Bowman. They had the stoop to themselves. "You ain't from Ranfield city hall. You ain't from Ranfield. Where is you comin' from?"

Bowman gestured vaguely. "I'm looking into the death of Mr. Urneg."

Tice drew himself up. "Why should I help you?"

"They've been trying to pin the death on someone from this neighborhood. I think the real killer is someone in Lapham."

"You got a name?"

"Gessler."

Tice shook his head. "Never heard of the gentleman."

"Mr. Urneg's nephew by marriage."

Tice smiled. "Everything always comes down to money, don't it? Even this race thing." He shook his head again. "What makes you think I could help you if I wanted to?"

"A young woman from this neighborhood worked for the Gesslers while they lived in Saxon Heights. She might have heard something or seen something."

"I'll ask around. But why should she stick her neck out?"

"There's a C-note in it for her."

"Money sings, all right." Tice grinned. "What's in it for me?"

Bowmen held up a twenty.

He thought at first that Tice was giving him the finger.

But Tice was displaying the ring on the finger. "Everything rolled into one. A spade with a diamond ring on a club finger that shows a heart problem." Tice took the twenty Bowman got up to go. "Take it easy."

"Yeah, I'll do that next time around."

The soft pounding wakened Bowman out of a dream about a lovely woman without mercy who demanded of her suitors their living beating hearts as valentines.

The pounding was not the beating of a heart but the knocking of a soft fist on the door.

He determined the time with one eye: 7:00 a.m. Who would be getting him up at 7:00 a.m.? "One minute." Bowman threw the covers off and swung around and erect and put on his robe. He padded to the door, holding the robe closed with one hand and finger-combing his hair with the other hand.

He opened the door on a thirtyish light brown woman with cornrow hair. She wore a maid's uniform and at first he took her for a worker here at the motel, though she carried no sheets or towels or dusting cloth. Then he knew who she must be.

His robe had fallen open and the woman stared at the scar on his chest.

He broke the spell. "Henry Tice sent you?"

"I'm Yevon Bowzer. My aunt heard Henry was asking about the woman who used to work for the Gesslers. My aunt phoned me, I phoned Henry. Henry told me where you were and what you wanted to ask me about, and here I am. Henry said something about one hundred dollars."

"That's right." He stepped back. "Come on in."

She stayed by the open door. "I'm fine here."

He didn't blame her. He knew if he looked in the mirror he wouldn't trust himself either. He got his wallet out of the toe of his shoe and a hundred-dollar bill out of the wallet. He handed her the bill.

She glanced at the bill and folded it into the pocket of her smock. "Can't stay long: got to get to my job. What do you want to know?"

"I want to know how the Gesslers felt about Mrs. Gessler's uncle."

"Mr. Urneg? The man who died when somebody chucked a rock at his car?"

"A concrete block."

"Was that it? Why, they both felt very bad when they heard what happened."

"No, I mean before he died. Did they ever talk about him in your hearing?"

She thought back. "Whenever Mrs. Gessler got a letter from Mr. Urneg from one of those faraway places, Mr. Gessler asked her to save him the stamps. He said Uncle Corey was making him a nice little collection."

"That's it? No talk about the money and property Mrs. Gessler would inherit when Mr. Urneg died?"

"Can't say I heard a word about that kind of thing."

"Why did you leave?"

A sudden smile broke up the smooth face. "You been talking to that Mrs. Lindsay? Well, it didn't happen any way near like what she might say."

"What might she say?"

"That Mr. Gessler and me fooled around."

"Then how might she have got the notion?"

210

"Well, it was true that Mrs. Gessler was jealous. Is jealous. But Mrs. Gessler is jealous of every woman Mr. Gessler looks at—the women who consult him, the women at the places where he shops and eats, any woman he has anything to do with. And I was right there and Mrs. Gessler just naturally took every nice thing Mr. Gessler said to me the wrong way. I guess I could've stood it a while longer, but the bus line dropped a few buses from its schedule on the Ranfield-Saxon Heights route and it got to be too much of a hassle getting there on time, so I up and found me another job and quit. Reminds me I better be going if I expect to catch this bus."

"Give me a chance to dress and I'll drive you. We can finish our talk on the way."

But she was already backing out. "We done finished." And before he could say more she was gone.

He told Loveday Fletcher about Yevon Bowzer. He and Fletcher were having coffee at a restaurant in the lower level of the Lapham mall.

Fletcher looked thoughtful. "I could always get the blahs and have to change something. Make an appointment with Cora Gessler and start talking about maids while she worked on my nails."

"Claws."

She glared at him. "It wouldn't be gossip for the sake of gossip. I'd be—Why are you shaking your head?"

"Keep your eye on the ball. The crystal ball, in this case, if Karl Gessler uses one. He's the one I want."

She looked at her watch. "Okay. I guess they're set up by now. Let's go."

They rode the escalator to the mezzanine. In among the mall's manicured little jungles, the psychics had their chairs and tables unfolded and were already in consultation with clients. Or—Bowman smiled to himself—with shills. Whatever, a hover of sheepish believers waited their turn.

"He's here," Fletcher whispered.

"Don't tell me," Bowman said. He surveyed the mix of palmists, numerologists, astrologers, and just plain tarot-pack fortune-tellers. "Let me tell you. The guy on the right in the first row."

"That's the one."

Had to be. Fletcher and Lindsay had spoken of the man's eyes. As the man looked up for a moment, his gaze swept past Bowman, and Bowman could almost believe that those eyes had the ability to pick one car out of thousands streaming past in the night. Gessler's foreknowledge that Mr. Urneg would be driving under the Edgeware Street overpass at that hour seemed a less mysterious matter: the engineer would have phoned his niece to say he was coming to see her and her husband, now that he had returned from his long stay abroad. But the eyes seemed eyes that might well wilt mums.

The man had no obvious gimmick, just spoke softly in a low vibrant voice that carried past his table only as a mesmerizing hum.

By a strange coincidence, he imagined Gessler would say, Gessler just happened to sit facing the PnailPhile.

The PnailPhile, as the painted-nail pennons of the *P*'s whimsically signified, offered nail and tip sculpturing, nail extensions, nail wrapping, manicures, and whirlpool pedicures. The display window featured an array of nail polish bottles.

Bowman's gaze lit on a bottle of fluorescent polish.

That cleared up how Gessler had, without benefit of psychic perception, locked on the target. Dabs of fluorescence on the Cadillac's roof and fenders would have enabled

Gessler to pick Mr. Urneg's car out of the stream of traffic. Bowman visualized Gessler stealing onto Mr. Urneg's Lapham property earlier that fatal evening and, a shadow among shadows, daubing spots of fluorescent polish on the Cadillac parked alongside the Morocco rococo house.

"I'm getting in line."

Before Bowman could snap to and take that in, Fletcher had moved too near Gessler's table for Bowman to draw her away without drawing Gessler's attention.

Shaking his head, Bowman returned his scrutiny to the PnailPhile. Someone was rearranging the window display. A woman with long blond hair and smooth white skin and huge dark glasses moved bottles of concealing cream and wrinkle lotion behind the bottles of nail polish. She had to be her own best ad for the wrinkle cream someone had told him Cora Gessler whipped up.

Some of Gessler's clients must have been among Mrs. Gessler's. Cora Gessler would have picked up gossip by and about them. She was in a position to tip her psychic mate off to bits of information about the clients. A new client sat down. Gessler's eyes went casually to the PnailPhile. Bowman's gaze shot there.

The woman put a bottle of concealing cream to the fore; she paused to light a cigarette, then, gracefully as a gesture of salaam, her hand touched her neck and descended to sweep out palm down at her waist.

That translated as: the dame got a burn on her neck when she was waist high.

As he watched her, she turned his way. Why did it seem to him that she recognized him? It could have been simple startlement. At any rate, she turned quickly away and pulled back from the window into the dim recesses of her shop.

His gaze shot to Gessler's table. The client's hand had

213

gone to her throat. Fletcher, up to bat next, looked impressed.

Bowman looked for the blond woman in the PnailPhile to appear again when Fletcher sat down, but the woman did not show. A frown briefly darkened Gessler's brow. Then he bent his gaze on Fletcher.

Bowman felt an unaccountable chill.

Bowman let Fletcher walk around a bend before he caught up with her.

"Well?"

"He's sharp. He knew right away that I wasn't there for a reading. He even knew I'm with the *Courier*, though I wasn't the reporter who interviewed him at the time of Urneg's death."

"That's easy enough. There's the little cut of your face on the editorial page."

"Anyway, he asked me what I really wanted."

"And how did you answer?"

"I asked him if he had used his psychic abilities to help the police find his uncle-in-law's killer."

"And?"

"And when he said that he had tried on his own but could not get a clear enough picture, I told him I had a clear picture of the concrete block that killed Urneg if that would help."

Bowman's heart misbeat. "That was dumb."

She looked angrier than hurt. "Why dumb?"

"If he killed Mr. Urneg, he'd kill you to cover it up."

She waved that away airily. "Oh, is that all. Anyway, he said that was most interesting and might well be worth following up. So I told him he could see the photo at my place tonight."

"Now, that was really dumb."

"You mean you're not able to be there, close by?"

"Oh. Sure. That's different."

"I'm not *that* dumb."

"I didn't say *you* were dumb. Smart people do dumb things."

"You look like you can handle him. Or is that a dumb assumption?"

"I can handle him."

"Well, let's just hope you don't do something dumb."

Bowman grinned. "On that note of mutual confidence . . ."

Bowman got up from the couch in the sitting room and went into the bedroom at Fletcher's beck.

She stood at the window and pointed down through the gauze of the curtain.

A foreshortened Gessler got out of a car parked across the street and headed their way. He stopped short, almost as though he were aware of them, and they drew back. But the cant of his head and the twist of his trunk said that someone had called to him from the car. He turned and walked back to the car. The blonde leaned out to hand him a package.

A big red beribboned cardboard heart.

Fletcher giggled. "How tacky. He comes bearing a box of chocolates for Valentine's Day."

Bowman shook his head. Fletcher would be wise to take Gessler seriously. "Better test them for poison before you eat them."

Fletcher stared at Bowman. "You really think he'd do that?"

Bowman shrugged. "If he thinks you're a threat, poisoned candy is dandy."

She shivered. "I'm glad you're here. But get out of sight."

She took a key from the dresser drawer and unlocked the closet door. She swung the door out and gestured him in, but then raised a hand to halt him before he started. She kicked off her flats and stepped into a pair of spiked heels she grabbed from the closet floor. She wobbled a moment seating her feet and held on to Bowman.

It was a nice moment, too soon over.

"I don't usually wear these indoors because they dent the parquet and the linoleum, but just in case I have to stomp his instep—"

The intercom rang.

"Get in."

Bowman hesitated. His stepfather had locked him in the closet and told him not to stir or cry or the vacuum cleaner in there with him would swallow him up. Ever since, Bowman had hated confined spaces. He looked inside Fletcher's closet. No vacuum cleaner. On a shelf higher than his head stood boxes of file folders and stacks of rubber-banded reporter's notebooks. A clothes-hanger rod ran across under the shelf. Most of the hangers were in use, but he could squeeze in among the dresses and pant suits. There were a few bare wire hangers, and if he stirred he might not get swallowed but he would cause jangling. He grabbed the naked hangers off the rod and put them on the floor in a corner among paired shoes. He looked at the door lock. On the inside the door had a winged turn that worked the catch but had nothing to do with the dead bolt.

Fletcher took the key out of the lock and put it on the dresser next to the Urneg story file folder. "Don't worry, you can't get locked in."

Bowman drew breath, a long one, as though it would have to last him, then stepped into the closet and let Fletcher shut the door on him.

To peep through the keyhole he had to get down on one knee and twist his rump sideways. Could've been worse: it could've been a chimney and he could have had santaclaustrophobia.

He watched Fletcher run spikily to buzz Gessler in. Bowman and Fletcher stayed so still that Bowman could hear the elevator go down and come up.

Then he heard Fletcher let Gessler in.

"For me? How thoughtful. Come right in. Have a seat on the couch. Can I get you anything?"

"Just the photo, if you please."

"Of course. But first I'd like to know how you work with something like that. Does it give you visions? Put you in touch with the scene it depicts?"

"Get the photo and I'll show you."

"All right. No, don't get up; you needn't come with me, I'll—"

But Gessler followed her into the bedroom. Bowman saw her enter carrying the heart-box and saw Gessler hard on her spike heels.

"You know, Miss Fletcher, we've met before."

She turned to face him, holding the box to her breast almost as a shield. "You mean before this afternoon in the mall?"

"Much before."

"I'm afraid I don't—"

"I recognize you from a previous existence. You were Salome."

Fletcher let a few beats pass. "And you?"

His eyes widened. "I am always the same. I do not change from life to life." He spoke with the utter sanity of utter madness.

Fletcher sounded shaken but gamely trying for lightness.

"Reincarnation. That might make an interesting piece."

"Reincarnation is merely one aspect of divine power, which is the power to take life as well as to grant life. Put yourself in God's shoes. You see an ant in your path and you know that your foot may squash the ant. What are your options? At the last instant you see that your foot will indeed come down upon the ant, but you do not change stride to miss the ant. Call that: Fate, Doom, Natural Law. At the last instant you close your eyes before you determine whether or not your foot will come down upon the ant and you do not take note of what happens. Call that: Blind Fate. At the last instant you change stride to spare the ant. Call that: Grace, Mercy. At the last instant you see that your foot will indeed miss the ant, and you change stride to squash the ant. Call that: Evil, Malice." He paused. "Do you get the picture? Have you put yourself in God's shoes?" He paused again. "Wrong. You can't put yourself in God's shoes. You're the ant."

While he spoke he had edged nearer the dresser, out of Bowman's line of sight. Going for the folder, Bowman guessed.

When Gessler's hand came back in view it held not the folder but the key, and the key came straight at Bowman's eye.

With the key coming at his eye, Bowman jerked back without thinking to open the door. By the time Bowman recovered, Gessler had turned the key and the dead bolt had snicked into place.

Bowman turned cold inside. Gessler knew Bowman was in the closet.

Gessler was psychic after all.

Don't be dumb. He was just good at picking up cues. He caught Fletcher's nervousness and her too-carefully-not-looking-toward-the-closet. Before that, he caught the cushions on the couch, big-body—dented and body-heated.

Gessler was not psychic but psychotic.

He had left the keyhole unobstructed on purpose. He wanted the man the blonde must've told him about, the watcher in the mall, to see what he was doing and to feel helpless and afraid.

"What are you doing?" Fletcher's voice, trying to keep the panic out of itself. It had all happened so unexpectedly and so matter-of-factly that she was only now taking it in.

"Nothing to worry about." Through the keyhole Bowman saw Gessler's hand move as though to pat Fletcher's shoulder. The hand shot to her neck before she could think to use her spike heels.

She slumped and fell to the floor, the red box striking the floor, too, and breaking open to spill foil-wrapped bonbons. Gessler had pressed the carotid, Bowman thought.

Bowman hurled his body at the door.

Gessler glanced impassively at the thudding, then unhurriedly took a roll of tape from his pocket and bound Fletcher's wrists together behind her, stopped her mouth, and bound her ankles together. He lifted her and stretched her on the bed across from the closet in direct line of sight.

Bowman emptied his lungs in a shout. "Let the woman alone!"

Gessler took his time turning around. He faced the closet gravely, God deigning to notice an ant. "Or you'll do what? You don't have a gun." Easy conclusion. If Bowman had a weapon he damned well would have used it. "But even if you had one you could not stop me." Easy boast. But somehow chilling.

Bowman pressed his back against the closet wall and tried to kick the door. The closet was too narrow to allow him any real leverage.

Could he pick the lock? He felt for the wire hangers down in the corner. Straighten one out—and then what? He didn't know the first thing about picking locks.

He fingered the useless hanger. The shape of it stirred memory. *Granddad . . . campfire . . . pine needles . . . starry night.* They had got the rabbit with an arrow.

Almost of themselves, his fingers twisted the hook to free it of the spiral grip of the other end. They flexed the wire at the shoulders to break off the straight length. Arrows are arrows are arrows. This was his arrow, hot to the touch at the jagged ends. He stretched out of his stiffness to reach the stacks of rubber-banded notes on the shelf. Good strong quarter-inch width. One was not so strong; it snapped apart at first pull. But he had four good rubber bands. He passed loop through loop to make a foot-long chain of them. He felt the hanging clothing for a wooden hanger and tore off whatever was on the first one he came to. He slipped the end loops of the rubber-band chain over the ends of the hanger. A bowstring. He took hold of the hanger neck with his left hand and gripped the middle of the bowstring with the other hand and drew the bowstring toward the hook and beyond, testing the stretch, feeling the stored energy. He had his weapon. One end of the arrow was sharper by a tiny jag or two than the other. That sharper end would be the point. Even the blunter end could still pierce a rubber band and hang when it came time to shoot. He tore a strip of cloth off a dress and wrapped it around the bowstring at the center to serve as a slinglike pocket.

He put his eye to the keyhole. What had the bastard been up to meanwhile?

Gessler had fitted on what looked like steel-tipped false fingernails. He had set the two heart-shaped halves of the empty valentine box on the bed beside Fletcher. He now stretched out his talons over Fletcher in some sort of ritual-istic gesture, murmured some kind of incantation, and sud-denly brought the steel claws raking down Fletcher's body from neck to navel. The talons ribboned her dress.

Gessler looked around toward the closet. He cocked his head as though to catch an outcry.

Bowman did not want to give Gessler the satisfaction, but he did want Gessler to keep thinking him helpless. "You damn lunatic."

Gessler smiled and turned back to Fletcher. He brought his claws to Fletcher's breasts and made a parting gesture with both hands that sent the shreds of dress and slip to either side. This was only the preliminary, to bare the flesh. The next sweep would take the claws deep through the flesh.

Did Gessler mean to tear her heart out and carry it away in the heart-shaped box? For crazy use in his crazy reincarnation mumbo jumbo?

Bowman seated the arrow in the pocket of the bowstring, thrust the shaft through the keyhole, and took as much bow-string pull as he dared. Even all it had might not be enough, but the energy it had now felt like a lot and any more might mean the ruin of it.

Now he could not see his target and would have to shoot blindly.

But it had to be this way and it had to be now.

Slant it a bit more to the left. He loosed the shaft.

The keyhole served to guide the arrow. The scrape of metal against metal or the rubbery twang: something turned Gessler as the arrow flew. It got him in the throat rather than in the back.

Eye at the keyhole, Bowman watched Gessler arch away from life. The arrow tore loose of its own weight and arterial blood spouted before Gessler's hands could go to his own throat, the talons wrapping around his own neck. He staggered backward out of sight.

Bowman felt around for a spike heel. He held it by the toe and hammered at the door panel at the edge nearer the dresser. The spike heel focused the force; the wood gave.

He made holes in a circle big enough to pass his arm through, knocked out the circle, then reached out and spidered for the key. As he touched it, he heard the apartment door open and high heels walk in. Must be the blonde. But how—? Use your head. Gessler must've jammed the downstairs door open and must've managed to punch the apartment door's unlock button when Loveday let him in.

"How's it coming, Karl?"

He had heard that voice before. It froze him now with the icy realization of all it implied.

"Karl?"

He stirred himself to grab the key and bring it near the keyhole, but froze again just before the woman stepped into the bedroom.

The keyhole showed him the blonde. She stopped on the threshold. Her mirror shades swung from Loveday on the bed to the floor where Gessler would be lying just out of Bowman's field of vision.

She dropped the jerrican of gasoline she carried and ran to Gessler's body. Bowman could just see the curve of her back as she knelt.

Quick, before she looked around and noticed that the closet door had grown an arm. He had trouble lining the key up with the keyhole.

The scraping and rattling must've drawn the woman's attention. He heard a screech, then hands grabbed his forearm. It took all his strength to hold firm against their tug. Teeth dug into his fist as he twisted the key. He heard the dead bolt slide and he worked the inner winged turn and as the door gave he pulled his outside arm in and shoved hard. The swinging door sent the woman sprawling.

He strode over to her and put his fingers in her hair and pulled. The long blond tresses came loose. He looked down at cornrow hair and a dark scalp that lacked the concealing cream that whitened the skin elsewhere. The mirror shades glared at him and she made a move to gather and spring.

"It's over," he said.

And Yevon Bowzer did not get up. She bowed her head and wrapped her arms around her knees and sat rocking and moaning.

Even in death Gessler looked scary. You could explain anything away, and the eerie aura, the subliminal shimmer, might prove to be phosphorescent dye in Gessler's clothing and luminescent tint in his skin lotion, and droplets of atropine in the eyes would give them their strange stare. But Bowman still shivered. Part of the shiver was for a shameful thought that had just crossed his mind: looking at it selfishly, he had cause to be grateful to Gessler. He felt relieved when the M.E.'s people bagged the body and carried it away.

He glared meaningfully at Wilkes, though, because Loveday Fletcher, holding her dressing gown tightly about her, could not help staring in horrified fascination at the plastic evidence bag Wilkes was absently swinging. The bag held the blond wig, which Bowman and Wilkes and the M.E. felt pretty sure would prove to be the hair and scalp of Cora Urneg Gessler. The things people did for love could be more hateful than the things they did for hate.

Wilkes caught Bowman's look and reddened and put the plastic bag behind his back. Wilkes surveyed the bloody bedroom as though taking a mental snapshot to back up the police photographer.

That seemed to satisfy him. But when he turned again to Bowman he frowned. "I still don't know why you came here to stir up the Urneg case. You haven't been working for the insurance company. So who the hell is your client?"

"Me."

"I thought you said you never knew the guy."

"True. I never knew Mr. Urneg and he never knew me."

"Then why . . . ?"

Loveday Fletcher too looked at Bowman and seemed to wait even more curiously than Wilkes for his answer.

Bowman smiled at her. "Mr. Urneg checked the *See Organ Donor Card* box on his driver's license and kept a uniform donor card with it. I have his heart."

THE LAST MILE

A lightning flash imprinted on Mr. Crakow's retina a still photo of the man in the doorway. It was no one he knew or wanted to see. He started to close the door in the man's face.

"Hold on, Mr. Crakow. I'm from the warden's office. I'm driving you up to the prison."

Mr. Crakow frowned but held on. "They didn't say—I didn't expect—"

The man raised an eyebrow, then shrugged. "I guess the wires got crossed somehow. But here I am. I sure wish it was somebody else. What a night for driving—what a night for anything."

Mr. Crakow eyed the night indifferently. "Come in."

The man came in dripping, his eyes darting about and taking everything in. All that he saw had a dusty look except for the twin-framed photos on the closed piano.

"Nice place you have here."

Mr. Crakow pointed to a chair. "Sit down, Mr.—?"

"Amber. Ken Amber."

"Sit down, Mr. Amber."

"Thanks, but—" Amber looked at his watch.

"Yes, of course. I'll be with you in a minute." Crakow started toward the hall closet, stopped himself, made for the foot of the stairs, stopped again. "Excuse me if I seem confused, Mr. Amber, but I was planning to take the train, and—"

"It's better this way. You'll avoid the reporters. Most of them are going by train." Amber's mouth twisted. "By bar car, I should say."

Mr. Crakow's eyes widened. "Oh? I didn't realize. It's a big thing, then?"

"Big is right. First execution in a long time. It should make headlines."

The old man looked suddenly younger. "Then it's really going to come off? He's going to die after all?"

"After all the delays and appeals, you mean?" Amber appeared to hesitate, then to reach a decision. "Mr. Crakow, I shouldn't be telling you this, but you'll find out anyway soon enough. And it's better if you're ready to take the shock." He stopped as though he had already gone too far.

The old man looked suddenly older. "Go on, tell me. I can take it."

"Well, the wise money says there will be a last-minute reprieve."

Mr. Crakow nodded slowly. "I had a feeling."

That feeling had been with him ever since he had heard the Governor on the radio, his voice full of the famous ahems and harumphs, saying that he would ahem give full harumph consideration to what was ahem literally a harumph life-and-death matter.

"So it's likely you'll take the trip for nothing."

Mr. Crakow pulled himself straighter. "I'm still going."

Amber let out a sigh. "Good. I'm on your side. It'll make a good—I mean, it should be a dramatic confrontation. You showing up to witness the scheduled execution of a vicious killer—and the warden having to say there'll be none. Your reaction to that should make a banner headline. Do you know what you're going to say?"

Mr. Crakow shook his head. He moved toward the stairs. "I won't be a minute. I just want to throw a few things in a bag in case I have to stay over."

"Sure. Take your time."

Amber waited till Crakow was upstairs, then he strode to the piano and slipped the photos of the girl and the woman out of their frames and into his pocket. When he heard Crakow's footfalls on the treads, he remained standing in front of the piano to block the empty frames from view, striking a pose of thoughtful, patient, compassionate waiting.

Crakow toted an old airlines carry-on bag.

"I'm ready if you are, Mr. Amber. Although maybe you'd like some coffee before we go."

"No, thanks. I'd like to get rolling. We can always stop along the way for coffee—or something stronger if you feel the need for it."

Crakow opened the front door to the driving rain. Amber made a dash for his car and Crakow switched off the lights and double-locked the door. Amber slid behind the wheel and opened the passenger door for Crakow, who squeezed in beside him. He sat with the flight bag on his lap, his gnarled hands gripping the handle.

Amber started the car but did not release the brake. He eyed the flight bag, then searched the old man's lined face. Water-streaked shadows hid any expression.

"You're not planning to do anything foolish, I hope? I can tell you right now they shake you down before you go in."

For the first time there was a slight smile in Crakow's voice. "I'm not carrying a weapon, if that's what's on your mind."

"That's all right, then." But Amber sounded almost let down. Then he saw Crakow's hands tighten on the handle, and he grinned to himself. Bare hands were a weapon. Of course the guards would not let Crakow get anywhere near the condemned man, but a lunge at him by Crakow would be newsworthy. VICTIM'S DAD LUNGES AT REPRIEVED CON.

Amber waited till they were out of city traffic and on the highway before he set to work on Crakow.

"Tell me, Mr. Crakow, why were you so bent on witnessing the execution? Are you that vengeful?"

Crakow's voice was rusty with disuse but iron-hard with feeling. "I want justice. Is it being vengeful to want to see justice done?'"

" 'An eye for an eye.' Is that it?"

"How can there be an eye for an eye? No matter how much he suffered he could never pay enough for what he did."

"Justice can't bring back your daughter, sir. Or your wife. Your wife died soon after it happened, didn't she? Of a broken heart?"

"The doctors say there's no such thing as a broken heart." Crakow's voice was dead.

"Getting back to the likelihood of a reprieve. Have you thought yet what you're going to say?"

Mr. Crakow shook his head wearily. "If you don't mind, I'm tired."

He closed his eyes and pretended to doze. The hypnotic hum of the tires and the metronome beat of the wipers turned it into a true doze.

It was nearly dawn when he opened his eyes. The rain still fell. Amber still hunched over the wheel, peering through the sweep of the wipers.

At his stirring, Amber turned his head and forced a smile. "With us again?"

Crakow looked for road signs. "We must be nearly there."

"Only a few miles more. What are your thoughts as the execution approaches? What are your feelings?"

"My own."

That hit Amber like whiplash. He recovered. "They can't

stay yours alone. People are going to want to know.”

"What people? The People versus William Hamilton? You say it's all fixed. If the people have nothing to say, the people have nothing to hear.”

Amber brightened, though he put commiseration in his voice. "Well, that's the word I get. The fix is in. They'll wait till the last minute to make it look good. They keep a line open between the warden and the Governor, you know, and at the very last minute there'll be a phone call.”

Again it was impossible to read Crakow's face, but again Crakow's hands tightened on the handle of the bag. It was obvious that Crakow had worked with his hands most of his life. Amber wondered briefly what line Crakow had been in before retiring on disability.

"You must be feeling bitter. I mean, it isn't everyone who'd want to see a guy die in the chair, but he killed your daughter—and in effect your wife. And now that you know he'll probably be pardoned you must be tasting gall. Am I reading you right?”

Crakow turned his eyes from the road to Amber's face. "All these questions. You're not from the warden. You're a reporter.”

Amber was a bad loser but good at pretending he was a good loser. He gave Crakow an ingratiating grin. "I've only been doing my job. In my sort of work you sometimes have to hand people a line.”

Crakow took one hand from the handle of the bag and put it on the handle of the door. "I'm getting out right here. I don't want to ride with you any further.”

Amber did not slow the car. He smiled. "You'll never make it there in time on foot.”

Crakow flung the door open and leaned partway out.

"Hey!" Amber braked in panic, sluing the car. "You

could've got us killed! It's lucky I'm a good driver!" Crakow got out stiffly. "Are you sure you know what you're doing? It's another full mile."

Crakow slammed the door shut. Amber rolled down the window and tried one last time, for the record.

"I hate to leave you out here in this downpour."

"I'm used to bad weather."

Amber shrugged. "All right."

He rolled up the window and drove off.

Crakow watched the car vanish around the bend, then squished onto the shoulder. He looked up and around. He opened his bag, took out his linesman's belt and spurs, and put them on. He hooked a testing phone on the belt and started climbing the nearest pole.

As he climbed, he felt the painful play of muscles at work, muscles long unused. Then he disconnected his body from his thoughts. By the time he reached the top, he knew what he was going to say. When the warden got on the line he would say, "No, Warden. I've ahem decided not to harumph order a stay."

HANGOVER

A force of screaming furies, tormentors straight out of a TV commercial, hammer-and-tonged in Bill Dunn's head. At the peak of the ill-tempered blacksmithing a chilling realization plunged him into wakefulness. He had spent the night before bending his elbow—and someone's ear.

For nearly three years he hadn't touched a drop, knowing his tongue would loosen—and his neck tighten. Now, after holding out against temptation in that desert of a thousand days, he had succumbed to the devils of memory and thirst.

And what he had feared would happen had happened. He had spilled his guts to some sympathetic listener—he didn't know who—in some sleazy bar—he didn't know where.

Foggily, he could see himself and a stranger sitting in a booth guzzling and talking. He was doing most of the talking. The other limited himself to encouraging nods and grunts. A man's face began to take shape in his mind. Spongy features arranged themselves into a cunning, fawning expression. The eyes had a drinking-in-every-word look, as Dunn sober visualized them watching Dunn drunk.

Why wouldn't they have that look? It wasn't every evening a solid citizen confided that his wife's death wasn't the accident it seemed. How the sympathetic listener's ears must have flapped, fanning in the details!

The little furies brought the anvil chorus to a crescendo. His eyes watered. He had managed to weep at his wife's funeral. But the moisture now was caused by mental anguish and acute physical pain.

Just possibly, however, things weren't as bad as they seemed. The man might have been too drunk himself to re-

231

alize what he had. Or he might have put it all down to the solid citizen's liquid expression of maudlin feelings of guilt, not something to take very seriously. Dunn winced. Things were probably worse than they seemed.

He hoped he hadn't told the man his name, where he lived, where he worked. He thought he had come home by himself. He prayed that the man hadn't tailed him. He had to find the man before the man found him. Otherwise, he was in for blackmail or a murder charge.

Dunn had always been one for slow thinking out and great patience in working out the details of a problem. But this called for quick thought, and fast action. He pulled the clock on the dresser into focus, and straightened with a suddenness that brought a cringing recoil. He reached for the phone with care. He dialed his office, gritting his teeth at the horrendous ratcheting each time the dial spun back.

Though he felt sure his secretary's solicitude was not phoney, her alarm at Mr. Dunn's calling in sick tried his nerves.

He said through his teeth, "Thank you, Miss Stizza. I know I'll be fine tomorrow." He hesitated. "By the way—"

He closed his eyes at her eager, "Yes?"

"If anyone should make inquiries of a personal nature about me, you won't—"

"Of course not, Mr. Dunn."

He hung up gently on a hurt and puzzled and loyal Miss Stizza. He made his way to the bathroom. A cold towel lessened the throbbing. Wearing a damp turban, he downed aspirins and black coffee, and gathered himself for the hunt. He half-expected the phone to ring before he set out. But it didn't.

It wasn't easy to track down a foggy image of a man.

It had been the foggy image of a woman that jounced him off the wagon to begin this mess. Michaela. He had killed his wife to be free to marry Michaela, only to have Michaela throw him over for a richer man. And the woman he had seen yesterday afternoon, making memory and thirst too strong to resist, hadn't even been Michaela—merely someone who looked somewhat like her. But that was beside the point.

The point was to find the man. That difficulty troubled Dunn more than what would probably happen when he found the man. It seemed to him that his drinking companion of the night before had been slight of build. This meant Dunn could deal with him in the same way he had dealt with his wife. His murder could be made to look like an accident.

It was evening now, and in this part of town the streetlights were dim. But bars were frequent, spilling pousse-cafes of neon, on the asphalt. Dunn had been at it since the neons began flickering on. He had thought it useless to start earlier—he would have missed the night bartenders, and one of them might remember seeing Dunn and his friend and might be able to tell Dunn the name of the friend.

He soon found it was the bartenders he would have to look to. In the first bar the steady customers were already working at getting unsteady. To pass the time, they punched the windbag about tonight's heavyweight title bout.

Dunn ordered a beer and sat waiting for an opportunity to edge into their talk. But they ignored him. Maybe it was because he was a stranger. Maybe it was because they thought him a suffering mortal whose right to be alone to commune with his soul they respected. The furies in his skull were not yet still and, as he could tell from the bar mirror, the hangover still showed.

So it was to the bartender he spoke.

That became the routine. Dunn stopped in at a bar, failed

to spot his friend, ordered a beer, tried the place on for a feeling of familiarity while taking token sips and fighting down his greed for a real pickup, and looked for recognition in the eyes of the bartender.

When he found none he inquired anyway if the bartender had seen a slight, spongy-faced man of about fifty at any time during the past ten hours, saw the eyes widen or narrow and the head shake *no,* and shoved off from his full glass of beer, to stop in at the next bar with the same lineup of questions waiting to be asked.

He came almost to believe that there was no trace to find of a listening stranger with spongy features that arranged themselves into a cunning, fawning expression, and that he had been talking to a grotesque distortion of himself in some mirroring surface.

Then he found the place. It looked like all the others, had the same beery, smoky atmosphere, the customary clientele. But when he passed through the swinging doors and crossed to the bar he knew he had been here the night before. He failed to spot his friend, and found the varnish of the woodwork of the booths too grimy to give back any likeness of himself. He ordered a beer.

The bartender's nod held recognition.

Here too the talk was of tonight's heavyweight title bout. The bartender drew Dunn's beer while watching a fat man flatten the air to show how the champ should do it. The bartender cut the foam, set the glass before Dunn. His eyes met Dunn's and he jerked his head the expert's way and smiled.

Dunn smiled back. He put down a five-dollar bill as though he meant to take out the change in drinks. He tried to sound off-handed as he asked if a slight, spongy-faced man of about fifty had been around.

The bartender looked hard at Dunn and thought a while

before he answered with a touch of suspicion.

"Yeah, I know who you mean. You and him was cozy last night over in the corner booth. What you want with him?"

"I borrowed something from him and forgot to give it back. I was pretty drunk."

"Yeah? What?"

After only the merest pause, Dunn reached into his pocket and brought out his silver lighter. He kept his fingers over his brazed-on monogram. He made it flare and go out.

"This."

"Where'd Pete ever get a nice lighter like that? Let's have a look at it."

Dunn pretended he hadn't heard the last part, pocketed the lighter.

"He said he found it."

Dunn hoped he hadn't stirred resentment in the bartender. But the bartender suddenly smiled at something. For an instant, Dunn thought the man he wanted might be standing right behind him, having heard words that would have made Dunn out a liar. But the bartender was smiling at something he saw in his own mind.

"Yeah, like I said, you and Pete Otis was sitting together over there. I sure had to laugh at the way Pete kept nodding his head and tossing them down."

Dunn stood up abruptly, frowned at his watch. "It's later than I thought. Got to go. Where does Pete live?"

The bartender shrugged. "Rooming house somewheres on Eighth, I think. Too bad you can't stay. Pete's pretty near a regular. He'll probably show up here around ten. If you want to, you can leave the lighter with me, and I'll give it to him. He probably didn't even miss it."

Dunn pretended he hadn't heard, nodded a preoccupied

farewell, scooped up his change, and left.

Once outside, he took out his penknife and pried his monogram off the lighter. He hesitated, then pocketed the fancy silver cutout with the rest.

His head felt suddenly clear, his brain sharp.

William Dunn's watch read nine-twenty when, standing in a dark doorway near the corner, he saw Pete Otis coming. That made this the perfect time and place for the job.

He let the man move unseeingly past him, scrutinizing him from head to foot. This was the man, all right. Dunn stepped out after him, and touched him lightly on the shoulder. The man turned with a start and almost instantly his face broke out in a smile.

"Ah, it's you," he said loudly.

Dunn read a lot into that smile—it looked both guilty and gloating, he thought—and the aggressive tone of the man's voice.

He handed Otis the lighter. Otis took it in wonder and turned it over. He looked up to Dunn for explanation. But by then Dunn had glanced both ways to make sure that no one was coming, and was slicing down with the edge of his hand on the back of Otis' neck.

The instant his victim sagged and went limp he caught him by the shoulders and lowered him to the sidewalk. If a man wanted to sit slumped on the curb that was his business. He was careful in picking up the lighter not to smear Otis's prints, and dropped it in the curb-sitter's pocket.

It cost him a slight pang to sacrifice the lighter. He lifted the body to its feet, walked it to the corner.

Otis was even lighter than his wife had been.

He propped the body up against a corner lamppost. Passing cars were infrequent here, so he couldn't afford to be choosy. But he had to wait for a driver not overly careful about slowing for a turn.

He let one car pass, two. Then a car came squealing around the corner at a furious spree. Before it straightened enough for its headlights to catch them in its sweep, Dunn hurled the body directly in its path. The toppling form flung out its hands realistically, like a man suddenly aware of oncoming death and trying to wave it away.

Then the screeching impact, glass and metal meeting flesh and bone.

The detective was in the middle of a yawn, and failed to complete it properly. "Say, would you mind telling me again how it happened?"

Dunn began again, careful not to let fear or irritation but only the shock natural to a man reliving sudden death show in his voice. Really, it had worked better than he had dared to hope. The driver had panicked, making this a hit-run. So Dunn could mean it when he said he didn't mind telling the detective again exactly how it had happened.

". . . So I saw him ahead of me on the street and shouted to him to wait—"

"You shouted to him?"

"That's right. And he stopped, and turned and waited for me to catch up with him. He recognized me straight off. I handed him back his lighter and he thanked me. Then he seemed to remember something and asked me the time. I told him—"

"You told him?"

"That's right. And he said, 'Good Lord, I got to hurry to a radio and hear the fight—' "

"Hear the fight?"

Bad echo in here.

"That's right. And that's when the guy started to run across the street."

The detective gave Dunn a look too long for comfort. He nodded slowly to himself. "We really have to look into this one. Suppose we begin by you turning out your pockets."

The monogram in Dunn's pocket felt as heavy as his heart, and his heart was stone and a force of furies was hammering insistently away at it.

"Why?"

"All that shouting and telling and hearing. I understand this Otis was as deaf as a post."

PLAY DEATH

Addison Burke watched the little girl next door bury her doll. She scooped out the hole with a toy shovel, heaping the earth on one side, she placed the doll in the hole, took a last long look at the secret smile on the doll's face, then began to shovel the dirt back.

Each shovelful onto the doll was a slow, scraping drumbeat; there was something terrible about it, and Addison stirred. The little girl stopped shoveling suddenly, her eyes following his shadow back up to him. It was too late to draw his head back across the fence. Their eyes met.

He smiled. The little girl stared somberly. That was natural; kids breathed being into inanimate objects, made living things of them, took them seriously. The doll had "sickened" and "died" and the child was laying it to rest, that was all.

His smile died. Why wasn't the child weeping? Shouldn't that be the most enjoyable part of the play funeral? Children loved to shed hypocritical tears. Instead, now that he looked more closely, the child wore faintly a secret, grave smile like the one on the doll's face. A fear grew in him as he stared at her. She couldn't know; she couldn't have seen him that day a month ago.

That day the sky had been a child's crayoning of summer heat. He was taking in the mail and sorting the letters as he walked. When he came to the bulky sealed envelope the trapped air in it startled him; giving to the pressure of his fingers, it cried like a doll. He smiled; he had never given thought to it before, but he supposed now that something of the sort was what made a doll cry on cue: *Mama!* He squeezed the envelope again and laughed. Then his own diaphragm

239

squeezed painfully as he noticed the writing on the envelope; he knew that arrogant hand.

It grew so still that he became aware there is never utter stillness; there was the cricketing outside, the constant sawing away at the air—then Genevieve's voice: "Anything for me?"

He handed her the letter; the envelope cried once more. She held it lazily till she saw the handwriting, then ripped it open and read it quickly. His eyes were on her as she read.

When she glanced up at him, she shocked him with her casual statement: "I'm leaving you."

He snatched the letter—a few bold sprawling words to the page—from her hand.

She smiled. "I'll tell you what it says. If I meet him at the dock we sail away together. If I don't show up he sails alone."

His voice trembled like the pages in his hand. "You're practically inviting me to lock you in until the boat sails."

Her eyelids fluttered but she said calmly, "You can't lock me in forever. Once I'm out, I go away from here, from you, anyway. Either way you lose me. Why not be nice about it?"

Why not? To everyone he was that nice Mr. Burke. Everyone liked that nice Mr. Burke—and yet he felt sure everyone pitied and scorned that nice Mr. Burke because his young wife ran around. Suddenly he wasn't that nice Mr. Burke anymore, and there was no more anything for Gen.

He waited till evening to bury her. It was dark but the cricketing had quickened, even so; it had grown hotter and closer. He was dripping perspiration by the time he struck softer earth. No one had been witness to the burial. Wait, there had been one witness; in the tree . . . No, that could only have been a bird.

Yet now there was the little girl playing at burial, imitating the real thing. How could she have seen? No window in her house faced that part of his grounds, the fence was too high and on her side there was no tree she might have climbed. The fence itself, was there a hole in it? He drew back and almost at once he heard the slow, scraping drumbeat begin again.

Bending over, he moved along the fence. There it was—a knothole, just about at her eye level. A hole was always so inviting to a kid. He could see her now through the hole, rapt in her shoveling. Had he seemed that rapt to her? But then, what would such a little girl have been doing up and out so late? Still there had been the confusion attending the new arrival and it would have been easy for her to slip the parental eyes. That was it, then.

Even if the child never told of what she had seen, the burying of the doll would bring out the murder, sooner or later. Sooner, if the mother missed the doll and asked the child what had become of it; later, if the mother caught the child playing burial again. In any event, the child would say she was only doing what she had seen the man next door do. Then, though the mother might quickly dismiss this as a child's fantasy, in the mother's mind there would be the planted seed, the growing doubt, and there would be the reviving and sharpening of gossip.

Had Mrs. Burke really run away with another man? Or had that nice Mr. Burke murdered her and buried her in his garden? Sooner or later, polite but firm, the police would come; and to the happy amazement of all, they would find that, but for a little girl imitating something she had seen without understanding, that nice Mr. Burke would have gone on living the rest of his life in their midst at the scene of his secret crime.

For a moment he had an urge to vault the wall and wring the little girl's neck. It quickly passed—and not because he caught window vignettes of her mother tiptoeing from the crib to the kitchen. Even if the mother had not been in view he could never do that. Nor could he try to lure the child into his yard and contrive an accident, perhaps have her die in a fall while climbing the fence. No, he could never again reach the high point of fury.

He could kill only once—and that once was now in the past. Not quite true; he knew now that the moment of killing and the fear of unearthing were both ever-present, would always be with him. He straightened stiffly and walked slowly—more in weariness than in unwillingness—into his house and into the kitchen and began to stuff the cracks.

Dorothy noticed the man had gone away and she was happy—until she heard her new baby brother James whimper and Dorothy's mother come running to see what was bothering him. Dorothy heard—and yet did not let herself hear—the picking up and the crooning and the patting. Dorothy finished the shoveling, then firmed the mound and smoothed the earth over the doll's grave, patting it and crooning softly, "Rest quiet, James."

MRS. GRADY'S SWAN SONG

Mrs. Grady felt guilty. Not because she had skipped Sunday Mass, her feet having been too swollen for her good shoes, but because this was her last night on the job and though, as always, she would be leaving behind a suite of offices to which she had brought order out of chaos, she would be leaving behind a mess of unresolved lives that were—well, a mess.

Not that the owners of those lives knew Mrs. Grady. They would not have recognized her if they had passed her on the street or even in the corridors of the office building as they hurried out and she clumped in. Their worlds did not overlap. One world ended at 5:00 p.m., give or take a few minutes, the other world, Mrs. Grady's, began at 7:00 p.m. So none of the executives and secretaries daily occupying the Gammon, Inc. offices in the Gammon Building had any awareness of Mrs. Grady, the cleaning woman.

All they knew was that somehow, no matter how untidy the place looked when they left at the end of their workday, it looked fresh and tidy when they came back in the morning. If they thought about it at all they realized there had to be human hands setting everything right. But that the hands were Mrs. Grady's was one of the unknowns in a world where everyone takes too much for granted.

On the other hand, Mrs. Grady knew them all. Oh, did she know them! They had become more than merely nameplates on desks or titles on doors. They had become people whose ghostly but all-too-human presence filled the weary and lonely watches of her night. And they were all the more human to her by the frailties their unwary leavings spelled out.

Not every scrap of interesting information went into the office shredder to add itself to universal debris. People were people and therefore careless and forgetful. Many a clue of a business nature—scribbles dealing with upcoming mergers or divestitures and with contracts firmly in hand or falling through—lay open to Mrs. Grady's view once she smoothed out a crumple of paper or scanned a notepad.

If Mrs. Grady's mind had worked that way, her quick eye could have led her to a killing or at least a wounding in the stock market. She might have retired long before tonight and on much more than her Social Security. But she focused her quick eye on the human thing, not on the lucrative. Instead of following the fortunes of the business, anticipating the ups and downs of Gammon stock, she followed the fortunes of Gammon people.

Thanks to crumples of paper and indentations on notepads and peeps into drawers she knew their characters and their secrets.

She knew that Mr. Gammon himself was a piratical mean-spirited old man who popped B-complex capsules by the handful, no doubt trying to live up to his image of 30 years before. His portrait dominated the boardroom. That slit of a mouth had sucked in businesses and hirelings and had spat out juiceless husks: the artist had pretended to idealize him but the ruthlessness had come through.

Besides, she had other evidence. One of the firm's enterprises was airfreight and she had seen a memo from Mr. Gammon ordering hazardous cargo aboard passenger planes even if it meant the use of misleading labeling. "The name of the game is to ship the stuff, not to insure safety," the memo had said. And she had seen an entry in his tickler file reminding him to see about firing older employees just before they earned their pension rights.

Mrs. Grady had hoped Mr. Gammon would step down or move aside and let Mr. Riley become President or Chair of the Board. But that did not seem any more likely now than it had years ago. Without ever having met him, Mr. Riley had become Mrs. Grady's favorite.

She knew that he smoked too much. But he was neat about it. He was also thoughtful enough to leave his copy of the afternoon paper for her, as though he knew she could do with something to read on the long subway ride home, and the paper always had its front page first, as good as new. A little thing, maybe, but it loomed big in Mrs. Grady's mind and heart.

Mr. Hastings, on the other hand, another V.P., was her unfavorite. He regularly left remains of his snacks, circles and drippings, scatters of cigarette stubs and ashes, even heelprints on his desk, and word had got back to her that twice he had complained of the cleaning woman filching change and candy bars from his desk drawer. Of course that was only his greedy forgetfulness talking. As if she had need of his coins or his sweets!

Mrs. Grady earned her own keep and paid her own way. She had done so all her life and would continue to do so even after retiring. Let others do the same, and let others cast no names, and the world would be a better place.

She did not scant Mr. Hastings' office, even on this last night, but moved on as quickly as she decently could. Her cleaning routine brought her to Miss Vandeveer's desk. Miss Vandeveer, now, was a sad case, though Mrs. Grady would be the last to throw the first stone.

She knew that Miss Vandeveer had been having an affair with Mr. Cole, the office manager. Notes between them had turned up in their wastebaskets. Nothing would ever come of the affair but despair. Mr. Cole had desk photos of his wife and three kids, and Mrs. Grady had never yet found it necessary to dust the glass and frames.

It would seem that Miss Vandeveer had finally caught on. And finding out must have been shattering to her. Lately the poor silly thing had been building up a deadly supply of prescription sleeping capsules. Mrs. Grady sent up a little prayer.

Mrs. Grady worked Miss Vandeveer's drawer open and drew in her breath. Another little bottle with a fresh label. Today Miss Vandeveer had seen yet another doctor on her lunch hour, had gone to yet another druggist to fill yet another prescription. Mrs. Grady knew it would not be long before Miss Vandeveer nerved herself to give up on Mr. Cole and do the sinful foolish deed.

Sighing, she moved on to Mr. Degener's. She knew that Mr. Degener was a secret drinker. He kept his lowest drawer locked, but a sniff of the paper cups in his wastebasket, plus the empty packages of breath-disguising pastilles, told her there had to be a fifth or something in that locked drawer.

Shortly after Miss Vandeveer had come to work here, Mr. Degener had moved his desk around to give him a constant view of Miss Vandeveer. For a while Mrs. Grady had hoped Miss Vandeveer would be the one to wean Mr. Degener from his bottle. But the notes between her and Mr. Cole had begun and, to go by the number of cups, Mr. Degener had only got worse.

Shaking her head, Mrs. Grady gave Mr. Degener's desk a last fond wipe and moved on to Mrs. Fiore's.

Mrs. Fiore was a nice enough young woman, but anxious to get on. It showed in the mistakes she made in her overeagerness, mistakes she carefully buried at the bottom of her wastebasket. She was still too new in her job for Mrs. Grady to have a fix on her: bad luck, that. Since Mrs. Grady would not be coming here any more after tonight, Mrs. Fiore's character would remain a relative unknown.

But as if to tantalize Mrs. Grady to the end of her days something new and strange turned up this very night.

In Mrs. Fiore's wastebasket Mrs. Grady found wad upon wad of facial tissue. They did not have the exploded look of tissues someone had used for a bad cold but the soft damp look of tissues someone had used for a good cry.

It was payday, but there was no pink slip in the wastebasket, so the chances were they hadn't fired her. Besides, though her desk seemed in some disarray, there was no sign she had emptied it of her personal belongings. A quarrel, then, with her husband? Or some bad news? Or had Miss Moffett leaned on her?

In puzzlement Mrs. Grady moved on to Miss Moffett, who was Mr. Gammon's secretary.

Miss Moffett was the office's oldest employee, so you'd think Mrs. Grady would have a handle on her by now. The best Mrs. Grady could sum up was that Miss Moffett was a perfectionist intolerant of her own and others' imperfections. Though to tell the truth and shame the devil, she had always given Mrs. Grady the least trouble of any of the lot, even Mr. Riley.

But Miss Moffett's neatness smacked of prissiness. Mrs. Grady had her suspicions of that kind of personality. She guessed that if she had a look into Miss Moffett's head she would find all sorts of untidiness.

Tonight, though, with Miss Moffett as with Mrs. Fiore, Mrs. Grady ran into another surprise.

Miss Moffett's desk looked as if a genteel whirlwind had swept through it. Mrs. Grady had to smile. Wouldn't you know her last day would be the hardest!

It wasn't till she emptied Miss Moffett's wastebasket that

she figured out what it had all been about. There had been something of a search and something of a to-do. But for all the fuss the one place they hadn't searched was Miss Moffett's wastebasket.

Miss Moffett's pay envelope, still sealed and nicely padded, fell out. Mrs. Grady, gingerly picking it up, saw what had happened.

In turning to answer an intercom call—one from Mr. Gammon would make her jump and forget everything else—Miss Moffett had unknowingly elbowed her pay envelope into her own wastebasket. It had worked its way to the bottom, past lighter crumples of paper, and had buried itself there. By the time Miss Moffett remembered the envelope, it had vanished.

Now the damp facial tissues Mrs. Grady had found in Mrs. Fiore's wastebasket fitted in. Mrs. Fiore, being nearest, had come under suspicion and had wept. "Search my desk. Search me, if you want to!" And Miss Moffett had wanted to.

Mrs. Grady could see it and hear it, plain as plain. Now, more than ever, it seemed to Mrs. Grady that cutting her ties with Gammon, Inc. was just like swearing off watching a soap opera in mid-season. She could not leave all these loose ends behind, all these lives up in the air. She pressed her lips together. She knew what she had to do and she would do it.

Holding the pay envelope by the edge so as not to leave fingerprints, Mrs. Grady slit the flap carefully and shook out onto the desk Miss Moffett's take-home pay—$314.28. The $314 went under the top band of one of Mrs. Grady's support stockings. She put the 28 cents into Mr. Hastings' desk drawer, alongside his half-eaten candy bar. The empty pay envelope she stuck under the seat cushion of his visitor's chair, letting one edge peep out on the side nearest the wall. Sooner or later someone would spot it—not Mr. Hastings himself, she hoped. And then Mr. Hastings would have some explaining to do.

Well, she had brought some order out of chaos. But as Mrs. Grady finished up she thought about Miss Vandeveer and sighed. That bit of disorder remained. Then she brightened, her face polishing itself with inspiration. One thing more and her last night's work would be complete.

She drew two paper cups from the dispenser by the water cooler. Into one she poured all Miss Vandeveer's sleeping capsules. She carried them to Mr. Gammon's private washroom off his inner office, poured the same level of B-complex capsules out of his large economy size bottle into the empty cup. She poured the sleeping capsules into the B-complex bottle and shook well.

Mr. Gammon would not swallow enough at any one time to put him to sleep for good. But he would swallow enough to slow his thinking, to cause him to make humbling mistakes. If her mind had run that way, Mrs. Grady would have begun considering going short on Gammon, Inc. stock. What she was thinking, though, was that maybe at last Mr. Riley would be taking Mr. Gammon's place.

She returned to Miss Vandeveer's desk and poured the B-complex capsules into the bottles. The B-complex capsules should work like—what was the word these days?—uppers. At least Miss Vandeveer, if she took what she believed was a fatal dose, would merely have a spell of good health and a chance to get over Mr. Cole. And maybe Mr. Degener would help her.

Mrs. Grady paused on her slow way out. Was that all? Here, yes. Tonight and forever. She had made sure to wipe her fingerprints off the bottles before replacing them, the way all good criminals should. Still she frowned, sensing she had overlooked something. Ah, yes. The money. Her church opened early and on her way home she would stop in and put Miss Moffett's pay into the poor box.

She did not look back. There was nothing to look back to. A lifetime of cleaning—and cleaning at best was only a staving off; you could not hope to win in the end, not against wear, dust, time. But what she felt as she left was not sadness. She had done her best to bring order to her world.